UN
MOTHER

MW00489650

To my lovely Ali
I did it!

hope you enjoy it!

Emma Robinson x.

THE UNDERCOVER MOTHER

EMMA ROBINSON

Bookouture

Published by Bookouture in 2018

An imprint of StoryFire Ltd.

Carmelite House
50 Victoria Embankment
London EC4Y 0DZ

www.bookouture.com

Copyright © Emma Robinson, 2018

Emma Robinson has asserted her right to be identified
as the author of this work.

All rights reserved. No part of this publication may be reproduced,
stored in any retrieval system, or transmitted, in any form or by
any means, electronic, mechanical, photocopying, recording or
otherwise, without the prior written permission of the publishers.

ISBN: 978-1-78681-359-6
eBook ISBN: 978-1-78681-358-9

This book is a work of fiction. Names, characters, businesses,
organizations, places and events other than those clearly in the
public domain, are either the product of the author's imagination
or are used fictitiously. Any resemblance to actual persons, living or
dead, events or locales is entirely coincidental.

For Mum and Dad.
For everything.

CHAPTER ONE

Preoccupied with checking her phone for a message from her boss, the length of the queue she was in and the question of whether the baby needed one or two giant cookies for breakfast, Jenny didn't notice the woman's splayed palms until they landed squarely on her stomach. She jumped so high she nearly lost hold of her sandwich.

'Look at your beautiful bump! How long have you got?'

Jenny took a small step backwards. 'Five weeks.' It wasn't a problem that the woman was touching The Bump – although a bit of warning might be nice – but there was no time for a conversation about the delights of pregnancy today. Eva was an even-tempered boss, but she hated lateness more than a missing apostrophe, and Jenny needed her in a good mood. She pushed her sandwich along the counter and focused on the jar of cookies. *Avoid eye contact. Buy the sandwich. Get to work.*

But Queue Woman didn't get the message. 'Is this your first one?'

'Yep.' Jenny nodded. 'First one.'

Here came The All-Knowing Smile. She got it a lot now. Why *did* everyone assume they knew better than her?

'You've certainly got a lot of changes coming your—' Leaning forward, the woman scrutinised Jenny's sandwich. 'Is that bacon and *brie?*'

Jenny knew what was coming next. 'Actually, I've researched and apparently…'

Queue Woman snatched the sandwich out of her hands, scanned the selection on the counter and replaced it with a ham and cheddar panini. 'Thank God I was here. You nearly ate soft cheese!' The Smile again. Accompanied by a shake of the head. 'Pregnancy brain.' Leaning down, she stage-whispered at Jenny's stomach. 'Silly Mummy.'

Jenny looked at the ceiling. She just wanted to buy a sandwich – and a cookie or two – and get to work. At least in the office people still talked to her face rather than her midriff. They'd enjoyed their joke of pointedly counting off the months since her wedding and had then barely mentioned her pregnancy since.

But now she *needed* to talk about it. Maternity leave started next week and she *still* hadn't been able to pin down her boss about the plan for her column. Eva had evaded her questions, as if the 'Girl About Town' articles would write themselves. Admittedly, they wouldn't need to cover the column for long because Jenny was only going to be off for six months and she'd also pick up some of the work from home once the baby was settled. Writing when it slept.

Queue Woman was back at face level. Frowning.

'You look tired. Do you need to sit down?' She lowered her voice. 'My friend was about your age when she had her first baby and she said it was *exhausting*.'

Thirty-seven is not old! Jenny bit her tongue. Even her doctor had said her ovaries were chucking out eggs like the last day of the January sales and that she should 'get on with it' if she wanted a baby. Just showed how much he knew.

'No, I'm fine, thanks. Really.'

The queue began to move and Jenny bought the panini she hadn't chosen, three cookies and a large latte – decaf, to avoid another lecture. On the way out, her mobile buzzed in her bag. A message from Eva.

Come and see me as soon as you get in. Don't speak to ANYONE.

At last.

✦

If Eva asked for something to be done *soon*, it meant *now*. But Jenny's bladder, or the baby sitting on it, couldn't have cared less. Halfway back to the office, she had to waddle furiously into M&S to find a toilet.

Thank God. No queue. But the cubicles were built for toothpicks. Reversing in seemed easiest, but she still whacked her elbow on the wall trying to wriggle her maternity tights off her hips. These reinforced passion-killers had become a begrudged necessity. The other option was maternity trousers, but their elasticated front sections made her feel like an entrant to a pie-eating contest.

Maybe Queue Woman was partly right. Some things *had* changed in the last few months. For a start, Jenny's idea of a good time had become lying on the sofa watching *First Dates* whilst licking Marmite off the top of a crumpet. But she was pregnant, for goodness' sake; there was a small human being inside her. Once the baby was here, her body would return to normal and the rest of her life would follow. She'd be able to stay awake past 9 p.m., wear clothes that didn't resemble camping equipment and be out and about researching nightlife for 'Girl About Town'.

Finally, she escaped the cubicle. Only to be caught at the wash basins by another one of the 'It'll change your life' brigade. The Bump got another feel. A rather damp one.

'Oh, look at you! You're about to pop any minute!'

'Five weeks to go.' Maybe she should have a countdown display on her forehead?

Toilet Woman put her head on one side. 'Oh, I remember it well. Such an exciting time. Getting everything ready, reading all the baby books, thinking up names.' She motioned towards Jenny's cup and chuckled. 'Enjoy your hot drinks while you can. You won't be getting many of those soon.'

Why wouldn't she be able to have a hot drink? Because she might spill it over the baby?

'Sorry, I really need to go. I have to meet my boss and make a plan for my maternity leave.'

Toilet Woman did The All-Knowing Smile. 'You may feel differently once baby is here. I couldn't even *think* about going back to work and leaving mine.' She sighed. 'I just loved them too much.'

Jenny felt her morning sickness make a surprise return. Toilet Woman should meet her sister, Claire. The two of them would get along like a 1950s house on fire.

✦

The main office of *Flair* magazine was open plan. Deadline day on a weekly magazine meant a buzz of activity: boxes of beauty product freebies spilled over desks, last-minute telephone conversations hunting down the latest celebrity news, photos of interviewees being approved or rejected. Head-height cubicle walls hid people from sight, but you could hear every phone conversation, every sandwich being unwrapped, from across the room.

Jenny made straight for her desk and flopped onto her chair. She had given up five-inch heels in favour of flats around month six, but that didn't stop her feet from screaming.

There was a commotion going on at Lucy's desk; people were shaking her hand and Lucy was flicking that perfect hair of hers all over the place. Jenny spotted one of their regular freelance photographers, Brian, and beckoned him over.

She used her eyes to motion in Lucy's direction. 'What's going on over there?'

'Hmm? Where?' Brian dropped his head and stared at the sheet of proofs he was holding as if they were the most interesting thing he had ever seen. He was attractive if you didn't know he had the morals of a premiership footballer.

Jenny took the proofs from him and used them to point. 'Over there. Little Miss Shiny Shoes and friends.'

Brian followed the direction of her gaze as if he had only just noticed the Lucy Fan Club in action. 'Oh. That. Uh, Lucy just got a, uh, a promotion.' He picked up a stapler from the desk and studied it, opening and closing the part where the staples went in. 'You obviously haven't been told.'

Jenny took the stapler out of his hands. Her heart was beating faster. Maybe that was just the sugar rush from the third cookie. 'Told what?'

Brian ran a distracted hand through his hair. 'Why am I always in the wrong place at the wrong time? I try not to get involved with anything, but…'

Jenny grabbed his wrist with both her hands, as if she were about to give him a Chinese burn. 'Spill.'

Brian took a deep breath and let it out in one go. 'Eva has given Lucy "Girl About Town".'

Jenny froze, turned to look at Lucy, then turned back to stare at Brian. She let go of his arm. Maybe she'd misheard him. Or maybe he was confused. 'Girl About Town' was *her* column. 'Who told you that?'

Brian shrugged, held up his hands and backed away. 'Don't shoot the messenger.'

As if on cue, the phone on Jenny's desk buzzed. Eva's name flashed up on the screen. Jenny picked it up.

'I thought I asked you to come and see me as soon as you got in?'

CHAPTER TWO

It was a relief that she didn't have to try and squeeze into one of the designer chairs at the conference table, but Jenny's stomach flip-flopped to see Eva waiting for her on the sofa. With tea and biscuits.

This was going to be bad.

Eva never looked entirely herself sitting on the sofa. There was something about her sharp, tailored frame which fit much better behind her large desk. She patted the armchair to her right. 'Come and join me.'

Jenny stood her ground and folded her arms over The Bump: she needed to attack before losing her nerve. *You should always be higher up than the person you are negotiating with.* 'Why have you given my column to Lucy?'

Eva lifted the teapot and started to pour. 'I don't know if you've fully realised this, Jen, but you're about to have a baby. I've not had children, but I'm assuming it will be rather difficult to research and write a column aimed at single women when you've got a small person attached to you—?'

Not Eva, too? She was having a baby, not moving to another continent.

'I know what HR said about maternity leave, but I'm only planning on taking six months. And I might even be back sooner. I've told you that.' Eva hadn't been pleased about the pregnancy, but Jenny had assured her from the outset that the baby would have as little impact on her work as possible. To be fair, the pregnancy had been a bit of a surprise to Jenny, too – who would have thought they'd get pregnant on the first go? 'Have you told Lucy that her promotion is only temporary?' Her eyes began to fill up. Damn hormones.

Eva sighed and pointed again to the armchair. 'Sit. I don't want your waters breaking all over the rug.'

Jenny perched on the edge of the armchair.

'We both knew this was coming, Jen. And not—' Eva held up her hand to prevent Jenny from interrupting '—not just because you're pregnant. You're getting too old to be reporting on the singles scene. For goodness' sake, you haven't been single for almost two years now.'

Jenny would never admit it, but she knew that Eva was right. Hauling herself out to speed dating events and nightclubs had lost its appeal. It was far nicer to lie on the sofa with Dan and a takeaway. Plus, half her wages now went on age-disguising eye cream.

But why wasn't it possible to keep everything the same, for a little while longer at least? It wasn't as if she were ill or emigrating to Australia. She was just having a baby. A tiny little baby. This must be why everyone said, 'Your life will change' – because they were the ones who changed it for you.

'So, you're taking my column away from me permanently. And what will you give me when I come back?' Without 'Girl About Town', Jenny would only have the slush pile of interviews, product reviews and other random articles. She was happy to do her fair share of 'How to Shape Your Eyebrows for Success', but her column was her first baby. She had worked hard to get it.

Eva picked a piece of lint from the sleeve of her suit jacket. She collected up some papers from her lap and tapped them on the table to tidy them. 'I know you don't plan to take your full twelve months' maternity leave, Jen, but you haven't had the baby yet. And if you do… Well, a lot changes in this industry in twelve months. We'll have to discuss your role if and when you return.'

If and when?

Eva looked Jenny in the eye. 'You might prefer something you can do from home.'

What could she do from home?

'Or part-time.'

Part-time?

Eva looked as if these were random suggestions that had just popped into her head, but Jenny knew her better. She also knew that Eva wasn't keen on people working from home. Far better to have them under close surveillance, where she could ensure that they weren't taking too many coffee breaks.

Jenny's heart thumped. Lucy would be writing *her* column whilst she, Jenny, slaved away trying to drum up exciting adjectives for the latest shade of eye shadow, waiting for the day when she would become surplus to requirement. She needed an idea for a new column. And she needed it fast. *Think. Think!* Something she could research while she was at home with the baby. Something new, which the magazine didn't already cover. Something that Eva would go for. Most importantly, something she could come up with right this minute.

'How about a column for mothers?' Jenny blurted out.

Eva looked at her as if she'd gone soft in the head. 'Mothers? Hardly our demographic. Our readers want glamour and gossip – not dummies and diapers. Are those hormones doing something to your brain? Maybe you should be thinking about starting your maternity leave sooner rather than later.' She glanced at her paperwork – Eva's usual sign that you should leave.

But Jenny wasn't about to give up. 'No, no, wait, listen. I don't mean a boring, mumsy column – quite the opposite. More a kind of "Englishman in New York" slant – what it's like to find yourself in the world of babies when you are the least maternal person on earth.' Jenny's mind whirred and her mouth followed. 'Think "Lost in Mothercare". And, of course, I'd be the perfect person to write it. I mean, who is less prepared for motherhood than me? Can you imagine some of the messes I'm going to get into? Some of the crazy women I'm likely to meet in the next couple of months?

It'll be *hilarious!*' Jenny laughed, to illustrate her point. *Must not slip into hysteria.*

Eva looked up. 'I'm not sure…'

Jenny leaned forward, getting into her pitch. 'What do you think has happened to all of those women who started reading "Girl About Town" ten years ago, when I first started writing it? Lots of them have met someone, settled down – might even be pregnant as we speak. Do you want to lose those readers, or give them something that speaks to them where they are now?'

Eva had her head on one side, listening. *Keep talking.*

'I could be the intrepid explorer, taking them into new territory, showing them the way.' Jenny held out her arm as if she were about to lead an expedition to Planet Baby.

Eva nodded slowly. Then shook her head. 'And how are you going to find time to write this column? I've heard that women at home with children find getting things done a bit tricky. Let's face it, Jen, you have hardly been the most organised writer, even when you've only had yourself to look after.'

Jenny made a mocking 'pfff' sound through her teeth. 'I'm going to be at home all day, every day!' According to her sister, it was impossible to do anything for yourself when you were at home with a baby, but Jenny wasn't intending to turn into Claire.

Eva tapped her mouth with the end of her pen. 'Just say I let you have a go at this… what will you write about? What kind of things do new mums *do* all day? Will you actually have any material?'

Material? Where could she get material? *Think. THINK!* 'I'm starting an antenatal class next week,' Jenny lied. 'I'll have a whole list of topics for you after that.' She would have given Eva a couple of examples at this point, but she didn't have a clue what they might be. 'Look, while I'm on maternity leave, I'll write a blog, test out a few ideas, see what kind of response I get. I won't use my name, so there'll be no connection to *Flair* to begin with… I'll be an undercover reporter. That's it! I'll call it, "The Undercover

Mother"! Just promise me you'll look at it and consider turning it into a column?'

Eva stood up. 'Okay. If you manage to keep up this "Undercover Mother" blog, I'll look at it.' She walked to her desk and sat down. 'But no promises about a regular column.'

Jenny left Eva's office and walked towards Lucy, who was sitting at her desk, chatting to Brian about her promotion. *Traitor.* Hot pants and thick tights weren't a look that everyone could carry off, but Lucy managed it.

Jenny leaned in as she walked past. 'Thanks so much for taking *"Girl About Town"* off my hands, Lucy. I've been begging Eva for weeks to let me start an exciting new project, and now I can.' Without waiting for a response, she flounced off outside. Well, as much as you *could* flounce when you were carrying an extra two stone around your middle.

It wasn't until she'd walked out of the front door that she fished into her bag for her phone. She googled 'Antenatal classes'.

Now, how was she going to sell the idea of them to her unsuspecting husband?

CHAPTER THREE

Ever been to a singles night? Trying to look relaxed and cool whilst scanning the room for someone who might be your type? Antenatal classes are just like that. The only difference is, you are guaranteed to have at least one thing in common.

So far, I haven't had much luck finding my Mrs Right, although they are a pretty mixed bunch. One of them is intent on a completely natural birth – I'm pretty sure she'd give birth squatting in the hospital garden if they'd let her. Another is so keen to find out about the drugs available, I've begun to wonder if she took a sedative during the conception…

From *The Undercover Mother*

✦

'Tell me again why we have to go to an antenatal class when you said, and I'm quoting, that you had "no intention whatsoever of sitting in a room with simpering women talking about babies"?'

Searching the lounge for her car keys, Jenny lifted the cushions next to her husband and looked underneath them. 'Dan, I am a writer about to begin maternity leave. Eva has given my column away to someone younger than half my wardrobe and, when I go back to work, I am likely to be writing about the current must-have colour in nail polish, and not much else. I had to come up with something fast.'

Dan leaned over to the coffee table, located the keys and handed them to her. 'Yes, you've already explained that. But why antenatal classes and, more importantly, why do I need to go with you?'

Jenny sighed. For a very clever man, he could be rather obtuse sometimes. 'The antenatal classes are for research. You—' she pulled him up out of his seat '—are my cover.'

✦

It had been too late to book on to a full antenatal course, so Jenny had signed them up for consecutive Saturdays at the local clinic. As they entered, the door creaked and several expectant glances turned in their direction. Jenny scanned the pregnant women. Who looked the most normal? Who was most likely to provide her with interesting material? Who wouldn't bore the pregnancy pants off her? Meanwhile, Dan just collected a sheaf of papers from Sally, the woman running the group, and sat down on a random chair in the semi-circle. Already, he was not following the plan.

Sally started with the obligatory ice-breakers – they had to pair up and introduce themselves. Dan looked at Jenny with a pained expression: this was his idea of hell. She'd make it up to him later, she decided. If he behaved himself.

A smart woman with long auburn hair approached Jenny tentatively. 'Hi, I'm Ruth. Sorry, were you about to pair up with someone else?'

'No, no, please, sit down.' Jenny pulled out the chair next to her. 'I'm Jenny. Married to Dan.' She motioned in the direction of her husband, who was scrutinising a poster on the wall in an effort to avoid the pairing up. 'When are you due?'

Ruth held up crossed fingers. 'In six weeks, hopefully, if we make full term. We've had a long road to get here. We tried IVF, which didn't work out, and it's taken us a lot of poking and prodding to get this far. Sorry – too much information?'

Hopefully, this Ruth wasn't going to spend their entire conversation apologising. 'No, not at all. No such thing as too much information as far as I'm concerned.'

Ruth looked relieved. 'Oh, did you do IVF, too?'

'No,' said Jenny. 'But I'm always interested in a good story. I'm a writer.' Time to steer the conversation in a different direction. 'What do you do?'

'Oh. I work for a bank. I did wonder, seeing the people here, whether there might be others who are IVF?'

Jenny raised an eyebrow. 'Because most of us are so old, you mean?'

'No! Well, maybe.' Ruth tucked her hair behind her ears. 'Sorry. I'm so nervous. David and I never thought we'd actually make it this far. Sorry, I'm talking about myself again. Tell me about your pregnancy.'

Jenny was here to gain information, not give it out. 'No, no. Carry on. Please.'

Ruth didn't need much persuading. 'Well, after we'd failed IVF at the third go, we gave up and went on holiday. About three weeks after we got back, I was in the toiletries aisle at Sainsbury's, saw a packet of tampons and realised that I hadn't bought any since before our holiday. At first I thought my ovaries had given up altogether – sorry for the gory details – but I also had a tiny flicker of hope. So, I decided to do a test straight away, before the hope got out of control.'

'In the toilet at Sainsbury's?' Jenny's own experience of pregnancy testing was of holding Dan's hand as they waited – for the longest three minutes of their life – for the second blue line to appear.

'Classy, huh? Trying to hover over the toilet and urinate on that thin little stick without weeing all over my shoes was pretty tricky.' Ruth stroked her bump as she spoke. 'I couldn't believe it when I saw the result. I assumed the test must be faulty so I did the second one straight away. I even went and bought more tests. When David got home from work, there was a row of six positive pregnancy tests on the back of the toilet waiting for him. Oh, sorry! Sally's calling us back now, and I haven't asked you anything!'

Jenny wasn't worried about that. She was more concerned with getting the scoop on the funny side of pregnancy. Ruth didn't seem a likely prospect: far too positive and nice.

Dan sat back down beside her. 'How is it for you?'

She shielded her mouth with her hand. 'Exactly as I expected so far. You?'

'I had a good chat with David over there about a new shed he's building. Have you noticed that there are only four men between five women?'

'Are there?' Jenny did a quick count. He was right. Which one was on her own?

Antenatal Sally didn't waste any more time before getting to the nitty-gritty of labour: the contractions, the pushing the baby out, and then the placenta. She made a valiant effort to make it sound enjoyable, but Jenny wasn't fooled. If you wanted a baby – which she did – labour was something you just needed to do. Up until then, she had done her best not to dwell on the realities of it, but now Sally had laid them all out before her.

It was terrifying.

She wasn't alone. If the husbands were squeamish at the mention of the placenta, they looked even worse after a general discussion of some of the post-birth side-effects. The fatigue and 'baby blues' didn't seem to worry them, but when the conversation took a turn onto the subjects of hair loss, bleeding nipples and tearing of the front bottom, there was a lot of uncomfortable shuffling in seats.

Then they got onto pain relief.

'Whatever they're offering, I'm taking them up on it,' said a slim, well-spoken lady with a perfectly round, small bump. Her name-badge told Jenny she was called Antonia; the Boden dress and coordinating jacket told her a lot more.

'Surely it's better to be able to give birth without any drugs at all?' This one – Naomi, according to her badge – looked about ten years younger than the rest of them, and was wearing a voluminous smock top and bangles that chinked against each other every time she pushed her long hair back from her face. 'Women give birth all over the world without using drugs. I'm hoping to do the same.' She smiled at her partner and he squeezed her hand.

'Yes, and loads of them die in bloody childbirth,' muttered Jenny to Dan. Neither Boden nor Bangles were her kind of woman. Maybe she should give Ruth another go?

During the break, Jenny followed Ruth to the kitchen, determined to see what she could uncover. 'I'd kill for a black coffee.'

Ruth poked around the assortment of jars and plastic containers. 'You might be out of luck; I can't find any decaf.' Jenny opened her mouth and then shut it again: drinking coffee with caffeine here would be like eating a cream cake at Weight Watchers.

Ruth placed four mugs in front of the geriatric kettle, then slumped against the wall. 'First thing I'm going to have after I've given birth – a latte with extra caffeine. And a big slab of pâté. And red wine. I haven't eaten anything off the banned list since I did the test.' She wrinkled her nose. 'Blimey, I sound boring, don't I?'

It was *all* boring, in Jenny's opinion. The pain-relief discussion had petered out after Naomi's proclamations about a drug-free birth. Jenny had been rooting for Antonia to take her on, but even Naomi's speech about women in paddy fields had been met with nothing more from her than a well-bred roll of the eyes. They were halfway through the session and Jenny had nothing. There had to be *something* she could write about. *Just keep asking questions.*

'What do you think of the class?'

Ruth lowered her voice. 'To be honest, I only came to meet other mums. We've read about fifty baby books between us in the last few months. Unless they've discovered how to teleport the baby out of me, I doubt we're going to find out anything new. David will be able to get work as a midwife by the end of this pregnancy.'

'Could you ask him to have a word with Dan? He wants to treat the baby like a new DVD player – get it home and have a play with it, see what it does.'

Just then, the fifth mum-to-be of the group marched into the kitchen. Jenny tried to read her name-badge without staring at her ample boob area. That was an expensive-looking suit. Who knew you could get maternity clothes that made you look so professional?

'So, this is where they're hiding the hot drinks. I was hoping to find something better than the warm orange juice out there. Hi, I'm Gail. I work in investment.' She reached out and shook their hands firmly. Was she about to thank them for coming and whip out an agenda?

'How are you finding the class?' Ruth asked.

'It's pretty much what I expected.' Gail opened the cupboard doors and looked inside. Her short, maroon fingernails looked professionally manicured. 'Don't they have any paper cups? Those mugs are rancid.'

Was she looking down her nose at the mugs or at the two of them?

'Have you been reading baby books, too?' Clearly it was time for Jenny to feel the fear and read one of the manuals her sister had passed on. Pretending that she wasn't about to go through childbirth was probably not the best strategy.

'Just one. My mum bought it.' Gail took the mug Jenny offered, then put it down on the counter and pushed it away. *No wedding ring*. 'It covered the basics. I don't need detail. Not like those two in there.' She motioned towards the meeting room with her head. 'That young girl is clearly some kind of Earth Mother. No pain relief? How ridiculous. And Antonia seems to think she's a cut above the rest of us. No surprises there.'

Now *this* was more like it. Someone with an edge. Strong opinions. The possibility of friction. *Please*.

'You know Antonia, then?' Jenny couldn't picture this Gail being friends with the Boden-clad beauty. In her well-cut suit, discreet

make-up and expensive shoes, Gail looked as if she'd got lost o
way to a board room. Antonia would be more at home in Har
Nichols' Café.

Gail looked up sharply. 'No. I've never met her before.'

From the look on her face, she wasn't too keen on getting to
know her, either. *Interesting*.

Ruth filled the awkward silence. 'My husband is jealous that
your partner found a way to get out of all this today.'

This was getting better. *Gail* was the one here alone. What was
the story with the absent father? Gail was just what Jenny was
looking for. *Thank God*.

No such luck.

'I don't think he needs to be here. I'm the one doing it.' And
she left the room.

There was no way on earth that Jenny was doing this birth
business on her own and, from the look on Ruth's face, she felt
the same way.

Just then, Antenatal Sally popped her head around the door.
'Okay to come back and get started again?'

Jenny's heart sank. What else was there left to find out about
childbirth? From what she had seen, there was no one and nothing
there that was worth writing about. Gail was the one person with
an interesting angle, but she clearly wasn't a 'sharer'. Pitching this
'Undercover Mother' blog to Eva might just have been career
suicide. If Jenny wasn't interested in the minutiae of motherhood
herself, how would she write something that other women would
want to read? Was it too late to back out and beg for her old job
back?

CHAPTER FOUR

*Pregnant women are supposed to GLOW and BLOOM: I'm not
sure my body got that memo.*

*My skin is stretched as tightly as cling film, my nipples are as
big as tea plates and the weight and size of my bump makes me
walk like I've peed my pants. Ironically, I'm also getting undressed
in front of more strangers than the staff at a brothel – and, like
them, no longer care who looks at my lady parts.*

*At least my maternity leave starts this week: no make-up, no
bra, no clothes at all if I don't feel like it. That'll teach my husband
for getting me in this state…*

From *The Undercover Mother*

✦

Long blonde hair and endless legs: Lucy turned the head of every
man they passed on their journey towards the bar. Strangely, they
didn't seem as interested in the human cannonball waddling behind
her. Jenny tried not to mind.

The bar was very young and very bright. There weren't many
places Jenny didn't know in the area, but this one had only opened
two weeks ago and, as they weren't serving Gaviscon cocktails, she
hadn't yet been in. Lucy, however, was already on cheek-kissing
terms with most of the barmen. Once she had made it abundantly
clear that she knew absolutely everyone in there, the two of them
looked for somewhere to sit.

Instead of tables and chairs of normal height, there were high,
red leather bar stools around tall tables you could only fit a couple

of cocktail glasses on. Jenny glanced around to see if there were any comfortable sofas more suitable for a pregnant woman. There were none. And it wasn't as if she could ask Lucy to help. *Show no weakness.*

Lucy had hopped up onto her stool effortlessly and seemed unaware of Jenny's dilemma.

'I'm so sorry that I've taken your job like this.' As opening statements go, this wasn't the most tactful, accompanied as it was with the kind of smile beloved by toothpaste adverts.

Jenny cracked a huge fake smile. 'Please don't apologise. I was happy to give it to you.'

They both knew where they stood.

Then Lucy noticed that Jenny was still standing. 'Don't you want a seat? I thought pregnant women had to sit down all the time. Don't your ankles swell up or something?' She glanced down at Jenny's feet, as if expecting to see that she had grown hooves.

There was nothing else for it: Jenny was going to have get up on that stool.

Circus elephants sat on chairs with more grace. A sideways approach – left cheek first – didn't get her posterior high enough. Right side first? Same result. There was no choice but to back into it, bending forwards and then flopping her backside on at the last minute. How humiliating.

'Comfortable?'

'Perfectly. Thanks.' In the time her manoeuvres had taken, their drinks had arrived. Jenny picked up her mocktail as nonchalantly as she could manage. 'So, what can I help you with?'

Why had Lucy asked to meet off-site to discuss the column? Maybe she thought Jenny would be less likely to cry and tear at her clothes if they were in a public place. Clearly, she'd never seen her on a big night out.

'Eva thought it would be good for us to get together. Have a bit of a handover. She seems to think there might be some bad feeling between us.' Lucy paused, as if waiting for Jenny to reply. Jenny continued to drink. 'But I assured her that we were professional women. We don't bring our private lives to work.'

Jenny knew exactly which element of her private life Lucy was referring to. Mark McLinley. Ex-'View from the Boys' columnist and time-wasting pig. He'd left *Flair* around the same time as he'd left Jenny – so he could start working his way around the single females at his new magazine. There had been a rumour about him and Lucy spending a lot of time together recently. Jenny wasn't about to warn her what a mistake that would be. Let her find out for herself.

Instead, Jenny focused on work. 'I'm not sure that there's much I can tell you that you can't learn from reading the column.' And there certainly wasn't much that she'd be willing to help her with, anyway – professional woman or not.

'Well, that's what I thought. It's not rocket science, is it?'

Obviously Lucy was baiting her, but current hormone levels made it impossible not to bite. 'I wouldn't say that. There's quite a lot of background work. Networking, building your contacts, being the first to hear about somewhere new. Takes time, you know.'

Lucy didn't look impressed. 'Well, I've only known I'm going to be doing this for a month and I seem to have a good handle on things.' She blew a kiss at a passing waiter.

Jenny sucked up the last of her sickly sweet concoction, making a louder noise than was polite: soft drinks never lasted long. Lucy had known for a month? But Eva had only told Jenny this week.

'Another drink?'

'No, I'm fine.' The other problem with soft drinks: they were too boring to drink more than one. 'I've got a lot to finish before I leave today. If we're done playing nicely for Eva's benefit, I'll get back to it.'

'Sorry. No can do.' Lucy flicked her hair. 'Eva said she would meet us here to firm up on the last few details of the handover. She'll be here shortly.'

Jenny groaned. She was stuck. 'I'll have an orange juice, then.' If she had to stay for another soft drink, she may as well get the benefit of its laxative properties.

Lucy gave their order to a young waitress, who she treated like her best friend in the whole world. Maybe she *was* going to be good at this networking lark. She continued to smile broadly when she turned back to Jenny.

'This might make you laugh. There's a rumour going around that you're going to write a column about being a *mother*.'

Word travelled fast. Jenny folded her arms. 'Actually, that's true.' Lucy's smug smile was unbearable. 'Of course, it requires an *experienced* journalist to take the mundane and make it interesting.'

Lucy nodded. 'Of course. Of course. But *babies*? Will you have enough to write about to keep a column going? Don't they just lie there doing nothing?'

Jenny had had much the same thought herself at the antenatal class. But she didn't need to have enough to keep the column going for very long; just long enough to prove to Eva that she could carry on writing after she'd had the baby. As soon as she was ready, she would swoop back in and take back 'Girl About Town' from under Lucy's pert little nose.

'Oh, yes. You'd be surprised.'

Lucy lifted her gaze over Jenny's shoulder and towards the door. 'Speaking of surprises…'

'Jenny!!!!' They all came in together: Brian, Maureen, even Eva. One of the girls from advertising was almost completely obscured by helium balloons emblazoned with nappy pins and storks.

'Did you know about this?' Jenny hissed under her breath at Lucy.

'Of course! You didn't think I actually needed your *help*, did you?' Lucy leaned back on her stool as if she were getting ready to enjoy the show.

✦

In bed that night, Dan was moaning about going back to the antenatal class. 'After last week, you said it was a waste of time. You promised we didn't have to go back.'

Jenny stopped fighting with her maternity pillow and turned on him. 'That was before my lunch with Lucy. I need something juicy to get this blog going, and I haven't got a clue where else to get it.'

She didn't say that she was starting to worry that there was no such thing as juicy material in the maternity sphere. There *had* to be an angle. Ruth's story about peeing on her shoes whilst taking a pregnancy test was mildly amusing, but it wasn't going to have Eva begging for Jenny's return.

Dan got out of bed and helped her to fit the long, sausage-shaped pillow under her bump. 'Haven't we got to watch a video of a birth tomorrow? I am not looking forward to that.' He pulled the quilt over her.

Now that she was wrapped around the pillow, she wouldn't be moving again any time soon. 'Well, you'll have the live performance to deal with soon, so you'd better get used to the idea.' Actually, Jenny wasn't desperate to watch it, either; she'd never even made it through an episode of *Casualty* with her eyes open – and that blood was fake.

'What did you think of the other couples?'

Dan shrugged. 'They seemed all right.'

'Didn't you think the women were all rather...' She searched for the word. 'Mum-ish?'

Dan laughed. 'What did you expect? You're one of them now, Jen, don't forget. Can we go to sleep? I need at least eight hours if you're forcing me to watch one human being emerging from another tomorrow.' He gave her a goodnight peck on the lips and turned over with a long sigh.

One of *them*? Did he think she was going to change into some kind of matronly stereotype the minute she gave birth?

The more Jenny thought about writing the blog, the more she realised what a good idea she'd had. She'd show everyone how you could have a baby *and* a life.

Now she was still, the baby began its nightly exercises. She felt a small bump move across her abdomen. Was that a hand or a foot? It still filled her with wonder that there was a tiny human being in there. She wrapped her arms around her stomach. 'Hello, baby,' she whispered. 'We'll show them all, won't we?'

Closing her eyes, she tried not to think about the birth film. If only someone could invent Ruth's idea, and they could beam the baby out of her, *Star Trek* style. Up until then, she'd managed to avoid thinking about the actual birth, but tomorrow she was going to have to face it in full colour.

CHAPTER FIVE

Up until now, I've avoided looking into too much detail about the actual birth. So you can imagine my delight when Antenatal Sally started producing medical equipment which looked like evidence from a GBH trial. Long metal sticks to break your waters, forceps which belong on a BBQ and head thermometers that hook onto a baby's halfway-born head. (I had been hoping for a baby at the end of all this, not a nine-pound carp.)

There is even a device that gets suctioned onto a baby's head like a sink plunger to pull them out if they get stuck. Now I've got a vision of my baby's birth turning into an ER version of The Enormous Turnip: one of these contraptions stuck between my legs whilst the doctor pulls it, and the nurse pulls him, and the cleaner pulls her and…

From *The Undercover Mother*

✦

Day Two of Antenatal and, due to the baby having an emergency need for a bacon sandwich, the class had already started when Jenny and Dan arrived. Antenatal Sally ushered them in.

'We're splitting into two groups to start with. Daddies over there, please.'

Jenny squeezed Dan's hand in an attempt to convey solidarity, then joined the other mums. Gail, Antonia and Ruth were on chairs; Naomi was perched on a huge inflatable ball, rolling her pelvis backwards and forwards. Jenny was tempted to give her a little nudge.

'We've got to sort these cards into priority order.' Ruth pointed at a set of laminated cards, curling at the edges. 'For the first few weeks after the baby's born.'

After the baby was born? Jenny was still getting her head around the whole birth thing. What else was there? She picked up the card nearest to her. 'Taking a shower? Is this a joke one?' Why the hell wouldn't you have time for a shower if you were home all day?

Naomi had started gently bouncing up and down on the ball. Her bangles jangled. 'Life can be unpredictable with a newborn. You can't cling to old habits. We need to *embrace* the changes.'

Jenny had an urge to embrace Naomi around the neck. Who'd made her a Motherhood Master?

Ruth picked up a card which read '*HOUSEWORK*'. 'I vacuum and clean every day. I can't imagine not doing that.'

Cleaning? Well, that one could scoot itself to the bottom of the list. Maybe there *were* benefits to some of these 'changes'.

'Just get a cleaner, darling.' Antonia didn't look like she spent much time with a duster in her hand. Gail raised a judgemental eyebrow behind her back.

'"Meeting friends" can go towards the bottom of the list.' Naomi stopped bouncing and sat cross-legged on the floor, her arms encircling her bump. 'Those first few weeks I want it to be just me, John and our baby, so we can really bond.'

Staying at home for weeks? Was she completely mad? That card was going right at the top of Jenny's list. 'I'll *need* to see other people. I'd go insane stuck indoors on my own every day.'

Gail nodded. 'Me, too. Although I'll only have two months to fill. Then I'm back to work.' She was dressed more casually today, but her smart trousers and collared maternity shirt were a far cry from the jersey dress stretched to breaking point that Jenny was wearing. She must have spent a fortune on her clothes.

'Goodness, that's early.' Antonia tucked her thick blonde hair behind her ears and then placed her hands back in her lap. Her linen dress barely creased. 'Geoff would *hate* me to have a job whilst the baby is small. What does your partner think about you going back so soon?'

Before Gail could reply, Antenatal Sally reappeared to see how they were doing.

Jenny had a sudden need to stretch her legs, which took her conveniently close enough to the group of dads to eavesdrop. They had a selection of baby catalogues and had had to make two lists: one for necessities, one for luxuries.

She saw Dan flicking aimlessly through a Mothercare catalogue. 'It's pretty pointless asking *us* to make these lists. I don't know about your wives, but mine has definitely been making all the decisions about *stuff*.'

Bloody cheek. He had chosen which cot they'd bought. She had merely *suggested* that the white one would coordinate with more bedding options.

Geoff agreed. 'And there's so much of it.' He turned the pages of a John Lewis baby book. 'A baby bath. What's the point when you have a perfectly good bath already? A changing table? As if Antonia is going to bother trooping upstairs every time it needs a new nappy.' He paused and looked closer at the page. 'What the hell is a top and tail set?'

David nodded. 'It all has to match too, according to Ruth.'

'Naomi and I have only got a small flat,' said John. 'I have no idea how we're going to fit all these things into it.'

'Well, you don't need a baby bath.' Geoff tapped the sheet of paper in front of them. 'Put that in the luxury list.'

David put his catalogue down and lowered his voice. 'Have you been pram shopping yet?' There was a unanimous groan. 'It would have been easier to buy a new car.'

'And cheaper,' said John. 'I'm trying to persuade Naomi to get a second-hand one.'

The other three laughed. Dan clapped him on the back. 'I admire your gumption, son. Good luck with that.'

Geoff went back to his magazine. 'What the hell is that?' he asked, pointing at a breast pump.

David peered over his shoulder. 'That, my friend, will ensure that you don't want to have sex with your wife for quite some time.'

Jenny crept back to the mums.

✦

When they joined up again, Sally handed out some more leaflets which she thought they might find useful. One of them was a series of eight different photographs of baby poo. The bacon sandwich Jenny had eaten suddenly seemed like less of a good idea. Number eight was bright yellow. Like psychedelic custard.

John was amused. 'Is this some kind of bingo game? Like those books your parents used to give you when you were on a long car journey and you had to tick the picture when you saw a cow or a letter box?'

'Not quite.' Sally smiled. 'Just wait, you will be amazed at how interested you will be in your baby's poo for the first few months of its life. You can tell a lot by the condition of a baby's poo.'

'You'll be in your element, Jen.' Dan nudged her. 'It's already like living with Gillian McKeith in our house.' Jenny hit him with the leaflet as the others laughed.

'Well, we've covered nearly everything now.' Sally was back at the front, with a TV screen on wheels. 'Get yourselves a drink and a biscuit and then we'll finish up by watching a film of a real birth.'

Time was running out if Jenny wanted to check out Antonia and Naomi. But Naomi had already begun an intense discussion with Antenatal Sally. Jenny overheard the words 'perineum' and 'olive oil' and shuddered, then followed Antonia out to the kitchen.

'I'm not looking forward to this at all.'

Although Antonia had reached the kitchen first, Jenny somehow seemed to be the one filling the kettle. Not for the first time that day, she longed fervently for caffeine. Or vodka.

Antonia wrinkled her nose. 'Me, neither, darling. It all sounds terribly messy. I'm assuming it's too late for us to back out?'

'Of the video? Or the actual birth?' Jenny was only half joking. Maybe her first instinct to avoid too much birth information had been a good one. Antenatal Sally was doing her best to be reassuring, but there was no getting away from the fact that the baby inside Jenny needed to make it to the outside. Perhaps sooner than she was ready for.

'I'm sure Naomi will know it all already. She's clearly a cut above the rest of us in the preparation department.' Antonia leaned back against the counter, her arms across the top of her bump. 'She offered to lend me some books about "hypnobirthing" or something. Not really me, sweetie.'

Jenny found the plastic container with the teabags. 'That's funny. That's exactly what Gail said about you last week – that you were a cut ab— that you knew a lot.'

'Oh, *did* she indeed? That's *very* interesting.' Antonia smiled to herself and tidied the cups on the worktop so that all of their handles pointed in the same direction. 'She's a curious character, don't you think? I'm surprised she has *time* to give birth with such a tight work schedule. Do you work?'

'I write for a magazine.' Jenny started to make tea for herself and Dan. She didn't want to talk about her job in too much detail. As soon as you told people you were a writer, they either clammed up completely or told you their life story. 'Do you want two cups? What's Geoff drinking?'

'Don't bother for him, darling. He can drink the insipid squash. We only just made it here on time today because he was out so late last night entertaining clients. Mind you, at least he's here. *Some* people don't seem to be able to get their baby daddy here at all.'

Ouch. Antonia wasn't afraid to go straight for the jugular. This was useful. A bit of tension made for good writing. Jenny just needed to direct it. 'What's this hypnobirthing of Naomi's?

'Goodness only knows. She kept talking about "visualising the pain" or some such hippy nonsense.' Antonia browsed the assortment of tea bags with a well-manicured finger. Nothing met with her approval. 'I'm not on board with all that "positive thinking" business. The only thing I'm positive about is that I want as much pain relief as I can persuade them to pump into me.'

Naomi and John chose that moment to appear in the doorway. Jenny clenched her toes: had they overheard Antonia's 'hippy' comment?

Antonia wasn't fazed. 'I wouldn't get too excited about the drinks menu,' she told them. 'Although there might be a couple of herbal sachets kicking around at the bottom which you'd like.'

Naomi didn't seem to be aware that she was being mocked. She couldn't have heard Antonia talking about her. 'Oh, thanks.' She let go of John's hand so that he could refill the kettle. 'This is wonderful, isn't it?'

'I'm glad someone's enjoying it. I need the loo, so I'll leave you to it.' Antonia winked at Jenny as she left.

Jenny took a big gulp of her tea. 'Mmmm, yes, it's really interesting.'

'John and I are so excited about it all,' Naomi gushed. 'The more we can find out, the better. I'd love to have done a longer course, but we couldn't really afford it. I'm a yoga instructor and am self-employed, so we're going to have to be a bit careful with money for the next few months till I can pick up my clients again.'

Of course she was a yoga instructor. And quite free with her personal information too, which might be useful. 'I see.'

'I can't wait to see the birth film. Although I have watched quite a few births online already.' Naomi's eyes shone.

Jenny gagged on her Rich Tea biscuit. 'Have you? Is it as bad as I'm expecting?'

'No, it's beautiful, isn't it, John?' She smiled up at him. John looked like a man who knew when to keep his mouth shut.

With her usual perfect timing, Antenatal Sally appeared at the door. 'I'm just about to press play!'

✦

Everyone sat in shocked silence, their expressions ranging from disbelief to abject terror. Everyone except for Naomi. She was beaming. Was she for real?

The birth film had left absolutely nothing to the imagination. Nothing Jenny wanted to imagine, anyway. A series of clips had followed an incredibly calm woman and her overly supportive husband at each stage of labour. It started in their home where they drank tea and chatted as if they had all the time in the world, and ended in a hospital delivery suite. Panting. Groaning. Unwanted close-ups of the baby's ridiculously large head emerging from between its mother's legs.

Jenny pressed her hand to her mouth. Oh God. This was real. No way out. Why had she watched it?

Antenatal Sally was still talking. Something about birth plans and what you should pack in your hospital bag.

'Take plenty of make-up, darling,' Antonia whispered. She didn't look as if she was joking.

'Did you just watch the same film as me?' Jenny whispered back.

'That sweaty woman looked horrific, sitting there holding the baby while her husband took *photographs*. Those pictures are going to be looked at for the rest of their lives. I do *not* want to look like that in mine.'

Jenny looked from Antonia to Naomi to Antenatal Sally and then back again. Were all of these women insane? Screw breathing, bouncing on big balls and make-up. The only thing that might get you through that experience was a whole load of alcohol. Could you pack vodka in your hospital bag?

A birth plan, though. That sounded good. Writing, at least, was something she knew she could do.

◆

When Jenny began the birth plan that evening, however, Dan was less than enthusiastic. 'Can't we just wait and see how it goes?'

Clearly, he hadn't been listening to Antenatal Sally. If they didn't get this written properly, who knew what might happen? 'We need to tell the medical staff what we want.'

Dan's expression was pained. 'Can't we just ask them to do what they usually do?'

Jenny told him to sod off and leave her to write it on her own, then wrote a beautiful two-page birth plan. That felt better.

Next up, a blog post about the antenatal class. Ruth, Gail, Antonia and Naomi might not be Jenny's first choice in friends, but the class itself had provided material for a decent blog. She was still miffed at Dan's comment that she was now 'one of them', but nevertheless it would be useful to stay in contact with the other four women after the birth. She'd swapped numbers before they left that afternoon, and had arranged to meet up with Ruth for a decaf coffee and full-fat cake next week. Now she just needed to write the blog in a style that would get Eva on board.

She sat back in her chair. Antenatal class completed. Birth plan written. Blog page set up and ready to go. All that was left was for the baby to arrive and, despite the scary video, she felt a lot more prepared now than she had been before the class. What else was she going to need? A birthing ball, a TENS machine, a back massager and some oil. Maybe even one of Naomi's 'wild-birthing' type books.

It was all going to be okay.

CHAPTER SIX

Packing a bag for the hospital is something I spent way too much time on. Paper knickers? They might be fine for paper dolls, but a woman whose backside needs its own postcode has got no chance of pulling them on. I even packed snacks in case I got peckish during labour. Snacks! I'd have been better off packing a bottle of gin and a klaxon to get the attention of the elusive consultant on the labour ward.

There is a conspiracy to not talk about the realities of childbirth. Admittedly, I didn't want the horror stories, but I wish someone could have warned me how it might go. How ridiculously smug were my plans to be walking around the room, stopping only to allow my husband to rub my back with a wooden massage roller and tell me how amazing I am. In actuality, if he had come anywhere near me with that thing I'd have whacked him – or myself – around the head with it...

From *The Undercover Mother*

✦

The contractions started on Thursday evening. Jenny was naively expectant.

'This must be it!'

It wasn't too bad: just a niggle, really. Where was her notebook? She needed to be ready to note down anything funny or interesting that was bloggable.

Dan made himself useful, bringing her a hot water bottle and writing down the times of the contractions as they got closer together.

It was starting to get uncomfortable. She was expecting pain, of course. Even Antenatal Sally had admitted that much. Time to crack out the TENS machine and hook herself up.

Now it was really beginning to hurt. Maybe she would be one of those women who had a really fast birth?

'How far apart are they?'

Dan checked his notes. 'Ten minutes. When you get to five minutes, I'll call the hospital.' Thank God. It wouldn't be long now.

But then the contractions got further apart again. Then closer. Then further apart.

This wasn't right. There was no pattern to them at all. And why was it going on for so bloody long?

Dan created an Excel spreadsheet of her contraction times. He even had time to make a graph.

The pain was unbearable. Jenny tore off the useless TENS machine. 'Call the hospital,' she growled.

But the midwife on the end of the telephone wasn't even interested in talking to them until the contractions were regular and only a few minutes apart. 'Take some paracetamol,' she advised.

'What does she tell people with a broken leg?' Jenny spat. 'Kiss it bloody better?'

When she couldn't bear it any longer, they decided to drive to the hospital. 'Bring the novelty handcuffs from my hen night,' she told Dan, 'and I'll chain myself to the reception desk if I have to.'

On the drive there, Dan tried to make Jenny laugh by suggesting they make a detour to buy a Dictaphone, as she wasn't making notes any more. He wouldn't be making that joke a second time.

The corridor which led to the maternity wing was eerily quiet. Jenny was only halfway along it before she had to lean against the wall as another contraction seared her body. Dan looked worried. 'Are you okay?'

'Just. Need. To. Breathe.'

A capable-looking woman appeared at the end of the corridor and came to take her arm. Jenny let out a long sigh of relief: everything was going to be all right now. They would take her to the Acorn birthing suite, let her splash around in one of the birthing pools she'd heard about, plug in her music and everything would continue as planned.

Except, it didn't.

The small room on the maternity assessment ward contained a bed and a rather scary-looking trolley full of electronics. The midwife asked Jenny a few questions, took her temperature and frowned. 'We're just going to run a few routine tests: urine sample, bloods. Nothing to worry about.'

Dan had to help her to the toilet and wait outside for her. Her wee hitting the cardboard bowl made the noise of a torrential storm. So romantic.

Then they had to wait for an interminably long time back in the assessment room. The pain was getting worse and it had spread to her back. Jenny nudged Dan in the direction of the door. 'Ask them when I can go to the water birth room. We might not get in otherwise.' She knew she would feel better if she could just get into a nice warm pool.

The midwife came back in. 'Sorry, no water birth for you. Your white cell count is up. Might be an infection. We need to get you up to the consultant-led ward.'

✦

Every contraction was more painful than the last. Jenny begged for an epidural. They had promised pain relief: why weren't they giving it to her? They could take a leg. A kidney. Anything. *Just make it stop. Make it stop now.*

A midwife leaned in towards her. 'We need to give you something to speed things up.'

Anything to get it over with. But then she heard the midwife warn Dan: 'The pain is going to get a lot worse.'

This couldn't be happening. She'd read the leaflets, done the pelvic floor exercises, even written a beautiful birth plan. Why was it going wrong? Dan looked terrified. There was a steady stream of people coming to look at her nether regions, but she didn't care. Why was no one listening? Couldn't they see the agony she was in? As if in a nightmare, she opened her mouth to tell them how she felt, but nothing came out. Bodies moved around, but no one was looking at her. *Look at me. Listen to me.* Where was Dan? He was there. Then he wasn't. Then there was nothing but pain. Tearing pain.

There were voices. Loud voices. 'Heart rate is dropping. We need to move.' Everything sped up. There was movement, a lot of movement. They were wheeling her down for surgery.

✦

When she woke, Jenny was in a very quiet room with a faint beeping in the background. The walls were white and she was covered in a pale blue sheet. Her head felt weird. Foggy. Like it was filled with cotton wool. Dan was standing in front of her holding a baby. A sleeping baby dressed in a yellow babygro. She was sure she had seen that babygro before. Dan was smiling. 'Hey,' he whispered. 'This is Henry.'

Henry? That was the boy's name they had chosen: Elizabeth for a girl; Henry for a boy. Was this their baby? Dan brought him a little closer to her. It *was* their baby. They had an actual, real-life baby.

The relief on Dan's face was almost tangible. 'Are you feeling okay? We're still in the recovery room, so take your time.'

Was she feeling okay? Physically, she didn't feel anything but exhausted. But something wasn't right. Wasn't she supposed to be the one holding the baby? Wasn't this the moment when Dan should tell her how amazing she was? Where she should sit up drinking tea and eating toast whilst everyone cooed around her?

'I think I'm going to be sick.'

Expertly, a nurse slipped a bowl under her chin and held her hair out of the way. 'It's the anaesthetic. It can affect you like that.'

✦

The ward was quiet. There were four beds in this section, and the other three were unoccupied. The nurse had placed Henry next to her on the bed and then wheeled them both to the ward, while Dan followed behind, looking like he'd just escaped a train wreck. Maybe the jubilation would come later.

Dan kissed her and stroked Henry's cheek with his finger. 'You did it, Jen.'

She didn't feel like she'd done anything. She felt like it had been done to her. Tears rolled down her cheeks. 'It wasn't supposed to be like this.'

Dan nodded and bit his lip. 'I know. I know.' He took her hand and kissed her palm. 'I know.'

The nurse had told her to get up and move around as soon as she could. Easy for her to say: she hadn't just been cut across the middle and had a small human being removed. Jenny had managed to prop herself up in bed and had tried to breastfeed Henry, but nothing seemed to be happening. The nurse wasn't concerned. 'It's fine, don't rush it. Sometimes that happens after a C-section – it takes a while for the milk to come in.'

Dan left her to go to the toilet and she lay and looked at her new son. Her son. He was very pink and wrinkled. She marvelled at the length of his fingers, his tiny fingernails, the soft curve of his top lip. Who knew this perfection had been inside her all this time? She breathed in his warm scent. Then, for a reason she couldn't explain, she licked him. A tiny lick on his cheek.

Dan reappeared beside her. 'I never knew he'd be this beautiful.' She started to cry again.

✦

Jenny and Dan's parents came to see their new grandchild and were all suitably gaga about how tiny and beautiful he was. Dan just kept staring at him, holding his fingers and then kissing Jenny again.

Jenny could now tentatively walk around the ward, even whilst holding Henry, if someone else lifted him from his cot first. Everything was going well. *Just don't think about the birth. It's all fine now.*

Then her sister arrived for a visit.

It started off all right. Claire cradled Henry in her arms and Jenny felt something surge in her chest. That was her baby. She'd made that.

'He's gorgeous,' Claire said. 'It seems so long ago that mine were this small. You blink your eyes and they're teenagers. You've done well. How are you feeling?'

'A bit shaky.'

It didn't feel like she'd 'done well'. She was supposed to have given birth effortlessly in the morning and been back home that same afternoon. Maybe she should call Antenatal Sally and ask for her money back.

'Hmmm. As you've found out, babies don't often follow the plan. Are you also beginning to see how unlikely it is that you'll manage to write this blog you're so intent on?'

Jenny shot Dan a death stare. What was he thinking, telling her sister about that? He made a 'Cup of tea?' sign and disappeared in the direction of the ward kitchen. *Coward.*

Claire was still looking at Jenny, expecting an answer.

'What do you mean?' Oh God, she was already sounding like a stroppy teenager.

'Ah.' Her sister smiled that smile. The 'face of experience' smile she had been doing ever since she'd started proper school and Jenny had still been in nursery. 'You've already seen how the birth hasn't gone according to plan. You're not going to be able to drive for six weeks now, you know. Just wait and see how much time you actually have when you get this little man home.'

Claire stopped short of wagging her finger, which was lucky for her as, still high on morphine, Jenny would have bitten it off.

She wanted to mimic her sister's 'Just wait and see' back at her in a stupid voice, but thought, as she was a mother now, she should find a slightly more grown-up way to convey her displeasure. Not trusting herself to say anything which wouldn't result in a full-scale family row in the first hours following her son's birth, she contented herself with another death stare.

Claire rocked Henry back and forth. 'I'm trying to decide who he looks like.'

'Oh, that is so ridiculous. They all just look like babies,' Jenny lied. Henry looked exactly like Dan. She wasn't going to give her sister the satisfaction of saying that, though. She also wouldn't admit that she had scanned his face for some small part that looked like her.

'Well, Mum said he was gorgeous and she was right. You need to take it easy once you get home, you know. Obviously, I managed a natural birth both times with mine, so I have no idea what a C-section is like. But I know you mustn't lift anything heavier than your baby.'

What did Claire think she was going to do when she got home: start weight training? 'I know, I know.' Jenny crossed her arms. 'They've given me a leaflet.' A leaflet she hadn't bothered to read when she saw it had diagrams of body parts in it.

But Claire was now talking directly to the baby. 'Oh, Henry. Your mummy has no idea how you're going to change things, does she? Silly Mummy thinks she can keep everything just as it was. Isn't that funny?'

Dan arrived with the drinks just in time to save Claire's life, and then the bell rang for the end of visiting time.

✦

Once Dan had gone home, Jenny shuffled out of bed and over to Henry's cot. How was it possible that she was so in love with this tiny creature? Of course, she'd assumed that she'd love him, but this was completely different to what she'd expected. It was like falling in love for the first time. Her heart surged when she looked at him.

Perhaps it was because he was such a good baby. *Look at him, just lying there asleep.* Everyone said how difficult newborn babies were, but he was an absolute angel. The recovery from the C-section was something she hadn't factored in, and breastfeeding was proving rather more difficult – and more painful – than Antenatal Sally had led her to believe, but she was sure that would fall into place soon, too.

She turned on her mobile. Messages of congratulations started to ping through. Good news obviously travelled fast. There were messages from Naomi and Antonia, and even Gail had sent a brief, 'Congratulations'. What about Ruth?

Ruth's due date had been over a week before – maybe she was currently in labour. Or maybe she was so fed up with being overdue that she couldn't bear to think of someone beating her to it. That was understandable. What could be more irritating than the advice of ingesting raspberry leaf tea, pineapple, curry or taking long walks? Or the inevitable nudge-nudge suggestions of what could be done in the bedroom to help get things moving, when you felt as interested in that idea as swimming the Channel? Jenny hoped Ruth was okay. After the struggle she'd had to get pregnant, she was the one of the five of them who really deserved to have a wonderful birth experience.

So. Jenny's sister thought she wouldn't manage to write the blog, did she? The first thing she was going to write about were the lies and propaganda of the antenatal class. Antenatal Sally had seemed so nice, so knowledgeable, so trustworthy. But it had all been lies. 'Just breathe.' Bullshit. 'You can have the birth you want.' Bollocks. 'Just keep walking around and the baby will be in the right position.' Buggering, bollocking bullshit.

Jenny was going to stick a big, fat pin into the antenatal class lies. Why hadn't anyone told her how excruciating the pain was? Why hadn't anyone warned her about all the possible outcomes that would be completely beyond her control? How come no one had floated the idea that she might end up kneeling on a hospital bed, flashing her backside to the world out of the back of her hospital gown and begging someone to give her pain relief, a general anaesthetic, smack her round the head with a plank of wood? If she had known these things, maybe she wouldn't have this massive sense of failure now. She felt a fool. A huge fool for believing the hype. For believing that this experience was going to be anything in the realms of beautiful.

But then she looked at Henry again. Dan was right: the birth might have been ugly, but Henry was the most beautiful thing she had ever seen. She held her hand to his chest and felt him breathe. The hard part was over. Now she just needed to get home, and life could get back to normal. She would prove to Claire, Eva and the rest of the 'your life will change' brigade that she could continue to live her life in exactly the same way and just take Henry along with her. Look at her now, merely hours after the birth, sitting with her newborn child and about to read something on her Kindle. She could just as easily whip out her laptop right then and start the first article.

This was going to be a breeze.

CHAPTER SEVEN

If you visit a new mother, don't take flowers. My house already looks like a satellite office for Kew Gardens, and every time someone arrives with another bunch, I have to haul myself into the kitchen to find a vase. If you want to bring something, make it cake. Or dinner.

I was a little surprised at how many people wanted to come and see the baby. It's surreal making polite conversation with your mum's dog-walking friend when you haven't showered in two days and you've got your milky boobs out...

From *The Undercover Mother*

✦

On the day Dan had to go back to work, Jenny cried in bed for about an hour.

The last couple of weeks had been a blur of feeding, pooping and crying; sometimes all three at once. After pretending to be an angel for the first few days – just long enough to make her fall desperately in love with him – Henry had turned into a demanding dictator. She bathed him, held him, flopped out her boobs on demand, but nothing was ever enough. She'd always sworn she'd never let a man treat her like this, and yet this one had her completely at his beck and call. And he only weighed eight pounds.

How would she survive without Dan? Nothing had fazed him. Whether it was getting up in the middle of the night, changing an explosive nappy or feeding Jenny chocolate digestives whilst she wept, he'd just taken it all in his stride.

And now he had left them to go back to work. Jenny was suspicious. It wasn't that he'd exactly skipped out of the door that morning, but he hadn't looked devastated, either.

'We can do this,' she said to Henry, trying not to dribble snot and tears onto his babygro. 'You just need to work with me.' And work with her he did. If by 'work with me' she had meant, 'wee all over the changing table'.

It felt like they'd just dozed off again when the doorbell rang. It was a huge bouquet from Eva, with a card that read: '*Congratulations on adding to the next generation! If you change your mind about the blog, we can find you something else when you return.*'

Well, if anything was going to get Jenny out of her pyjamas and in front of the laptop, it was the thought of the 'something else' Eva would otherwise fob her off with. Anyway, it was a good thing she was up as she needed to shower this morning. Gail was coming, even though she was now more than a week overdue. She was the only one of them still pregnant: Antonia had had to have an emergency C-section three weeks before her due date, and Naomi had gone into labour five days ago, pulling off the perfect birth twelve hours later. According to Naomi's 400-word Facebook post, baby Daisy had been delivered in water, accompanied by some kind of whale music. Naomi and John were now in their post-birth bonding period. Meanwhile, Jenny was in her post-birth pyjama period. Why had she invited someone here on her first day flying solo?

She'd invited Ruth too, but Ruth hadn't even replied to her text. Two weeks ago, Jenny might have been irritated by that. Now she assumed that Ruth was lying prone somewhere under a heap of dirty babygros and would call when she escaped. She *must* have had the baby by now.

Maybe it was good that it would be just herself and Gail: she could really get to know her and assess how useful she would be for blog fodder. Remembering the smart clothes Gail had worn to the antenatal class, Jenny decided that she would also need to change out of her pyjamas.

✦

At about ten o'clock, Henry fell asleep, feeding. Jenny placed him in his baby chair as if he were an unexploded bomb and crept up to the bathroom, carrying him in it. She knew she wasn't supposed to, but how else was she meant to shower? Gail was due at eleven, so if Henry stayed asleep, Jenny should be showered and dressed in plenty of time. Easy.

Henry decided to wait until she was naked, wet and fully lathered before beginning to wail like an air-raid siren. Throwing open the shower cubicle door, she tried to make it across the tiled floor as quickly as her tender stomach and wet, sliding feet would allow. Carefully, she crouched down beside him, trying to see through the face wash that was stinging her eyes, and attempted to pacify him without having to pick him up and cover him in Radox. When no amount of shushing and chair rocking would do, she gave in and picked him up. With a deadly accuracy, he found her nipple and helped himself to a quick snack. This in turn made her yelp in surprise and pain, which started him crying all over again.

This time, it was impossible to calm him down. Which is why, an hour later, she opened the door to a punctual Gail with wet but unwashed hair and wearing only a dressing gown.

Gail, on the other hand, was wearing yet another combination of shirt and tailored trousers; she wasn't dressing down on maternity leave. 'Interesting look you're going for there.'

'I call it post-natal chic.' Jenny ushered her in. 'It's surprisingly wearable.' Normally, she would be mortified for anyone but her closest friends to see her like this. But Henry had finally gone back to sleep in the last few minutes and rather than use the time to get dressed, she had been hovering at the door, waiting to let Gail in before she rang the doorbell. She was terrified that any sudden noise might wake him. 'Can you watch Henry for two minutes whilst I go upstairs and change into something less comfortable?'

When she got back, Henry was still sleeping. Gail was sitting on the sofa, checking messages on her mobile. When Jenny walked in, she clicked it off and looked up. 'So, an actual baby, then. How was the birth?'

Despite her promise to smash the maternity code of silence and proclaim to all other women how awful childbirth really was, Jenny knew that she couldn't do that to Gail. It would be cruel when she had no way of backing out. 'Don't ask me that question. Maybe ask Naomi – she seems to be better at it than me.'

Gail smiled. 'Yes. I've seen the birth report. Have you heard anything from Antonia about her birth?'

'Only that she had a C-section, same as me, the day before yesterday, and that she had a baby girl. They've called her Jessica.'

Gail tapped her short, glossy fingernails on her mobile case. 'So, no more swanning around having lunch for a while, then? Still, I'm sure she'll have an army of people waiting on her. Although I can't imagine Geoff changing many nappies.'

Jenny was impressed that Gail could remember Antonia's husband's name. 'No, he didn't seem to be particularly hands-on. Unless he was googling birth facts on his phone the whole time. I think she said her mum was going to stay for a few days. Do you want a drink?'

'A cold drink would be good. I'll come out with you.'

Gail followed her to the kitchen, leaving Henry in the lounge on his own. Jenny had no idea what accident could possibly befall him sleeping in his baby chair, but she wasn't about to find out. She sloshed orange juice into two glasses in record time and practically pushed Gail back into the lounge. Was he still sleeping? Breathing? Yes, he was.

'Have you heard from Ruth?' Gail sat back down on the sofa. 'She's the only one who didn't comment on Naomi's post.'

'No, I haven't. I was going to ask you that. I don't even know whether she's had her baby or not.'

Gail shrugged. 'Maybe they're busy seeing relatives.'

'Maybe. Dan hasn't heard from David, either, so that could be the case. Speaking of the New Dads, have you banned your partner from working away until the birth? I met a woman at the hospital whose husband was working in the city and didn't make it back in time. She was not impressed.'

Gail put her glass down on the coffee table and adjusted the collar on her shirt. 'Joe? No, I haven't. It doesn't matter if he's not there.'

'Really?' There was no way Jenny could have got through her birth experience without Dan's calm reassurance. At one point, he had actually needed to remind her to breathe. 'Surely you don't want to do it alone?'

'No. My mum will be there.'

Her mum? Jenny was close to her own mum, but she was glad she hadn't been there for the labour. For a start, she might have been a little shocked to hear the full repertoire of her daughter's bad language.

'Doesn't your partner – Joe – *want* to be there?'

Gail sighed, irritably. 'It's more about whether he'd be any use. Not everyone is like you and Dan. Lots of people choose different birth partners now.'

Jenny resented Gail's tone. 'Oh, I know that. Naomi talked about a doula and Antonia planned to have a private midwife. I don't know if she did in the end.'

'An extra midwife would have been rather redundant in the circumstances, though, wouldn't she? I'm not surprised Antonia was "too posh to push" in the actual event.'

Jenny bristled. 'The baby was three weeks early, so I'm guessing it was probably an emergency operation, like mine. And she's still in hospital.' She waved a hand around her navel. 'Plus, this is no walk in the park, believe me.'

Gail held up her hands. 'Sorry. I wasn't suggesting it was.'

'Have you asked Joe whether he wants to be there?'

'Very briefly.' Gail's tone made it clear that this topic was over. 'So, any top tips you want to share?'

'Yes,' said Jenny. 'Go back in time and hire a surrogate.'

✦

Gail had left and Jenny was making a salad for lunch when Henry woke up with a yell. She attempted to keep cutting tomatoes with one hand as she jiggled him in the other arm. It was impossible. What could she prepare one-handed? Maryland cookies.

The card from Eva's flowers mocked her from the sideboard, so she returned to the sitting room with Henry and the biscuits and turned on her laptop. Then Henry opened his mouth and deposited a pool of undigested milk into her lap. *More washing.* No, she was not going to be side-tracked. Just mop it up with a baby wipe and carry on.

What should she begin with? Maybe just a sneaky look at Facebook. There were a couple of photos of a fresh-faced Naomi holding baby Daisy, and a post from Lucy raving about a new club she had reviewed for the magazine.

Even though Jenny was viciously jealous that Lucy had her job, the last thing she felt like doing right then was shuffling around a packed dance floor.

Obviously, that would change soon.

Gail hadn't been a great source of ideas for *The Undercover Mother*. In her defence, she hadn't had her baby yet, but Jenny had the impression she wasn't really a sharer. It also seemed pretty pointless trying to cultivate a relationship with someone who was going back to work in a few weeks. For the next six months, Jenny needed someone to meet up with during the day who could regale her with the hilarious mishaps of life with a newborn. Perhaps she should try Ruth again – if she could ever get hold of her.

Bored with Facebook, she checked her emails. Unlike her working days, there were only five waiting unread. Two were baby congratulations from former contacts, two were advertising special offers on shoes.

But the last one was an email from Ruth and David. The subject read: '*Our Sad News*'.

CHAPTER EIGHT

For the first few days, The Boy slept for hours on end and I congratulated myself on having given birth to such an easy baby. Within two weeks, that babymoon period was over and so was any hope of a complete sleep cycle.

Even getting him to go to sleep is a Herculean feat. We take it in turns to walk up and down the hallway, rocking and shushing and praying for his eyes to close. Even when we've cracked it, the job isn't over – we still have to lower him into his Moses basket. Seemingly, his bottom has a pre-installed parking sensor: if it gets within 15mm of the mattress, it causes his eyes to open and his mouth to follow.

I can't understand it. Right now, I would give anything for someone to feed me warm milk, tuck me up in a cot and sing me a lullaby. I'd even settle for a glass of water and a park bench if you could guarantee me an uninterrupted six hours…

From *The Undercover Mother*

✦

When fitting a child's car seat, you must make sure the seatbelt passes through all the correct guides. It must go through the blue guides if it is a rearward-facing seat, and through the red guides if it is a forward-facing seat. It should not be yanked several times whilst you swear like a navvy. You should not need to cry about being a 'prisoner in your own home'.

Henry was six weeks old and, if life was going to get back to normal, Jenny needed to be able to take him out on her own. At last she was feeling up to driving and Dan had shown her again and again how to do this. So why was it so difficult? *Damn thing.*

Fumbling with the stupid seatbelt, she tried not to think about the fact she hadn't yet driven alone with Henry in the back. Already, it had taken about two hours to get ready to leave the house. Nappies, wipes, spare baby clothes for sick/poo/dribble emergencies; she used to pack less for a weekend away. Thank God for breastfeeding – how women managed to also coordinate sterilised bottles was beyond her – but she was also mildly terrified about getting her boobs out in public. They hadn't seen sunlight since Ayia Napa, circa 2001.

The seatbelt clicked into place and Jenny kissed Henry in triumph. They were on their way.

When she got to the café, Antonia and Naomi were already there, both looking remarkably slim. Jenny felt ashamed of her maternity leggings and was glad they couldn't see she was still wearing her post-birth knickers. Her mum had bought her the waist-hugger pants after the birth, as normal knickers were too uncomfortable on her scar. 'I'm not wearing those bloody things,' she'd scoffed. But then she'd tried them and *crikey* they were comfy.

'Hello, ladies,' she said, taking the obligatory look at their newborns and making the appropriate remarks about cuteness, whilst being secretly pleased that Henry was obviously far more attractive than Jessica and Daisy. 'How are you both?'

'Bloody knackered, darling.' Antonia kissed Jenny on both cheeks, leaving an aroma of expensive face cream. Jenny smelled more like nappy cream. 'That bloody woman at antenatal didn't tell us that they never bloody sleep.' But she didn't *look* like she hadn't slept; there were women on the front covers of magazines who looked less glamorous.

But thank God Jenny wasn't the only one struggling with a persistent insomniac. 'You, too? I think I was up about forty times last night.' Although 'up' seemed rather a strong euphemism for the state of half-conscious, semi-prone staggering from cot to bed that had been her nocturnal activity.

'I think we're all rather sleep-deprived. Wine?' Antonia raised a perfectly proportioned eyebrow and a waiter appeared.

If only. 'I still don't know if I'm allowed to or not while I'm breastfeeding.' The NHS leaflet said *no,* but Jenny's desperate Google research said *yes.* Last night she'd considered drinking four fingers of whisky in the hope it would filter through her boob to Henry and make him sleep. 'Better stick to orange juice, please.'

'Actually, you *are* allowed a glass of wine, although *I* am completely abstaining.' Naomi flicked a plait over her shoulder and fiddled with the leather thong around her neck. It appeared to have something hanging from it that was indented with a baby footprint. Obviously, she was going to be an expert on breastfeeding as well as birth. 'Have you tried fennel tea? It helps with your milk.'

Antonia adjusted the neckline of her wrap dress. 'You're doing better than me. I managed about five days before I couldn't bear the pain any longer.'

'It's a lot more difficult than I thought,' admitted Jenny. 'My nipples feel like I've massaged them with broken glass.'

'Really? But it's easy.' Naomi leaned forwards to fold back a crocheted pram blanket and stroke baby Daisy's cheek. 'Daisy latched on immediately after birth.'

Antonia rolled her eyes at Jenny.

A smart, trendy pram appeared next to them, followed by an equally smart, trendy Gail. 'Hi, all. Where are we parking these things?' She slid into the seat next to Jenny. 'Have you ordered?' She nodded at a waiter and mouthed, 'House red.' Then she turned back to the others. 'Sorry I'm a little late. I had a call from the office.'

Jenny felt like she'd stepped into the twilight zone. No one would guess that these women were brand new mothers. Antonia looked like she belonged in a Maybelline advert, Naomi was bossing the breastfeeding and Gail was already taking work calls. Meanwhile,

Jenny wanted a round of applause for getting out of the house fully dressed. What was she doing wrong?

'How are you managing to work already?' she asked. 'I can't seem to get anything done and I'm trying to write a… uh… novel whilst I'm on maternity leave.' She had decided not to tell them about the blog just yet. They might start acting differently if they knew she was using them for research. 'Sometimes I'm still in my pyjamas at ten o'clock.' Or twelve.

Antonia shuddered. 'Last week, a colleague of Geoff's collected him for a breakfast meeting before I'd brushed my hair and done my make-up. I was mortified.'

Jenny tried to imagine Antonia with messy hair and no make-up. *Nope. Can't do it.*

'My mum visits most days and I have some time then,' said Gail. 'She's cooking all my meals and watching Jake if I want a nap.'

'I would kill for an afternoon nap.' Jenny had often had a little 'disco nap' if she had a big night out planned. That had gone out of the window, along with hot cups of coffee. At least she knew now what Toilet Woman had meant about enjoying hot drinks whilst she could.

'Has anyone heard anything more from Ruth?' asked Gail.

'I have,' Jenny said.

David's original email had been brief. *'We're very sad to tell you that our little girl didn't make it. We will be in touch soon.'* It was a week later that he'd sent another email, explaining what had happened. The baby hadn't moved for almost a day and Ruth had been concerned. The midwife had come to visit and hadn't been able to find a heartbeat. Ruth and David had had to go into hospital to get the confirmation of what they already knew: the baby's heart had stopped. The doctors thought that the umbilical cord had somehow been obstructed and the baby had been deprived of oxygen. In all other respects, she'd been a perfectly healthy baby.

Jenny had sent Ruth and David an email saying how sorry she was and had then called her a couple of weeks later. 'We only had a very brief conversation.'

'How is the poor darling?' asked Antonia.

Jenny shrugged. 'I'm not really sure. She sounded strained on the phone, said she was just taking things a day at a time. Actually, I'm going to see her soon.'

'We mustn't lose touch with her.' Naomi was emphatic. 'I'd hate her to think that we didn't want to see her. Can I come with you?'

'She may not want to see you,' warned Gail. 'She certainly doesn't want to be seeing small babies right now.'

'I wasn't planning on taking Henry,' Jenny replied, quickly. Did Gail think she was stupid?

For a few moments, they were quiet. Naomi glanced at Daisy, Gail rocked Jake's pram and Antonia readjusted the blanket covering Jessica. *Ruth should be here too.* Jenny watched Henry's lips twitching in his sleep and tried to imagine how it would feel to... She stopped herself. It was too painful. *Don't think about it.*

Instead she focused on how she was going to get blog material out of these three. Where would she find any humour? There was nothing funny about women who had babies and managed very well. Plus, it was making her feel more than a little inadequate. *Just change the subject.*

'Anyone started a diet yet?'

'I don't think we should be dieting so soon, should we?' Naomi smoothed her loose smock top across her flat stomach. 'Anyway, I think the breastfeeding is doing its job. I seem to be losing the weight without trying.'

Avoiding the urge to stick her fork in Naomi's eye, Jenny sat up and tried to suck her belly in. 'Not for me. Breastfeeding makes me want to eat anything I can get my hands on. Speaking of which, are we going to order some lunch?'

They had only just ordered their meals when the babies started to wake up to be fed. Hot and clammy, Jenny realised that she was going to have to feed Henry. In public. At home, she could strip to the waist and have several attempts at sticking him on and off before she found a position that didn't make her toes curl; here, she would just have to go for it. Pulling her breastfeeding top apart, she held her breath and pinned him on as quickly and about as accurately as a tail on the donkey. Nose to nipple. Nose to nipple. Agony.

Watching her wince, Antonia raised her glass to Jenny. 'You're a brave woman to keep at it, darling. I remember that torture only too well.'

'Are you sure he's latching on properly? It shouldn't be painful.' To prove her point, Naomi lifted her smock top and slipped Daisy onto her own breast as easily as the stupid bloody video Antenatal Sally had shown them. Jenny added Naomi to her list of people to kill.

'Yep. That's what the health visitor said.' Jenny yelped as Henry's gums clamped round her sore nipple. How come Naomi looked so bloody serene? If it wasn't for the outline of Daisy's head under her top, you wouldn't even know what she was doing. Jenny gritted her teeth. 'She also said my nipples would harden up eventually and it would stop hurting so much.'

Gail grimaced. 'Oooh, hard nipples? Something else to look forward to.' She straightened her blazer. 'Piles, stretch marks, wetting yourself every time you laugh. Childbirth really is the gift that keeps on giving.'

'How do all these movie stars look so glamorous only days after giving birth?' Jenny had tortured herself looking though old copies of *Hello!* magazine at the baby-weighing clinic the day before.

'They have staff,' Gail replied.

Antonia leaned forwards. 'I read somewhere that they have liposuction straight after the birth.'

'Really? Can that be true? I wish I could have had a bit of that.' Jenny could understand why she'd put on weight around her belly – to cushion the baby – but why had the size of her backside increased so much?

'What about me?' said Gail. 'I'm going back to work soon, and I can just see the looks from my staff when I roll in on the Monday morning. I don't think I'm anywhere near fitting into any of my work suits.'

Jenny had further depressed herself by trying on a pair of work trousers the previous week. The two sides of the zip had been so far apart they needed a passport to meet up.

'Are you really going back so soon?' asked Naomi. 'I thought you might have changed your mind.'

Gail shook her head. 'A large part of being an investment fund manager is meeting with financial analysts to stay on top of the market. If I'm away too long, I'll be no good to my clients. Frankly, I also need the money. Especially if I have to go out and buy a set of fat suits.'

Jenny wanted to ask about Joe: wouldn't he be supporting Gail for a while? In all the communication they'd had so far, Gail had barely mentioned him. Could she ask?

Just then, the food arrived and Jenny tried to jiggle Henry around a bit so that the waiter could put her plate down without getting a full frontal. She may as well not have bothered, as Henry chose that moment to fall asleep and drop his head back dramatically, exposing her oversized nipple to anyone who cared to look.

Jenny pulled her top back over her chest then, as if holding a live grenade, placed Henry back into his pram. Sitting back, she realised her shoulders were hunched up almost to her ears and tried to make herself relax. The other three seemed to be coping so well. Naomi was even supporting Daisy with her right hand whilst eating a superfood salad with her left. Jenny wanted to lie face down on the table and go to sleep. In a plate of chips.

Maybe she just needed a couple more weeks to get the hang of it all. So she wasn't a natural like Naomi. She would just have to try a bit harder. Henry was only six weeks old. In a real job, she wouldn't have even completed the induction period yet. It had probably been the same when she'd started on the magazine.

Except, on the magazine, she had been given some useful training, not left to fend for herself with a handful of baby manuals and a brief meeting with a health visitor. Why hadn't Antenatal Sally taught useful skills, like how to eat lunch with one hand, dress a baby octopus and survive on five hours' sleep? She should have ditched the antenatal class and spent a week on special ops with the SAS.

An alarm started to beep on Gail's mobile. 'That's my cue to go,' she said. 'I promised I'd dial into a conference call from home this afternoon.' She stood up and put a £20 note on the table. 'That's should cover my bill and a tip. Sorry I have to dash. I'll see you all soon.' She waved and was gone.

'I should go, too, really,' said Jenny. 'I promised to visit the girls at the magazine and introduce them to Henry.' This was a lie, but she had a sudden urge to be somewhere where she knew what she was doing. She could check in with Eva, see what she thought about the blog – and make sure that no one had started using her desk.

Antonia motioned to the waiter for the bill. 'Would you both like to come to me next time, ladies? It might be more comfortable than sitting around a table.'

Jenny rummaged around her cavernous changing bag, trying to locate her purse. She wasn't particularly thrilled about the thought of seeing them again so soon, but what else was she going to do for blog ideas? Plus, she wouldn't mind having a nose around Antonia's house: it was bound to be huge. 'Found it!' she said, pulling out her purse and bringing two nappies with it. 'It would be lovely to meet at yours. Just let me know when. Will you let Gail know, or shall I?' She stuffed the nappies back into the bag.

Antonia shrugged. 'Feel free to ask her, but she may be too busy having *important meetings*.'

Jenny glanced at her watch. It was 2 p.m. Eva was usually back in her office by now, which meant that Jenny could have an important meeting of her own.

CHAPTER NINE

When I was pregnant, I imagined our new family life as a romantic film montage: the baby lying between us in bed, or the three of us rolling around on the rug together, laughing, or my husband and me pushing a pram around the park with my perfect hair flowing in the wind.

Spoiler alert: it is not like this.

For a start, The Boy can't lie between us in bed because he rotates himself ninety degrees to stick his feet painfully between my lower vertebrae. We never lie on the rug together because it's covered in crumbs from the slice of toast I have been trying to eat since breakfast, and he regards his pram as solitary confinement, which means I have to balance him in one arm whilst trying to push the pram with the other. And in none of these scenarios is my hair looking perfect…

From *The Undercover Mother*

✦

As soon as Jenny walked through the door, women appeared from everywhere to worship Henry. Jenny knew how handsome he was, but it was gratifying to have it confirmed.

Eva came out of her office to find out what the noise was. 'Hello, stranger.' She stopped and looked at Jenny intently. 'You look different.'

If Jenny had felt self-conscious about her clothes over lunch, it was much worse now. 'Do I?'

Eva looked closer. 'Has your hair always been... *wavy*?' She said the word 'wavy' as if it was an insult.

Jenny's hand went to her head defensively. 'I usually straighten it for work.'

'Hmm.' Eva shrugged. 'How's life on the outside?'

Jenny smiled. 'Good. Good. Little bit repetitive at times. But good. Are you missing me?' She hoped fervently that the answer was yes.

'Every day. Although each month when Lucy files her column on time, my loyalties are divided.'

Jenny ignored this joke. What were deadlines for, if not to be met at the last minute? 'This is Henry.' She held him aloft proudly, like a homemade sponge cake, although she knew better than to expect any kind of infant worship from Eva.

'Ah. Very nice, well done.'

'Have you been looking at the blog posts? What do you think?' Jenny was proud that she had written anything at all. Sleep deprivation was not the mother of creativity.

'Ye-es. Shall we have a quick chat about it?' Eva motioned towards her office. 'Maureen won't mind watching the baby for a moment, will you?'

'Not at all, I've been waiting for a cuddle!' Maureen was Eva's PA and substitute mother to most of the office.

Jenny handed Henry over a little reluctantly and followed Eva.

'I like your writing, of course.' Shutting the door behind them, Eva cut straight to the point. 'And it *is* mildly funny. But it's just not very...' She paused for the right word. 'Exciting.'

Jenny laughed. 'I don't want to shatter any illusions here, but there aren't many James Bond moments for a stay-at-home mum.'

'Well, that's what I assumed when you suggested it. So what's the point? Why would people want to read it?'

'You should look at the comments.' Jenny had been surprised herself by the reaction she'd had so far. Other mums had been writing that they agreed with her, that she had made them laugh and that she had made them feel 'normal'. Although some of the comments included acronyms such as DD and SO and BLW and, at first, she hadn't had a clue what they were talking about. 'People like it because it's realistic – it's the same as "Girl About Town". Women read that to feel like they aren't the only ones meeting dodgy blokes and spilling wine over themselves in equally dodgy nightclubs. Mums are the same, although it's worse for them because it feels like every single thing they do is being judged.' Jenny had found article after article online that told parents exactly what they should, and shouldn't, be doing. When she got her column in the magazine, it would tell everyone they should do things their own way, and to stick a teething ring in the mouth of anyone who said otherwise.

'Ye-es.' Eva still didn't look convinced. Staring at Jenny, she stroked her lip. Jenny knew better than to interrupt: this was Eva's thinking face. Interestingly, it was quite similar to Henry's weeing face. 'I think we need more on the other mothers – your new crew. It worked perfectly in your old column, writing about the lives of the girls you knocked around with – really fleshed it out.' Eva sat back in her chair. 'That's what you need to do.'

'You must have read my mind!' Jenny lied, relieved that Eva was still sufficiently interested in her idea to make a suggestion. 'I've already got a group of women I met at antenatal and I was just going to ask your opinion on including more about them in the blog!' She beamed with fake confidence.

'How fortuitous.' Eva's eyes showed that she knew Jenny was lying. 'We have an advertisers' event next month. You could come along and work some magic on our corporate friends. If you can get some sponsors for your idea, we can talk.' She looked at Jenny's hair again. Then at her leggings. 'If you're feeling up to it.'

'Great idea.' Jenny's heart sank. 'I'll be there.'

A knock on the door and Lucy's face appeared, her annoyingly beautiful long hair swinging. 'Sorry to interrupt, E,' she said. *Since when was she shortening Eva's three-letter name?* 'But I wondered if you'd remembered to ask Jenny about her book?'

'Ah, yes.' Eva nodded. 'Thanks for reminding me, Lucy.'

Jenny wanted to ask why she wasn't shortening her new best buddy's name to 'L'.

Eva turned back to Jenny with a smile. 'I was wondering if you'd mind giving Lucy a copy of your contacts book.'

✦

Jenny slammed the cupboard shut and banged two mugs down onto the kitchen counter. She had completely forgotten to go to the supermarket after her trip to the office, and Dan was now eating a mixing bowl full of Shredded Wheat and Crunchy Nut Cornflakes for his dinner. He looked like he regretted accepting her offer of a cup of tea.

'Can you believe it? Not only has she stolen my job, she now wants a copy of my black book. My *bible*.' She paused for emphasis. 'It has taken me years to build that up. The names and numbers of everyone who organises any kind of social event in the city. Every bar owner, club manager and tour manager. I've even got personal mobile or home numbers for most of them.' A fresh wave of anger hit. 'When I started, all my predecessor left me was a sheet of A4 paper with a list of venues and her own unintelligible rating system. And Eva – I mean "*E*", apparently—' she mimicked Lucy's breathy, enthusiastic voice '—Eva thinks I should just hand it over to Lucy.'

'Mm.' Dan mumbled through a mouthful of cereal, then swallowed. 'Maybe she just thought you wouldn't be using it at the moment. You know, being on maternity leave.'

'That's irrelevant! The book doesn't belong to the magazine. It's mine! I kept those notes on everywhere I went, everyone I met.

That book, those names, those numbers – it's everything I've done as "Girl About Town". It's my life! It's who I am!'

Dan looked confused. 'You're a large, black address book with a silver star on it?'

Jenny laid her head on the table. 'You don't understand, either!'

'I'm trying, Jen. Really I am.' He laid down his spoon and put a hand on her shoulder. 'Don't bite me when I say this, but… do you really need it any more?'

Jenny's head shot up again. 'Of course I'm going to need it! What happens when I go back to work and she's already wormed her way in with all the people who used to save the best tables and seats for me?'

'Okay, Jen, humour me for a minute.' Dan was using the calm tone of a police negotiator trying to talk someone down from a window ledge. 'Because I don't understand what the problem is. Before we decided to have a baby, you were complaining that you were getting too old to write a "singles life" column. Right?'

Jenny gave a small nod. She didn't want to commit herself until she saw where he was going with this.

'But now Eva has given the column to someone else, you've decided that you don't want to lose it?'

'Yes. No. Well, kind of, but…'

Dan held up his hand. 'But you're writing a blog about being a mum, which you're hoping will become a column in the magazine and then you can write that instead?'

'Yes. But it might not work. Eva hasn't made me any promises. I might do all this work and she could say no.'

'Do you enjoy writing it?'

Did she enjoy writing it? It was new. It was challenging. She found herself thinking about it when she wasn't writing it. 'I think I do.'

Dan shrugged. 'Then we'll work it out. If Eva doesn't go for it, you can write the blog until it does take off, and we'll just have to live on bread and water for a while.'

'But it's a *blog*.'

Dan looked confused. 'I already said that.'

'I'm a journalist, Dan, not a blogger. I get *paid* to write. I'm a *professional*.'

Then Henry started to cry and Jenny stomped up the stairs, muttering about people changing your life for you without even asking.

✦

That night in bed, Jenny told Dan what Eva had said about the blog. 'I need to step it up a level,' she said. 'Eva looked decidedly unimpressed with it so far. I need to make it more exciting – especially now I'm competing with Little Miss Perky.'

Dan nodded, slowly. 'What did you actually say to Eva about your contacts book?'

'That I'd try and look it out for her. What else could I say?' She turned to face him. 'I'm not going to give her the actual book, though. I'll buy another one and copy some of it over. I'm not giving her *everything*.'

'Good idea.' Dan looked relieved that she hadn't recommenced her rant from earlier.

'Eva thinks I should write about the other mums in the blog. Like the Girl Crew I used to have for "Girl About Town".' She and her crazy friends from her twenties had had some good times together over the years. They'd visited en masse when Henry was brand new, but they were all still single and had been out until the early hours of the morning; they'd seemed oblivious to Jenny's own exhaustion. Obviously, she would just pick up with them again once she had got the hang of this motherhood business.

'That sounds like an interesting idea.' Dan was clearly keeping his language as non-committal as possible so that he didn't say the wrong thing. 'Will you be writing about personal stuff? Have you asked their permission yet?'

Jenny looked a little uncomfortable. 'Not exactly. I was planning on giving them pseudonyms and just writing about things that they do and say. If they know about it, they might not like it.'

Dan gave a lengthy whistle. 'I bet they wouldn't, particularly that posh one. Antonia, is it? Or that scary one who came on her own. She's got enough balls to have conceived without the absent boyfriend.'

Jenny sat up in bed, her creative brain whirring into action. 'Husband, you're a genius! You've got it! Posh, Scary…' She thought for a moment. 'Naomi is a yoga teacher, so she must be pretty sporty, and Ruth is ginger! Well, auburn,' she conceded. 'They're the flippin' Spice Girls!'

Dan sighed and turned over, realising Jenny would now be on a roll that could last some time. 'Okay, Baby Spice, I need to go to sleep now. Hey,' he turned back again, 'am I going to be in it, too?'

Jenny closed her eyes. 'Shush now, time to sleep.'

Dan was soon snoring, but Jenny's mind was racing. The Spice Girls angle could really work, especially as there were five of them. Perfect. Except for Ruth. She couldn't write about Ruth. Could she?

And then there was this advertisers' event to think about. As well as putting some impressive posts on the blog, she would need to get herself back into some kind of physical shape before then. Sexist as it was, most of the attendees at these events were men, and she'd have much more chance of winning their marketing pounds if she looked good.

If the look on Eva's face was anything to go by, she also needed to sort out her clothes and hair. She was in real danger of veering into 'She's let herself go' territory. She'd seen it happen to her sister. Within two months of giving birth, Claire had been living in jeans and sweatshirts, her hair in a permanent ponytail. Being a mum didn't mean you had to dress like one.

Last week, Antonia had texted Jenny for her opinion on two dresses she was thinking of buying for her first post-baby night out. Jenny would give her a call and ask where she'd found them. Job done.

CHAPTER TEN

My first mistake was eating for two during pregnancy. Or maybe for three.

Fat has accumulated in new places. As well as an ample bottom, and the extra inches around my middle, I've got the upper thighs of an Olympic cyclist.

Sporty, however, sprang back to slim within hours of giving birth, although I do wonder whether that's because she's a decade younger. She also swears by Buggy Bootcamp, which apparently involves exercising and pushing a buggy at the same time. The closest I get to that level of multitasking is eating a packet of biscuits whilst I push a trolley around the supermarket. Even Scary's bought a running machine so that she can work out without leaving Baby Scary, and Posh has a personal trainer at her glamorous gym. I've seen her on the way there in her designer Lycra and it just makes me want to reach for another Hobnob…

From *The Undercover Mother*

✦

The shopping centre was empty apart from a few bored assistants. Irritating piped music followed Jenny as she looked at the window displays, trying not to be intimidated by the flat-stomached mannequins. Everything was so short and tight. She wanted generous and forgiving. Was that too much to ask?

It had been a mistake telling Antonia she needed new clothes to accommodate her temporary shape. Because, of course, Antonia had offered to go with her. Antonia shopped in the kinds of places that made Jenny's credit card tremble in fear; and, more importantly, Jenny didn't want Antonia seeing her naked.

It wasn't vanity – Kate Moss had never been looking over her shoulder at Jenny in fear for her career – but pre-baby Jenny had known how to dress for her shape: fitted at the top, A-line at the bottom. Now, eight weeks after the birth, she had a lumpy, bumpy stomach to accommodate, too. Wearing anything remotely clingy made her middle resemble cake mixture. To be fair, cake mixture was what it had seen most of in the last few months.

Hence she was here an hour early. She could finish the trying on and be safely perusing shoes and bags before Antonia got there. Now she just needed to go in and start.

In the first store, the clothes were displayed so closely together she could barely make her way through. Henry's pram caught every dress they passed, and the assistant watched her pityingly as she careered into one clothes carousel after another, like an oversized ball in a pinball machine. In the end, she gave up and left. She hadn't liked their clothes, anyway.

The second one had more aisle space and she found a few things that might work. The days were gone when she could tell by looking at something whether or not it would fit. Now she didn't even know what size she was. To hell with it. She grabbed three different sizes in everything which looked roughly the right shape.

Changing-room cubicles aren't known for their spaciousness and this one would definitely not have room for a pram. 'Why don't you leave it outside the changing rooms?' suggested the assistant.

Jenny looked at her incredulously. Leave Henry outside, on the shop floor? Where did she think they were? The 1950s? 'It's okay,' she mumbled. 'I'll manage.'

The assistant appraised the pile of clothes in various sizes that Jenny had thrown hopefully across the roof of the pram. 'You can only take five items in.'

Only five? This was going to take all day.

She picked five hangers from the top of the pile, left the rest with the assistant and headed for the opposite end of the changing rooms. After a bit of manoeuvring, she managed to poke the pram half in and half out of the cubicle, leaving a gap in the curtain wide enough for her to see Henry, and anyone else in the changing room to see her cellulite.

First attempt was a dark blue skirt in the largest size. Far better for her self-esteem to have to ask for a smaller size than a bigger one. It didn't fit. She managed to get it on (the stretchy fabric lulling her into a false sense of security) by gradually wiggling it up past her hips. But then it wouldn't zip up. She sucked in her stomach as tightly as she could, but the cruel mirror showed that depriving herself of oxygen was having no effect. Even unfastened, there were stretch marks across the front of the skirt which made it look as if her hips were fighting to escape out of the side pockets. Carefully, she peeled it off again.

Maybe it was a tiny size on the wrong hanger? She checked the label. It wasn't. No way was she going up another size from that one. Maybe a dress would be better.

There was a dress, but only in the middle and smaller size. She called out to the assistant. 'Excuse me, could you bring me the larger dress, please?'

No response. Louder, she called again. Still nothing. The music was ramped up so high she probably couldn't hear her. To get it herself, she would have to get dressed again. Or just try the medium one. It was a different shape from the skirt. Maybe it would be okay?

This time, she managed to get it on and zipped up, at least. But that damn mirror made her look like a 'before' picture from a Weight Watchers advert. She couldn't wear this to the advertisers' lunch – it would put them off their sausage rolls. *Just get it off and get out of here.* This wasn't fun.

She wriggled the dress downwards but couldn't get it over her hips without straining the zip dangerously. It would have to go over her head. But she hadn't taken into account the increased size of her breasts.

She struggled to emerge, Houdini-like, from the bottom of the now-hateful dress. Was this a private hell or had she managed to draw a crowd? The pounding pop music and her face covered in material meant she had no idea.

Then Henry woke up and started to cry.

Rocking the pram with one hip, kneading breast flesh under and out of the unforgiving waistband… it was like being the warm-up act at a cut-price lap dancing club. Resisting the urge to fall down next to Henry and join in with his screams, Jenny swore in the most soothing tones she could muster. 'Sh, sh, it'll be o—bugger!… Mummy won't be long… bollocks!'

Something gave. She was out. And alone, thank God. She pulled her leggings back on gratefully and bolted from the store.

Maybe she did need Antonia's help after all. Right now, she needed coffee. No cake.

✦

The café was busy with shoppers starting their day. Jenny joined the queue and looked around to see if there was a table with room for the pram. Then she saw them, sitting in the corner. Antonia. And a handsome younger man.

They were deep in conversation. He had leaned in conspiratorially and she was hanging on his every word. Although all of the chairs and tables were full, this didn't seem like an idle chat between two strangers who had agreed to share. Smart and stylish as usual, Antonia had her hair swept back in a glossy ponytail. In a well-cut suit, the young man made a fitting companion. Would they want her to join them? Maybe not.

Jenny backed out of the queue and left the café. The man was probably just a friend Antonia had met by chance. There was no reason for suspicion. She would meet Antonia in half an hour, as agreed, and find out who he was then.

✦

A large latte, (skinny) muffin and thirty minutes later, Jenny arrived at the department store to find Antonia browsing in the underwear department, holding a cerise-pink lacy bra.

'Lucky Geoff – that looks sexy.'

Antonia turned. 'He doesn't deserve it.' She kissed Jenny on both cheeks. 'Hello, darling. Shall we get started or do you want to get a coffee first?'

Even Jenny couldn't manage another one so soon. 'I've just had one, but I'm happy to come with you. Haven't you had a drink?'

Antonia shook her head. 'No, I just arrived. But I don't need one, either. I had tea with my mother when I dropped off Jessica with her.' She put the bra back on the clothes rail. 'Let's make a start on finding you something fabulous to wear!'

Jenny trailed behind Antonia as she selected and rejected different outfits – she had a real knack for putting things together. Jenny made the right noises about the skirts, shirts and trousers, but she was more interested in finding out about Café Man. Why had Antonia lied?

This time, they left the pram outside the changing room and Antonia followed her in, holding Henry.

'I saw Gail last week.'

Jenny was the other side of the curtain, fastening buttons. 'Really? Where?'

'At one of Geoff's work functions. The company she works for looks after Geoff's company's investments.'

Jenny stepped out of the cubicle, wearing a trousers and shirt combination. At least it fitted, but it wasn't going to set the fashion world alight. 'Really?' she said again. 'How come you've never seen her before? I thought she'd worked for that company for years.'

Antonia looked her up and down. 'Put that on the "maybe" pile. Try something more fitted. I've seen her once or twice.'

Something didn't add up. Gail had denied knowing Antonia at the first antenatal class. Jenny retreated into the cubicle. 'Did you say hello?'

'No. She was with a man. They were deep in conversation. I didn't like to interrupt.' Antonia sounded bored with the whole subject.

Jenny stuck her head out from behind the curtain. 'That could have been Joe! Did he look like he could be her boyfriend?'

Antonia laughed derisively. 'I doubt it, darling. He was about thirty years older than her. Anyway, it was a corporate event. He was more likely to be her boss.'

Jenny returned to trying to squeeze herself into the bodycon dress Antonia had persuaded her to try. This was an exciting piece of news. 'Yes, but you were there with Geoff. It could easily have been Joe!' She came out wearing the dress and turned around to get Antonia's verdict. 'Weren't you interested in finding out who he was?'

'Not really.' Antonia gave the dress the thumbs down. 'There is rarely anything to interest me at those things unless it comes in a glass bottle. Speaking of which, it's lunchtime. Shall we get ourselves a glass of wine when you're done? Jessica will be with my mother until this evening – I intend to make the most of it.'

Jenny flicked through the other clothes she'd brought in with her. 'Is this the first time you've left her?'

'No, both sets of grandparents have looked after her. We're also trying to find a reliable babysitter. Geoff says we should just use an agency but I'd rather find someone that's been recommended. Do you know anyone?'

Just the word 'babysitter' gave Jenny butterflies in her stomach. Before Henry had arrived, she'd waxed lyrical about how handy it was that her mum lived so close – she could drop him at her parents' house any time she needed to go out. But that was then. Now, just leaving him in the next room made her feel like she'd lost a limb.

'No, I don't know any babysitters. My mum said she'd have him any time.'

And that 'any time' needed to start soon. When she visited Ruth next week, it would be beyond insensitive to take Henry with her. She'd call her mum and do a trial run tomorrow. Or maybe Saturday, when Dan would be with her. Or Sunday.

CHAPTER ELEVEN

My mum has a black belt in worrying. Every time she calls my mobile, she checks I'm not driving before she starts the conversation. When she hears an ambulance, you can see her do a mental headcount of every member of the family and their whereabouts. Whenever my sister and I roll our eyes at being told to 'give three rings when you get there', she always says the same thing: 'You wait until you're a mother! You'll understand!'

And she's right.

It began the minute we left the hospital and drove home as if we were balancing three dozen eggs on the car bonnet. When I put our new baby in the crib beside our bed for the first time, I made Mr Baby get out of bed twenty times to check that he was still breathing.

The first time I left him with Mum, I spent the whole two hours convinced that some freakish accident was going to occur. (Quite what natural disaster was going to hit my mum's three-bedroom semi on a Saturday afternoon, I couldn't tell you…)

From *The Undercover Mother*

✦

'Jenny, love, I have looked after a baby before.' Her mother's tone was somewhere between comforting and irritated.

'I know, I just…' Jenny trailed off. She couldn't explain why the thought of leaving Henry for a couple of hours while they popped to IKEA was filling her with such terror. She turned to Dan. 'Maybe we should just take him with us?'

Dan took her hand and led her purposefully towards the front door. 'This was your idea. You said you needed to start getting used to leaving him. You can't take him when you go and see Ruth, can you?'

Blinking back tears, Jenny turned her head back towards Henry. Her mum smiled encouragingly and waved at her. 'He'll be absolutely fine. Don't rush back,' she called.

✦

Halfway to IKEA, Jenny remembered that she hadn't told her mum about the burping. 'We have to go back.'

Dan showed no signs of screeching into a U-turn. 'Why?'

'I haven't shown her the leg thing I do when he has wind.'

Dan smiled. 'She's had two children of her own, Jen. Plus, she's looked after your sister's kids. I'm sure she'll work it out.'

'No, no.' A rising, irrational terror bubbled in her throat. 'She won't. It's a new method. I only just learnt it this week. She'll just put him over her shoulder and rub his back and… and…'

'He'll burp?'

Jenny wasn't going to be put off that easily. 'But he might not and then he'll be in pain and then he'll cry and I won't be there and…'

'Jenny. Stop.' Dan had the calm tone of a relaxation tape. 'We are only going to be a couple of hours. Your mum has successfully raised two children without the modern burping method, and Henry will be absolutely fine.'

Jenny took a deep breath. 'Okay,' she agreed. But she was far from convinced.

✦

Wandering around IKEA, she tried not to run through worst-case scenarios in her head: Henry writhing in wind-induced pain, desperate for someone to lay him on his back and rotate his legs; an unattended Henry rolling off the sofa onto a hard wooden floor; her mum tripping and falling whilst holding him, and throwing him up into the air.

Jenny picked up kitchen utensils and put them down again without even looking at them. She felt on high alert, like a gazelle listening for dangerous predators, ears almost twitching. Why was this so terrifying? Mothers left their babies all the time. Surely they didn't all feel like this?

After the third time she'd checked her phone for an emergency message, Dan took the multicoloured chopping board set she was holding and put it back on the shelf. 'Shall we go and get some meatballs?'

✦

Whilst Dan queued, Jenny looked for a table. In the far corner, she spotted a familiar face.

'You've caught me.' Gail closed her laptop. 'I'm supposed to be looking for a cot mattress, but Jake fell asleep so I'm having a sneaky catch-up on some financial briefings. Funnily enough, I've just sent a text to Naomi. Jake's had wind and she mentioned some massage techniques that might help. All alone?'

'Dan's in the queue, but we've left Henry with my mum.' Jenny raised her fists in a cheer but her voice wobbled. Seeing Jake asleep in his pram made her feel worse.

Gail was sympathetic. 'First time? It gets easier, I promise. First day back at work I cried the whole way there.' She zipped her laptop into its case and slid it onto the shelf under Jake's pram.

Gail's thick, shoulder-length hair was twisted and pinned up with a large clip and her lack of make-up made her look less intimidating than usual. But crying? That was a surprise. Jenny perched herself on the chair opposite.

'Well, that makes me feel a little less pathetic. Thanks. How are you finding it, being back at work now?'

'It's fine. I'm so busy I don't have time to think.' Gail re-adjusted Jake's blanket. 'When I leave, though, I'm desperate to get home and see him.'

Now she was there, Jenny could ask Gail about the man at her work function. 'I went shopping with Antonia last week. She mentioned she saw you and Joe together.' Somehow, in the intervening days, Jenny had convinced herself that the man Antonia had described had to be Joe.

Gail looked startled. 'Did she? Where?'

'At a work event. She was there with Geoff and she said she saw you with a distinguished-looking man.' Antonia hadn't said distinguished either, but Jenny didn't want to say 'old'.

Understanding dawned on Gail's face. She unclipped her hair and brushed it through with her fingers. 'That wasn't Joe. That was my boss. Which I'm sure Antonia realised.'

'Oh.' Jenny was disappointed. 'She did say he might have been your boss.'

'I'm sure she did. Did she enjoy herself, dutifully following her husband around?' Gail's voice developed an edge any time she referred to Antonia.

'I was a little confused.' Jenny made herself more comfortable on the hard plastic seat. 'You told me at antenatal that you didn't know each other, but she said she's seen you at work events before.'

Gail tapped the table with her nails. 'I said I didn't *know* her and I didn't. There are lots of wives at these things. I can't be expected to remember all of them. I'm there to network, not chit chat.'

Jenny was more interested in finding out about Joe than Antonia. 'Anyway, how is Joe? Enjoying fatherhood?'

'He's not particularly hands-on. You probably guessed that from his absence from the class.'

'I thought you said he was working?'

'I lied. He just refused to come.'

Was Gail going to talk about him at last? Jenny tried to make it easy for her. 'I'm sure that's not unusual. I had to drag Dan there kicking and screaming.'

Gail looked her in the eye. 'Joe and I, we're not really like you and Dan.'

Jenny was all ears. She had tried to discuss the existence of Joe several times with Dan, forcing him to give an opinion, even though he had zero interest. His conclusion was that 'Joe' was code for 'sperm donor' and didn't actually exist. Jenny thought that maybe Joe had been a one-night stand and that it hadn't worked out. Or they had been a couple, and he'd given her an ultimatum: if you have the child, I'll leave. Or maybe he was her gay best friend and they had decided to conceive a child together, like Madonna and Rupert Everett in that film – what was it called? *The Next Best Thing*. Then Dan had suggested Jenny needed to go back to work and apply her brain to something more useful.

'What do you mean?' Jenny tried now to sound nonchalant.

'Jake wasn't planned.'

'Oh.' Jenny thought briefly of Ruth and her IVF. And her tragic loss. Fertility was such an unfair lottery.

Just then, Dan appeared, greeted Gail and turned to Jenny. 'Your meatballs are served, my lady.'

'You can have this table – I need to brave the search for the cot mattress.' Gail pinned her hair back into place and took hold of Jake's pram. 'Try not to worry about Henry. I'll bet he's being spoiled rotten at your mum's. I'm sure they miss us much less than we miss them.' She kicked the brake off to release the pram and waved with her fingers. 'I'll catch up with you soon.'

✦

When they collected Henry from her mum's, Jenny's sister was there, too. Henry was asleep on her lap. Jenny tried to resist the urge to snatch him from Claire's arms, but she only lasted about thirty seconds.

'Missed him, have you?' asked Claire, as Jenny scooped Henry up and nestled her face into his neck. He smelt vaguely of her sister's perfume. 'So, how are you finding being a mum? Isn't it the most wonderful thing you've ever done?'

Did she never let up on this saintly mother theme? Jenny did think being a mum was pretty wonderful but she wasn't about to admit it to Perfect Pants. 'Yeah, it's pretty good. Don't forget I have a very good career, too. I'm not just a mum, you know.' Even as she said it, she felt guilty. How could she refer to the way she felt about Henry as being 'just a mum'?

'Oh, you are still planning on going back to work, then?'

Jenny noticed that Dan had retreated to the kitchen to help her mum make tea. 'Of course. Why wouldn't I?'

'I suppose everyone is different.' Claire was using her 'If you don't think like me, you're wrong' voice. 'Though I have never understood why a woman would have a baby and then leave them with someone else so she could go back to work. I wanted to be there for my children.'

If Claire was so intent on 'being there' for her children, why wasn't she watching them play football or at a dance practice on a Saturday afternoon, rather than sitting there preaching to Jenny about not missing out? *Try not to rise to it.* 'I will be there for my child, thank you. I just want to write, too. Am I not allowed to do both?'

Claire laughed. 'Of course you're *allowed* to do anything you want. I just don't want you to miss out. This time goes by so quickly.' She reached out and patted Henry. 'He's a lovely little boy.'

Perhaps her sister was trying, in her own judgemental style, to be nice. 'Thank you. We are pretty besotted with him.'

Besotted was the right word. It had been so hard to leave him that afternoon. Hopefully Gail was right and she'd get used to it. It was unlikely that *Flair* magazine would open a crèche.

'So, who will look after Henry when you go back to this great job of yours?' Claire wasn't giving up. 'I hope you're not expecting Mum to do it every day?'

'I'll be able to work from home and email my column.' This was a lie. Eva would never go for that. Jenny waved her mobile at Claire. 'It's called modern technology.'

At that moment, the phone pinged with a new message. It was Lucy. Just what she needed.

Reminder about the ads evo. Stupid woman always used her own abbreviations. *Meet you there? Mark coming. Did you know?*

Claire had launched into a long story about someone she knew who had gone back to work two weeks after having her baby and who was now having some kind of maternal guilt therapy. Jenny wasn't listening.

Mark McLinley was going to be at the advertisers' event.

Mark's magazine, *Suave*, was owned by the same parent company as *Flair*. He liked nothing better than an industry schmoozing event, so of course he was going to be there. Jenny should have expected it.

If she hadn't been anxious about going before, she certainly was now.

There was a large mirror over the fireplace. When Claire broke off from her story to go and remind their mum not to put milk in her camomile tea, Jenny stood up and appraised herself. The prospect of facing a room full of advertising executives when she was two stone over her fighting weight had been bad enough, but now she had to see Mark, too? She was going to need more than an Antonia-inspired outfit if she was going to show her ex-boyfriend how wonderful her life was without him. This called for more than industrial-strength Spanx.

She sent a text to Naomi. Jenny had no idea what the hell Buggy Bootcamp was, but Naomi looked good on it. When Naomi had invited Jenny to try a new group with her, Jenny had laughed. Suddenly it wasn't such a funny idea.

She had three weeks.

CHAPTER TWELVE

Going to the clinic to have The Boy weighed always leaves me slightly depressed. Maybe it's a repressed fear of Weight Watchers, or possibly it's the conveyor belt of mothers and babies reminding me that I am 'one of them' now. My attitude is not helped by the health visitor repeatedly calling me 'Mummy', as in: 'If Mummy could just bring baby over here?' and 'Does Mummy have the baby record book?' I want to ask her if she's talking to me or The Boy because if it's to him, she should expect a very limited response.

Posh doesn't take Baby Posh to the clinic any more because they made her feel guilty about not breastfeeding. She also didn't like their suggestion that she might need to eat more herself. Instead, she weighs Baby Posh by holding her whilst standing on the scales at her exclusive gym. With both of them on there, I bet they still weigh less than I do...

From *The Undercover Mother*

✦

The weather was clear and crisp. People were jogging around the perimeter of the park; others were sitting on the benches, chatting. A squirrel ran across their path. Jenny started to relax a little. Maybe this wasn't going to be so bad, after all. Buggy Bootcamp was surely an ironic title. No one was expecting aerobic activity from people who had recently given birth. She mocked herself for being so frightened on the way over there.

Then she saw them.

In the distance, a circle of mums. They were limbering up. They were stretching. They were wearing Lycra.

'Let's hurry up,' said Naomi. 'We're going to miss the warm up.'

Warm up? Jenny hadn't bent her body into shapes like that since Year 9 PE lessons. Was it going to get more difficult?

'I'm not sure this is a good idea.'

'You can't back out now. Come on.'

Naomi picked up the pace and Jenny had no choice but to follow. Purposely pushing the buggy firmly over any large bumps, she prayed for Henry to wake up and save her. Or for a wheel to fall off the pram. Whichever.

A tall, blonde woman in a vest and leggings turned to them with a smile. 'Hi. You must be our new ladies. Welcome to the group. We're just waiting for a couple more and then we'll start the warm up.'

Start the warm up? So what were they doing now? Warming up for the warm up? Jenny turned around to speak to Naomi and found that she was standing with her legs splayed, rocking from knee to knee. Jenny tried to do the same but her thighs weren't happy about it. She jiggled Henry's pram again. *Now he sleeps.*

The other buggies were very different from hers. They all had three wheels and tyres that looked as though they belonged on a small car. She had seen buggies like that when they were buying Henry's pram. The shop assistant had told them how they were suitable for 'all terrains'. Dan had laughed uproariously when Jenny had asked whether that meant both carpet and lino.

Two more all-terrain buggies appeared, followed by more Lycra. It was time to start the warm up.

It wasn't as if Jenny had never been to an exercise class before. Over the years, she had pretty much tried them all: either from choice, or as research for the column. She had tried Zumba (couldn't follow the routines), step aerobics (kept falling off) and she'd even tried the cycling one, where she just got shouted at by the man at the front whatever she did. But she had never really stuck at anything because, basically, she hated exercise.

Now it was serious. She needed to do something about this flabby expanse around her middle. There was no way she was going to stand alongside Lucy at the lunch with a muffin top.

It started out simply enough, with a walk along the path. Then the pace picked up until they were actually jogging. Jenny sent a silent apology to her breasts. As if they weren't getting enough abuse as it was. Thankfully, the jogging didn't last long and they collected around the instructor, who took them through some bending and stretching. Jenny leaned over to Naomi. 'This isn't as bad as I thought.'

Naomi looked puzzled. 'The warm up?'

'Oh, yes, the warm up.' Jenny felt a rise of panic.

'Okay, ladies, now we're warmed up and ready to go. Let's get those bodies back to their best!'

They actually cheered.

What followed was torture. Jumping and hopping and lunging and skipping: Jenny could only assume the session was being sponsored by Tena Lady. The only reason she stayed was that her car was a long walk away. If she left, they would all watch her traversing the length of the park with her tail between her legs.

Naomi, on the other hand, seemed to be in her absolute element. She called out to Jenny mid-star jump: 'This is great, isn't it?'

Jenny tried to smile back, but she found it was quite difficult to smile when she was trying to remember how to breathe.

Then, praise the lord, Henry woke up and started to cry. It was more of a gurgle, but Jenny seized it as an opportunity to stop. Unfortunately, this strategy didn't work.

'As we've got one awake, this is a good time for us to do our arm exercises.' Instructor Woman beamed at Jenny. 'Use your baby like a dumb-bell. He'll love it. Just make sure you support his head.'

Who was going to support *her* head? And the rest of her.

Childbirth had taught Jenny that even awful experiences come to an end, and eventually they were 'cooling down' and saying their goodbyes. She listened politely as Instructor Woman gave out information about all the different classes and different times.

She'd be coming again when hell froze over.

✦

'Wasn't that fun?' said Naomi, for probably the seventh time that morning. They were sitting on a bench, enjoying the sunshine. 'Shall we make it a regular thing?'

'Hmm. Maybe. I'll have to see how it goes.' *Hell. Freezing. Over.* 'That was more strenuous than I expected it to be.'

'Really?' Naomi looked surprised. 'I was disappointed that they didn't push us harder.'

Jenny wanted to push Naomi a little harder.

'So how are you and John finding parenthood?'

Naomi fiddled with the straps on her changing bag. 'Yeah, it's great. Being a *parent* is great.' She emphasised the word 'parent'.

'Everything okay?'

'I guess we're just getting used to it all.' Naomi stopped fiddling with her bag and looked at Jenny. 'Daisy wasn't planned, did I tell you that?'

First Gail, now Naomi! She would google later and find out just how many pregnancies were unplanned. 'No, I didn't know.'

'John and I met when we were both travelling last summer. It was just a fling, really. But I got to bring home a souvenir I hadn't purchased.' She leaned into Daisy's pram and untangled the pram toys so that they were once more hanging in a neat row. 'Not that I regret it for a second.'

'Wow. I thought Dan and I had been quick off the mark, but I think you beat us. How did you end up getting together?'

'We had swapped emails, and I contacted him after we got home. He was amazing.' She rubbed her eye.

'And now you're living together and you have a baby. Great to get a happy ending.'

'Mmm. Yeah.' Naomi retucked the blanket around Daisy. She got up and started to stretch. 'Fancy going for a quick run before you go?'

Jenny pretended to consider it. 'If "quick run" is code for cake, then yes. Otherwise, I think I'll leave you to it.'

She watched Naomi run off, pushing the pram. She wasn't even doing the half-jog mum-run; that was proper marathon-runner-in-training stuff. How had she got a body like that so soon after the birth? Whether it was the downward dog or the fact she was a decade younger, she'd popped back like a piece of elastic. Whereas Jenny's body felt like a pair of Lycra leggings which had visited the washing machine too many times: there was definite saggage.

Her boobs were starting to feel a little heavy, so she took out her phone, intending to look at the app which told her whether it was time to feed Henry, which boob she should use and that also allowed her to log how long he fed for each time. It was comforting to have the confirmation that she was doing it right.

She'd had two text messages: one from Lucy, one from Ruth. She opened Lucy's first. It was a photo of her. With Mark.

Look who I bumped into at Murphy's!

Jenny's stomach flipped. Was Lucy trying to psych her out? What were they saying about her? Lucy looked fantastic. So did Mark. Jenny looked at Naomi in the distance and then down at her own wobbly stomach. Maybe she should have taken Naomi up on the offer of a run. Or maybe Naomi could just body-double for her at the event?

Mark McLinley. At one point, Jenny had thought she was actually in love with him. They had had a great time together:

swanky lunches, product launches, concerts – all on his expense account, of course. It had been fine for quite some time. Until her thirtieth birthday had made her begin to talk about their future. Then she hadn't seen him for the expensive dust coming off his Italian leather shoes.

She opened Ruth's text.

Hi Jen. Yes, all still okay for tomorrow. 2pm? x

That was good; she'd been worried that Ruth might cancel. At least her impending face-off with Lucy and Mark would give her something to talk about. Something other than babies. She needed to steer away from that.

Somehow, Naomi had completed a whole circuit of the park and was back at the bench.

'I thought you were leaving?'

Jenny hadn't even got around to checking the app, but her burning boobs told her that it was time to wake Henry for a feed. 'I was. Just got caught up.' She waved her phone at Naomi. 'I got a text from Ruth. She's still on for tomorrow.'

CHAPTER THIRTEEN

Smug parents like to evangelise on how they 'got' their baby to nap to a schedule/sleep through the night/love broccoli, but they are delusional: it's all down to luck.

Fertility is the biggest lottery of all. How can some of the best candidates for parenthood be the ones whose reproductive systems are on the blink? And don't get me started on birth. Sporty waxes lyrical on how her positive mental attitude and breathing techniques brought about Baby Sporty's beautiful birth. But if you discover that your pelvis is a bit wonky, there ain't no amount of hypnochanting gonna get that baby out.

I might write my own baby manual for expectant mothers, entitled 'Cross your fingers and hope for the best'…

From *The Undercover Mother*

✦

The upside to Henry having been up four times in the night was that he slept most of the morning. Naomi was collecting Jenny at 1.30 p.m., which gave her time to research some other parenting blogs.

There were tons of them out there. The writers seemed to span a wide range of types. There were the worthy-hipster-organic ones, the scatty-messy-funny ones and the perfect-crafty-baking ones. Were there any mothers not blogging about their daily life? Jenny took heart from the fact that no one seemed to have her 'lost in a foreign land' angle and, she reminded herself, she wasn't competing for best blogger; she just needed to sell Eva on the idea of a magazine column. Surely the number of blogs out there added weight to her case?

Another reason for staying glued to her laptop screen was that she was trying not to succumb to watching daytime TV. Somehow, she'd managed to pick up a minor addiction to watching posh people looking around huge houses in the country. Thankfully, she hadn't slipped into watching poorer people taking chunks out of each other live to the nation, but that was merely a flick of the remote control away.

✦

When Naomi arrived, she had Daisy in the car. Jenny felt the colour drain from her face. Even if Naomi hadn't been googling 'Bereaved parents – what to say' the night before as Jenny had, surely she realised you didn't take a baby to visit someone who had just lost theirs?

She did. They dropped Daisy to Naomi's mother-in-law, who had her front door open as soon as they pulled up.

Naomi jumped out. 'I won't be long.'

Jenny watched Naomi with John's mother through her peripheral vision. Dan always said she was nosy, but Jenny preferred to see it as taking an interest in other people. 'You're not actually listening to me at all,' Dan would say, as she tried to catch the conversation of a couple at the table next to them in a restaurant, or behind them in a queue. Once, there had been a mother and daughter having such an interesting conversation about an affair that Jenny had surreptitiously followed them around Marks & Spencer for about fifteen minutes. 'I'm a *writer*,' she would argue. 'You never know when you might hear a good story.'

Naomi was back in the car within four minutes. She closed the car door hard and they drove the next five minutes in stony silence. Jenny had to say something.

'All okay? Daisy settled?'

Naomi tapped the steering wheel irritably. 'Yep.'

Jenny tried again. 'John's mum looks nice.'

'Does she?' Naomi continued to tap the wheel. 'She'll be in a different outfit by now.'

'John's mum?' She had looked perfectly presentable. A cream twinset was a classic for a woman of her age.

'Daisy. She will have changed Daisy into something pink and covered in disgusting nylon frills the minute I turned the corner.'

Dan's mum was like that about putting vests on Henry. Even when it was about a hundred degrees.

'I hate clothes like that, too,' Jenny said. 'And tops with cartoon characters. Still, if it makes her happy, what's the harm? She probably enjoys dressing a baby girl.' Jenny was often envious of the rows of baby girl's clothes. There was so much more choice.

Naomi wasn't listening. 'Last time we left Daisy with her, she said that she wouldn't take my expressed breast milk and tried to give her formula. *Formula!* She spat out the word 'formula' as if it were 'whisky' or 'arsenic'.

For most people, Jenny knew, this wouldn't be a huge issue. But Naomi was practically a breastfeeding evangelist.

'She didn't drink it, of course. Refused it completely.' Naomi sounded proud. 'But that's not the point.'

'Of course, of course,' Jenny soothed. 'But you know what grandmothers are like.'

'She wouldn't *be* a grandmother if it weren't for me. I was the one who made that decision. She should be grateful.'

What decision? Hadn't Naomi said she got pregnant by accident? But one glance at Naomi's face confirmed that now wasn't the time to ask.

✦

Ruth and David lived on a new estate of executive homes in a tall town house. The kitchen took up the whole of the ground floor and they sat there, at a large round table, with their tea and a plate of homemade cake.

Ruth looked well. Tired, but well. She'd had her thick, dark red hair cut into a short, blunt bob and it suited her. She'd lost some weight (well, of course, they'd all lost weight since they'd last seen each other) and it showed in her face. She wore a little make-up, a navy striped top and jeans. She looked good.

Ruth pushed a plate towards them. 'Please, take more cake – I've made enough for twenty visitors and David has eaten quite enough lately.' She hadn't eaten any herself.

Jenny plunged straight in. 'We're all so sorry, Ruth. I don't know what to say to you. It's just so unfair.'

Ruth nodded. 'Yeah. You know, I'd really begun to think that we might actually get to be parents this time. Should never have given in to the hope.' She gave them a watery smile and then shook her head as if to remove her thoughts. 'Anyway, it's good to see you both. It's been really quiet around here since David went back to work. All my closest friends and family are about three hours away.'

Jenny felt terrible that they hadn't been to visit Ruth before now; she had assumed that they would be ensconced in a private family huddle. 'We would have come sooner if we'd known you didn't have people around.'

'They all came down when they heard. And they were great at sorting stuff out. Like sending the lovely pram back.' Ruth bit her lip and Jenny's heart flinched for her. 'But since they went home, it's been pretty much the two of us, barring a visit from the girls I work with. Honestly, it's fine.' Ruth waved a hand as Jenny tried to apologise again. 'Anyway, it's given us some time to get on with the job in hand – getting ourselves pregnant again.'

Jenny could tell from Naomi's face that she was as surprised as Jenny was.

'You're trying for another baby?'

Ruth scooped a few crumbs from the table and dropped them onto her empty tea plate. 'It takes us a long time just to get pregnant, so if we want a baby we can't be hanging about.'

'Are you restarting IVF?' That seemed a lot to be putting herself through having just lost a baby.

'No.' Ruth shook her head. 'They wouldn't even consider us at the moment. No.' She sighed and sat back in her chair. 'We're hoping that having carried a pregnancy to term will make us more likely to fall pregnant naturally a second time.'

The clinical way Ruth phrased this seemed to come straight from the mouth of one of her doctors. There was also something in her tone which didn't sound convincing. What was she holding back?

✦

Before they left, Naomi went to the bathroom and Ruth started to wrap up some of the cake for them to take home to Dan and John.

'Dan will be very grateful. In fact, this might end up being his dinner.' Jenny collected their cake plates and put them on the kitchen counter. 'What are your plans for next week? Maybe you could come to me for lunch one day, if you're at a loose end?'

'That would be nice. But, be warned, I am a bit weepy at the best of times. The sight of Henry might make me sob.'

'You can sob whenever you want. There's a high chance I might even join you.' Jenny paused. 'How's David?'

'He's okay. We're both getting there. Trying to focus on the future.' Ruth gave what Jenny's nan would have called a 'brave soldier' smile.

Jenny squeezed her hand. 'I appreciate we don't know each other that well, Ruth, but I'm pretty good at eating cake and listening. You can talk to me if you need to. Any time. About *anything*.' Her journalistic instinct was twitching. Obviously she wasn't going to write about Ruth's terribly traumatic experience, but she wanted to be her friend. And there seemed to be something unspoken behind her words. What wasn't she telling them?

Ruth gave her a furtive glance and lowered her voice as they heard Naomi coming back down the stairs. 'I'll come and see you as soon as I feel ready. We'll talk then.'

✦

Because Jenny's mum and dad were away, Claire had looked after Henry. Stupidly, she told her sister all about Ruth.

Claire was sympathetic. 'It makes you so grateful, doesn't it?'

'It really does. I can't imagine how it would feel to lose Henry.' Since she'd been back, Jenny had already squeezed him about twenty times.

'And yet you're planning on going back to work and leaving him.'

How had she not seen that coming?

'You don't miss a trick, do you?'

Claire held up her hands. 'I just think you've waited a long time to have a baby. Why not take the time out of your career to enjoy him?'

Waited a long time? Did her sister think she'd been merely marking time as a writer whilst secretly pining for a husband and children all these years?

'I'm not *you*, you know, Claire.'

'What's that supposed to mean?' Claire could give it, but she couldn't take it. 'I have a rather good life, I think. My children have certainly never wanted for anything.'

She was right there. In the motherhood business, Claire was a professional. Organic meals, cakes for the PTA, school project creations of which Michelangelo would be proud. Claire was the Usain Bolt of the mothering world: no one else came close.

'You're a fantastic mother. Really, I admire you. I honestly do. It's just… I mean… Don't you ever get a bit… bored?'

'Bored?' Claire looked at Jenny as if she were speaking Swahili. 'How could you be bored watching their first steps, hearing their first words? I don't think you realise what you might miss out on.'

Jenny gave up. There was no point having this conversation with Claire – she'd never had a career that she loved; she just wouldn't understand. Whilst her sister had stayed home surrounded by papier mâché and cupcake cases, Jenny had been out meeting people and visiting great places. It was a lot to give up.

✦

But when Jenny went to bed that night, Claire's voice was in her head. *You will miss out on so much.* She had stopped listening to her sister about twenty years ago, but her warnings now made Jenny feel uneasy. What if she was right?

She dug Dan in the ribs, but he mumbled and rolled over. There'd be no point asking him, anyway – he'd just say that she should do whatever she wanted to. And she knew what she wanted to do. She wanted to write. And to be with Henry.

She would just have to do whatever it took at that advertisers' lunch to prove to Eva that *The Undercover Mother* would work. It had to.

CHAPTER FOURTEEN

Breastfeeding is one of those things that, as a woman, you assume will come naturally. Like breathing. And shoe shopping.

After my general anaesthetic, The Boy was so zonked he couldn't keep my nipple in his mouth, so a helpful midwife hooked me up to a dairy-farm-strength breast pump. It nearly turned me inside out to extract about 3ml of yellow milk, which I tried to feed to The Boy from a cup. It was like trying to get black coffee down the neck of a drunk.

Three months on and my milk ducts have got the hang of things. Now I wake up in the morning looking like a boob-double for Katie Price. Apparently, the more frequently you feed, the more milk they produce. As her baby feeds more often than a giant panda, Sporty's milk ducts must be working twenty-four-hour shifts...

From *The Undercover Mother*

✦

The conference room at the hotel was predictably anonymous and corporate. Along one side stretched a table covered in sandwiches and mini quiches. Dotted around the room were men, and a few women, wearing suits, holding paper plates and trying to look interested in the person they were talking with.

In the past, Jenny had hated these events. Right now, she was looking forward to a free sandwich and some adult conversation.

'Hi, Jen. Glad you could make it.' Eva joined her at the food table, not carrying a paper plate. 'There are quite a few advertisers of women's products here today. Might be a worthwhile day for us. Have you seen Lucy yet?'

Jenny shook her head; her mouth was filled with two cocktail sausages. She hadn't wanted to put more than three on her plate in case she looked greedy. Breastfeeding made her want to eat all the time. It was nice to have something to blame.

Eva was scanning the room. 'Maybe she's running late. I know she was out until the small hours this morning at that new club opening. Oh, there she is. Over talking to Mark McLinley. I'm not sure I want the two of them talking – go and split them up.'

Jenny nearly choked on her last mouthful. Mark was there already? She couldn't face that yet. 'I'll go and catch up with her in a minute. I've just seen Jack Jenkins, the sales rep from CleanWare. I'm sure their products would appeal to the *The Undercover Mother* audience.'

Eva gave a snort of surprise. 'Good luck.'

Jack Jenkins was not a nice man. When he looked at you, you wanted to go and take a shower afterwards. He was dressed in a suit just a little too small for him, the buttons of his shirt barely meeting across his stomach. Not that Jenny was one to judge, but he could easily have passed for five months pregnant.

'Well, hello, Miss Jenny. I haven't seen you at one of these things for a while. You're looking—' he paused '—well?'

She knew a euphemism when she heard one, but she couldn't afford sarcasm right then. If she could get even one person there to tell Eva that they thought her motherhood column was a good idea, she would have a fighting chance of getting it off the ground. 'Thank you, Jack. I could say the same to you. How's business?'

He held out a pudgy hand and twisted his wrist. 'You know how it is – ballooning targets, squeezed budgets.' He had been giving this same old story for years. He was well-known by the sales team back at *Flair* for waiting until the last minute to place his advertisements, and then negotiating an incredibly low rate. Jenny felt sorry for them having to deal with him every month – at least she only had to play nice when asked to attend these networking events.

'I've got a new column pitch which you might be interested in.' She tried to look as excited as possible, maybe a little flirty. *Demeaning but necessary.* 'It's aimed at new mothers.'

Jack blanched as if he'd just swallowed a dodgy vol-au-vent. 'Mothers?'

Jenny nodded enthusiastically. 'Yeah, a humorous column. We're all in this together… isn't it funny? That kind of thing.'

'Funny?' He looked like he'd never heard of the word.

'It's going to be great. I've already started a blog and the feedback has been immense.' She had an idea. 'Hey, maybe you could advertise on my blog? Get in at the ground level before everyone else?'

She could almost see the oil coming out of his pores. 'Sounds great, really. But not sure it's our kind of "thing".' He did those annoying air quotes that made Jenny want to snip off the ends of his fingers. 'Sorry, Jen, I've just seen someone I need to catch up with. We'll talk later, yeah?' And he was gone.

Jenny put another sausage in her mouth. She looked around to see where Lucy and Mark were. She didn't want to talk to either of them until she'd got something positive to say.

'Jen! How great to see you!'

She swallowed the sausage whole and a rather unattractive sucking noise came out of her mouth. 'Mark! What a nice surprise!'

'I told you he'd be here.' Lucy was right at his elbow. *Cow.*

'Did you? I'd forgotten.' Jenny smiled at Lucy with her mouth and killed her with her eyes.

'The memory is the first thing to go when you have a baby, so I've heard.' Mark smiled. Lucy laughed raucously.

'Totally untrue,' said Jenny. *It's the patience with twats that goes first.* 'How are you?'

'Oh, you know, keeping busy. I got the editor's job.'

'I heard. Congratulations.'

'Thanks. I've been trying to tempt this one—' he smiled at Lucy '—to come over to my rag, but apparently she's just been given a plum job at your place.' He raised a provocative eyebrow.

Jenny gritted her teeth. 'Yes, I'm working on a new project.'

'So I hear. So I hear.' Mark and Lucy exchanged a look which made Jenny want to smash their faces into the quiche Lorraine. 'A parenting advice column, isn't it?'

Lucy sniggered.

'No. It's a humorous column, actually. I'm exploring new media. You know what they say about print nowadays.'

Mark rubbed his fingers and thumb together. 'It's still where most of the money is. Seems to me you'll be wasting your talents. You're a party girl, Jen. You're good at it.'

Jenny tried to hold his gaze but her face grew warm. 'Things change.'

'Not everything. Maybe you and I should have a chat sometime. We might be able to do a little something together?'

The last time they'd 'done a little something together' it had ended with her drowning her sorrows with a bottle of Gordon's, vowing never to call him again.

'Thanks, but I'm happy at *Flair*.'

'Like you said, things change. Just keep my offer in mind. Here's my card with my new office details, in case you've lost my number.'

Jenny hadn't *lost* his number. Her friends had made her delete it after a couple of drunken episodes when they'd had to wrestle her phone from her hands to stop her booty calling him at 2 a.m. But not taking his card would make her look like she still had it.

'Okay, but I really don't think I'll be needing it. Sorry I can't chat for longer, but there's a million people here I really need to see. Good luck with the new job.' She looked at Lucy pointedly. 'Both of you.'

She scanned the room frantically; she couldn't leave the two of them and then stand on her own like a lost puppy. Over by the buffet table was a new face. Young, handsome and conveniently placed near the Pringles. If old ad men like Jack Jenkins weren't going to bite, she'd go after young blood. *Watch me and weep, Mark McLinley.*

Striding over purposefully, she thrust out her hand and flashed a smile. 'Hi. Jenny Thompson. *Flair* magazine.'

He put down his plate and shook her hand, eagerly. 'Simon Clarke. Unlimited Faces. I'm here representing a couple of new make-up brands.'

'That's perfect! You have new products, we have a new column!' This was her chance. Jenny turned up the style dial. 'You show me yours and I'll show you mine.'

Simon might be young but he seemed willing to play. 'Well, I don't have any samples with me, but…' She saw him glance at her chest. Although this was totally inappropriate, Jenny felt a little pleased. She still had it.

'Well, that's a shame. I don't have any hard copies, either – but you can take a look at my… blog.'

This was supposed to sound a little flirty, but Simon was starting to twitch. And not in a good way.

'Blog?' he repeated, nervously.

He was looking at her chest again. That was a bit much. But she needed something to go back to Eva with. *Just keep going.*

'It's aimed at first-time mothers. It's funny. It's different. We've had a lot of positive feedback already. I can come to your office and show you.' She took out a business card and offered it to him.

'Mothers? With babies?' He looked at her boobs *again* and then at her face. 'Uh, I'm not sure that it really fits with…'

'Of course it does!' Jenny flicked her hair back; she was getting into her stride. 'Intelligent women. At home, with time on their hands. Who else can browse adverts like they do?'

He was pulling at the collar of his shirt. 'But our products are very glamorous and…'

Jenny's smile froze on her face. 'And mothers aren't glamorous?' She tried not to sound irritated. 'I'm a mother.' And he'd been looking at her boobs for the last five minutes. 'Do you not think mothers want to look good, too?'

He looked horrified. 'No, no, I wasn't... I can see you are...' Now he was desperately trying *not* to look below her neck. 'I just need to... Let me just take your card. I'll call if...' He took the business card that Jenny offered him and almost ran away.

Dammit. Jenny glanced around to see if Mark or Lucy had been near enough to witness her crash and burn. Eva had been caught by Jack Jenkins. She'd just have one more sausage and then go and rescue her.

'Excuse me.'

A waitress was hovering by Jenny's elbow. Was there a ration on how many sausages you were allowed? 'Yes?'

'Er, I just thought you might want to know. You've got, er...' She waved towards her own chest. 'You've got... something, er... down your top.'

Jenny looked down. Her face got very hot. On her chest were two huge milk stains.

✦

Twenty minutes later, she was semi-prone beneath a hand-dryer when Eva came in to the Ladies'. With nothing much to do whilst drying, Jenny had sent a picture of the milk stains to the other mums; Antonia had sent back a picture of her Jimmy Choos covered in baby sick.

'Should I even ask?'

Jenny stood up and surveyed her bra region in the mirror. 'Bloody breast pads leaked.'

Eva shuddered. 'A "no" would have sufficed. How are you getting on?'

'Great.' Jenny lied. 'I've been giving my card out and I'm sure I'll have some leads for the ad team once we have a launch date for the column.'

Eva looked sceptical. 'Really? Who?'

'Well, there's no point giving you names until...' Jenny trailed off. She was tired. She was wet. And she didn't have the energy for this right now.

'Look, Jen, I know this isn't the place, but we need to have a chat. The blog. It's not really cutting it. Your writing is good, of course. It's the *content*.'

Jenny just nodded.

'We've got a planning meeting in a couple of weeks. Come to that. Maybe there's something else we could give you. Monday 24th, 10 a.m.'

◆

Getting stuck in traffic was the perfect end to the day. Jenny turned on the radio and then turned if off again; she wasn't in the mood for the DJ's bright, chirpy voice. The tissue she had stuffed into her bra was a poor replacement for a breast pad and she could feel milk soaking through her top again.

She didn't want Eva to be right. It had surprised her how much she enjoyed writing the blog. Admittedly, it was less *Eat, Pray, Love* and more 'Eat, Play, Sleep'. With a lot more poo. But it was fun finding the humour in it all, and the comments she'd had from complete strangers had really made her day.

But none of this would matter to Eva: she had to think of the commercial side of things. And it seemed that she might have already decided that *The Undercover Mother* was never going to bring in the marketing bucks.

Maybe Jenny was fooling herself with this whole thing. Maybe they were right about motherhood addling your brain. Was she wasting her time? Or did she just need a new angle? Up until then, *The Undercover Mother* had been about the realities of living with a new baby. But maybe she just needed to widen her net a little. Start to write a lot more about the personal lives of the mothers themselves.

Like the mothers who were having problems with their in-laws. The mothers whose partners were not on the scene. The mothers who might have started an affair. Everyone liked to lift a rock and look at what was crawling underneath.

It was time to go deep.

CHAPTER FIFTEEN

To prove their lineage, newborn babies are supposed to look like their fathers. Apparently, newborn Baby Sporty looked so much like Mr Sporty's dad that, when she looked downwards at her bald baby, Sporty felt like she was breastfeeding her father-in-law. Scary tells us that her son bears a real resemblance to his dad, although she hasn't been forthcoming with any evidence. And I am quite happy that The Boy looks just like Mr Baby.

Posh, however, seems equally pleased that there are very few traces of Mr Posh in her baby anywhere. A few thousand years ago, that could have caused a lot of talk cave-side...

From *The Undercover Mother*

✦

'Bugger!' Jenny jumped up, almost rolling Henry off the sofa they were lying on. She must have dozed off whilst trying to get him to take a nap. He woke up and started crying. 'Bugger, bugger, bugger!'

The lounge was carnage and so was she. One side of her face was bright red and indented with the shape of the teething ring she'd somehow fallen asleep on. There was no time now for the shower she had planned to take whilst Henry slept – her flattened hair would just have to be scraped into a ponytail; she couldn't keep her hat on in Antonia's house. Now, where was the damn changing bag?

Although the changing bag was huge and purple, it was surprising how often she lost it. Oh, how she longed for the days when leaving the house had just meant grabbing her keys, purse and phone. Now even a trip to the shops involved a level of packing and preparation which would have impressed Edmund Hillary. Plus, Edmund Hillary didn't get to the front door of Everest and discover that one of his crew had pooped in their nappy and had to be stripped off and changed before they could start again.

✦

Antonia's lounge looked exactly as Jenny would have predicted: neutral, classic and expensive. It took her a few moments before she realised that, apart from baby Jessica lying on a play mat in front of the sofa, there was no baby paraphernalia anywhere. Jenny put Henry down on the mat beside Jessica as she took in the room.

Naomi was sitting cross-legged on a voluminous sofa, feeding Daisy. 'Nice here, isn't it?' she whispered. 'This is the grown-ups' sitting room. There's another "family room" with all the baby stuff.'

Antonia came back in with Jenny's tea (bone china mug – no chips), looking immaculate in white linen trousers and a navy top. With freshly washed hair.

'Jessica has been fine. Not a whimper.' Naomi placed Daisy next to the other babies on the mat.

'That's a relief. I don't know what it is with her at the moment. Every time I leave the room she gets upset.' Antonia knelt down and pressed her nose onto Jessica's, before sitting back on her heels and looking at Jenny. 'I can't believe it's taken so long for me to invite you over. It's just going to be the three of us. I did invite Ruth, but she understandably said she wasn't up to it. And I shouldn't think that…' She was interrupted by the doorbell and looked surprised. 'I'll just go and get that.'

When Antonia opened the door, they heard her say: 'Oh, you came?'

'I thought I was invited?' Gail followed Antonia into the living room and nodded at Naomi and Jenny, before turning back to Antonia with a bemused expression.

'Yes, yes, of course you were.' Antonia was back in hostess mode. 'I just thought you were back at work.'

'Only part-time right now. We've been at Baby Sign.' She laid Jake down on the mat with the other babies.

When the others didn't question what the hell that was, Jenny asked, 'Baby Sign?'

Gail sat down next to Jenny. She smelled of freshly ironed cotton, and her crisp white shirt next to Jenny's crumpled one made them look like before and after pictures on a washing powder ad.

'It's a sign language course for babies.'

Jenny nearly snorted her tea through her nose. 'Seriously?'

But Gail wasn't joking. 'Who knows if it works? But you have to take them to something. It might as well be something productive.'

Jenny hadn't even considered taking Henry to a baby group. She looked to the others for support, but they were both nodding.

'We go to baby massage,' said Naomi. 'It's a wonderful time of bonding. Organic oils, obviously.'

Even Antonia was at it. 'I'm taking Jessica swimming at my gym.'

Sign language? Baby massage? Swimming? Jenny looked at Henry, kicking his legs on the expensive-looking quilt. Why hadn't she known she was supposed to be taking him to these places? What else were they missing out on?

Whilst Antonia made Gail a black coffee, Naomi extolled the virtues of baby massage until Daisy saved them by rolling onto Henry's arm.

'Crikey, she's rolling already?' Jenny had had an email from a baby website which said: '*Your baby might try to roll this week!*' She'd spent the last two days trying to tempt Henry onto his side by calling his name, shaking rattles and, she was ashamed to admit, lying down next to him with her boob out, asking him if he wanted any milk.

'Yep. She's never in the same place I left her.' Naomi moved Daisy back to where she'd started.

Gail nodded towards Henry. 'He looks exactly like Dan.'

For some weird reason, Jenny loved it when people noticed that. 'I know. I sometimes wonder if he got any of my genes at all. Does Jake look like Joe?'

Gail held her son's kicking foot. 'He does, actually.'

Antonia reappeared with the coffee. 'Does he?' She looked at Jake and then at Jessica, who was wriggling towards him. 'Jess doesn't look anything like Geoff, thank God.'

Antonia was right: her little girl was fair like her rather than dark like Geoff. She also had Antonia's blue eyes and perfect nose.

Jenny had read about this when she'd been trawling for blog ideas. 'I thought all babies were supposed to look like their father?'

Gail nodded. 'I heard that, too. Cave dads needed proof. No Jeremy Kyle DNA tests back then.'

'I also read that one in ten doubt they are the father of their child.' As she said it, Jenny realised how tactless that sounded after Antonia's comment. 'But surely that can't be true?'

'Well, I think it's entirely possible,' said Antonia. 'Affairs happen all the time. Goodness, at least three of Geoff's colleagues have been caught out.'

'Do you think the women know when their husband isn't the father?' Jenny's journalistic instinct was twitching like a rabbit's nose.

Antonia shrugged. 'Maybe they don't want to know for sure.'

'What about the other man? Surely he'd want to know if the baby was his?' Jenny pressed.

'Really?' Antonia raised an eyebrow. 'Isn't that a little naive? Do you really think a man who sleeps with married women wants to be saddled with a child?'

'I think *that's* naive.' Gail tapped her fingers on her folded arms. 'Fatherhood can change a man.'

Antonia turned to look at her. 'Really? Have you got an example? Is Joe a hands-on dad?'

Jenny winced at Antonia's tone, though she was also desperate to know what was going on, even more so since Dan had interrupted her conversation with Gail in IKEA.

But Gail met Antonia's eyes. 'I've told you before. Joe works away a great deal.'

Before Antonia could ask anything else, Naomi interrupted. 'John's a great dad,' she said.

And then she burst into tears.

✦

Once Antonia had brought in a box of tissues and made another cup of tea, Naomi was more composed.

'We're okay, really. It's just that he works so much that sometimes I feel like I'm doing this on my own.'

Jenny knew better than to mention Naomi's helpful in-laws. Unfortunately, Antonia didn't. 'Doesn't his family live close to you? Can't they have the baby?'

Naomi grimaced and fiddled with the beads around her neck. 'That is part of the problem. His mother visits us all the time.' She paused for emphasis. 'All. The. Time.'

'Is she still doing it? Can't you just tell her that you're busy, or going out?' Gail was unlikely to put up with such behaviour.

'I do. As often as I can, but she just turns up unannounced.' She mimicked a high old-lady voice: '*Only me, Naomi! I was just passing and thought I'd see if you needed anything.*' She dropped the impression. 'Then she comes in and starts—' she waved her arms in the air '—tidying up, folding washing, clearing the draining board.'

'That doesn't sound too terrible to me.' Jenny had a Kilimanjaro of dirty crockery waiting for her at home. 'Why don't you leave her downstairs with the baby and take the opportunity to go and have a sleep or a shower?'

Naomi shook her head again. 'That would be like admitting defeat – she already thinks I am some kind of hippy with no idea how to raise a child.'

Jenny almost blushed. She'd referred to Naomi as a hippy more than once. But no one could say she didn't know how to raise a child. She was practically a baby whisperer.

'If I hear one more time, "*John liked to nap straight after lunch. John was always better if I left him to sleep in his own cot. John didn't like being held like that…*" I am going to… to… flip.'

Antonia smirked seductively. 'Maybe try telling her a few things John likes nowadays that she might not be aware of, and see how she likes that, darling.'

Naomi smiled a watery smile.

Jenny thanked her lucky stars that Dan's parents lived in another county. They were nice, but she couldn't imagine having them hovering over her every day. It was unlikely to ever be a problem; if they suggested visiting more than twice in a month, Dan would threaten to turn out the lights and lie down behind the sofa.

Gail was more forthright. 'If you can't tell her, then John needs to. He's not a little boy, for goodness' sake.'

Naomi shook her head. 'That's never going to happen. John isn't one for standing up to people. He'd no sooner tell his mother not to come around than take on a rabid dog. Plus, he says she's just trying to help.'

'You have to do something, though.' Antonia put her mug on the table. 'You can't have her popping in like that forever. You could be doing *anything*.' She raised an eyebrow. 'I mean. Can you imagine if you were—'

'—cleaning the toilet?' finished Jenny, in an attempt to lighten the mood. Not that she was likely to be found cleaning. Or the thing that Antonia was suggesting.

Naomi nodded. 'You're right. I agree completely.' She paused. 'Maybe it would be easier if I didn't live so close to them. I mean, familiarity breeds contempt and all that.' She leaned forwards and started to fiddle with the straps on Daisy's dungarees. 'Actually, I've been thinking of leaving. Moving back home to Bristol.'

That was a surprise. Moving? Naomi had mentioned in their WhatsApp group that John worked for his father. 'How will John get to work from there?'

Naomi was still adjusting Daisy's straps in an attempt not to meet anyone's eye. 'I meant just me and Daisy.'

There was a silence. No one knew what to say.

'That's a bit drastic, isn't it?' Jenny felt the need to fill the silence. 'Leaving John just because he has an overly familiar mother.'

'It's not just that. I don't think it's working out with me and John. Whatever we had when we met doesn't seem to be enough. We hardly spend any time together at all.'

'It's a bit like that for all of us, though, isn't it?' Jenny hoped this was true. 'New baby, being knackered, not sure what we're doing. I shouldn't think any of us are winning "Romantic of the Year" right now. I know I'm not. Most evenings I can be found snoring on the sofa, or going to bed early wearing M&S pyjamas and bed socks. Dan would need to be a serious fetishist to find that alluring.'

'Oh, we still have *sex*.' Naomi's expression suggested it was ridiculous to think that they might not. 'That's not the problem. I do love him. But I might have a better life back with my parents.'

✦

Jenny drove the long way home in the hope that Henry would fall asleep. With all the issues at work, she hadn't realised she had been neglecting his development. Was Daisy rolling already because the baby massage was expanding her mind? She had visions of Henry starting school alongside second-language-speaking, yoga-demonstrating geniuses whilst he had only just mastered a sippy cup. She was a terrible mother.

And wife. If Naomi and John were on the verge of splitting up and were still managing bedroom gymnastics, what did it say about Jenny and Dan's relationship? She'd been neglecting him, too. Once, a friend of hers had said she and her husband hadn't had sex in two years and Jenny had been shocked. Now she could see how easily that might happen.

It was difficult to have sex in bed at night. Not only was she exhausted by then, but Henry was sleeping in their room and it just didn't feel *right*. Morning sex was out because Dan left for work so early. In the whole work/life/baby juggling act, she couldn't remember the last time they'd even sat down and had a cuddle.

Time for some action.

CHAPTER SIXTEEN

When they gave me that 'Post C-Section' leaflet at the hospital, I didn't even bother to read the paragraph entitled 'Resuming your sex life' because at that time I felt as interested in solo space travel as I did in horizontal jogging.

Now it's difficult to find the time to do it. There are no more lazy mornings in bed at the weekend, no more drunken nights out, for fear of the hellish combination of hangover and crying baby. Even quiet nights at home with a takeaway and a bottle of wine are interrupted by unscheduled wake ups or a dirty nappy. Nothing kills the romance like a packet of yellow poo.

Maybe it's because Sporty is younger than the rest of us that her sex life seems to have bounced back into action as quickly as her body. Posh maintains that having sex is like doing the ironing. You really can't face it but, once you get the board out, it's not as bad as you thought...

From *The Undercover Mother*

✦

The lounge floor was completely clear and there were no piles of washing to be seen on either of the sofas. Music played quietly in the background and Henry was asleep in his cot. After a long shower, Jenny had dressed in the only slinky nightdress she could find that still fit. When Dan came through the front door, she was standing in the hallway with two glasses of wine. Ready for action.

'Get your clothes off.'

'Pardon?'

'Get your clothes off – I want to have sex.'

Dan looked at her suspiciously. 'What's happened?'

Jenny rolled her eyes. 'Nothing has happened. Henry is asleep. We need to have sex now, before he wakes up.' She narrowed her gaze. 'Don't you want to have sex with me?'

Dan's suspicion seemed to change to mild fear. 'Of course I do, but I've just got in. Anyway, are you going to be okay, you know, after the Caesarean?'

Jenny was starting to feel silly. 'I'll be fine. Come on, we need to do it now.' She gestured impatiently towards the living room.

Dan looked in confusion to where she was motioning. 'In there?'

'Yes, in there. Henry is asleep in our room.' She sighed. 'It's our sofa. It's not like I'm suggesting we do it on the front lawn.' What had happened to the days when they would fall through the front door and have sex on the stairs because they couldn't wait to make it to the bedroom?

Dan followed her into the lounge, taking his shoes off as he walked. He sat down next to her and kissed her. Jenny wanted to laugh; it was almost like they'd never done this before.

Now he was over the surprise, Dan seemed quite keen. 'I remember you,' he whispered.

It did feel good to be together like this. Concentrating on each other, touching each other, not merely passing on updates about nappy changes and feed times. Weirdly, she felt a little emotional. Like she had returned home after a long trip away.

Dan slipped his hand under her robe and onto her body. Sharply, he pulled his hand back. 'You're leaking!'

She could feel the milk running down her chest and onto her stomach. It wasn't a pleasant sensation. 'Bugger! I'll have to put my bra back on.' She ran upstairs to get her nursing bra and a couple of breast pads. Catching a glimpse of herself in the mirror on the way back, she wished she had been able to fit into her pretty underwear.

By the time she got back to the lounge, Dan had switched on the TV. He reached for the remote to turn it off but, by then, the moment had passed. A wave of exhaustion hit her and she yawned. Dan kissed her on the cheek. 'Are you sure you're ready for this? We don't have to rush it, you know.'

Jenny closed her eyes and lay back on the sofa. 'We do, though. We need to get back to normal. We used to have sex all the time.'

Dan put his arm around her and pulled her close. 'We weren't enslaved by the mini-tyrant upstairs in those days.'

All the rushing around, tidying up and force-feeding Henry so that he'd stay asleep had been for nothing. Jenny wanted to cry. Were they never going to have sex again? Watching her writhe on the hospital bed with her bottom sticking out couldn't have been the sexiest thing Dan had ever seen, but had it really turned him off her for ever?

'You don't seem bothered about this. Why aren't you bothered?'

Dan kissed the top of her head. 'I just accept that things are different now – at least for a while. I expected things to change.'

Jenny sat up. It was easy for him to talk about change. What *had* actually changed for him? 'You don't understand what it's like. It's different for me. I'm fighting to keep my job, my body feels ruined and I haven't had a night out in weeks. You get to be a dad *and* keep your career. It's easy for you.'

As soon as the words were out of her mouth, Jenny wanted to claw them back in. She had never seen her husband lose his temper. She had a feeling she might be about to.

'And I don't think that *you* understand that there are people who go to work every day and hardly ever see their child during the week. One of them even lives in this house. I go out at 7 a.m. and return at 7 p.m. If I'm lucky, I get to see Henry for twenty minutes a day. Other than that, I get picture messages showing me all the things I miss out on. No one gets to have everything, Jen. No one. I am trying to support you whether you go back to work, stay at home, write a column, write a blog – whatever you want to do. But you need to stop assuming that you're the only one who has to make sacrifices.'

He was right. She was being selfish. Something else to feel guilty about. 'I know. I know. I'm sorry. I just liked our life the way it was.'

Dan let out a long breath and then took her hand. 'So did I, Jen. But our new life will be great, too. We just need to work it out.'

Jenny wasn't so sure.

✦

After dinner, Jenny found her laptop and started to look for local baby groups. There were hundreds. Baby Gym, Baby Sensory, Baby Algebra. Well, maybe not the last one but, seriously? Maybe she should start with something a bit more manageable. The local church hall had a mother and baby group. She would try that. How bad could it be?

Dan turned one eye to her. 'How's the blog going?'

'Good. When I get a chance to write it. I'm not sure how keen Eva is on it, though. It's going to take a lot of persuading to get it into the magazine.'

'Have you given her your black book yet?'

Jenny had bought a new one and was transferring some of the names and numbers across. 'Not yet.' She tapped away at the keyboard for a few more moments. 'I have a couple of weeks till I'm next in. I'll get it done by then.'

✦

Having never been known for her punctuality, Jenny wasn't sure whether her colleagues were more surprised by the fact that she was *at* the editorial meeting or the fact that she was the first one to arrive.

It was good to be back in the office, if a little strange. A bit like visiting an old school or a childhood holiday resort. The sounds and smells were familiar but she didn't feel quite part of it. She couldn't even sit at her old desk because it seemed to have been organised to within an inch of its life into a pink in-tray and coordinating box files. A nauseating framed photo of perfect people stuck to the top of the computer screen confirmed what she'd suspected: Lucy had her desk, too.

At least Maureen didn't change. 'Jenny! How lovely to see you. Where's that beautiful boy?'

'At home with Daddy. Dan has the day off.' Jenny kissed her. 'Eva not in yet?'

'She had a breakfast meeting with one of the advertisers, she'll be in soon. I'm following your blog!' Maureen announced proudly.

Jenny grinned. 'Are you? What do you think?'

'I love it! Those women you're writing about – they're a mixed bag, aren't they? I told Eva how good I think it is.'

'Thanks!' Jenny hugged her. 'And thanks for telling Eva. I'm not sure she's convinced it will work.'

'Then you need to show her.' Maureen patted her hand, then looked up. 'Oh, my word, look who else is here early. I'd best get the kettle on. Morning, Brian. Coffee?'

'Yes please, Mo.' Brian turned to Jenny. 'Hello, stranger. What are you doing here? I thought you'd left?'

The butterflies in Jenny's stomach went crazy. Why would he think she'd left? Hadn't Eva told them what she was doing? 'I'm pretty surprised to see you here at this time, too. Since when did you get in before Eva?'

The photographer was his usual dishevelled self. He rubbed the top of his head and looked sheepish. 'I didn't stay at home last night.'

It had been a long time since Jenny had done the walk of shame, but she remembered it well. 'Lucky you. I won't ask for details.

How are things here?' She narrowed her eyes. 'Haven't you been told about the new column I'm writing?'

'Oh, yeah, the one about babies. I didn't know if that was a joke.'

A joke? But Brian was grinning. He was teasing her. Jenny smiled. 'You should have a look at it. I know you like pictures, but you *can* read, right?

Brian laughed. 'Yeah. When I have to. Eva not here yet?'

'Breakfast meeting, apparently.' Jenny tried to sound nonchalant as she asked, 'How's Lucy getting on with my column?'

'Lucy? She's brilliant. And she has a *ton* of good-looking friends.' Brian gave a thumbs-up sign. 'She's much better than you at hooking me up.'

Jenny wasn't going to bite a second time. 'That's because my friends have taste.'

Brian looked up. 'Speak of the devil.'

'Jenny.' Lucy stalked towards them. 'I didn't know you were coming in. Dare I hope you're here to deliver the contacts book?'

'I've come in for the editorial meeting, actually. But, yes, I have *my* contacts book for you.' She neglected to mention that this was a censored version. She groped around in her bag and handed over the book, resisting the temptation to hold it just out of Lucy's reach. 'I'll catch up with you both in a minute. I'm just going to help Maureen with the drinks.'

✦

The rest of the staff writers arrived in dribs and drabs and were similarly surprised to see Jenny there, until Eva swept in and they followed her into her office.

'Great to have you here, Jen,' she said, before launching straight into business. 'Going around the table. What have we got for next month's issue?'

Everyone gave in their story ideas, which were either accepted, rejected or tweaked to Eva's satisfaction. Lucy gushed about a new bar opening in town that was going to run singles nights on a Thursday. Jenny resisted the urge to tell her that the guy opening the bar was a complete letch who already had a string of failed ventures behind him. His was one of the names she had copied into the book she was giving Lucy. Let her find out for herself.

Finally, it was Jenny's turn. 'Okay. *The Undercover Mother* is going really well – I have about 6,000 followers now and it's growing daily. I'm getting a good idea of which stories work well and which don't. By the time I come back, we should be good to go.'

'Hmmm,' said Eva. 'So, what exciting topics do you have in the pipeline?'

In her peripheral vision, Jenny could see a smirk spreading across Lucy's face.

How she wanted to wipe it off. And she'd just thought how to do it.

'Actually, I am going to dispel the myth that mums can't have a social life.' She turned to Lucy. 'I can accompany Lucy to one of her events. Give her the benefit of my experience at the same time.'

✦

Jenny was regretting her rash comment before she even got home and told Dan about it. What had she been thinking? The last thing she wanted was a night out in a bar; especially with Luscious Lucy.

Predictably, Dan laughed when she told him. 'How are you going to stay awake long enough to go out?'

Despite her strict instructions that Henry was not quite ready for solid food, Dan had seated him in his Bumbo, where he was happily mashing a banana between his fingers. Jenny grabbed a wet wipe and started to clean Henry's fingers, much to his annoyance.

'Just because I have a baby, it doesn't mean I can't still go out and enjoy myself.' She bent down to kiss Henry's now-clean face and was rewarded with a chunk of banana wiped into her hair.

'In theory, you have every right to a night on the town,' Dan agreed. 'In reality, you're snoring on the sofa before the nine o'clock film is through the opening credits. What time are you planning on meeting her?'

'Ten o'clock,' Jenny mumbled.

Dan snorted. 'And were you planning on going in your pyjamas?'

Flip. What to wear was another problem. The shopping trip with Antonia hadn't included 'going out' clothes, and Jenny had no idea which pre-pregnancy outfits still fitted her. Or even if they were still in fashion.

'You think I'm not up to it any more, don't you?' she challenged Dan, not about to admit that she herself was uncertain she was still up to it.

Dan kissed her on the cheek before picking Henry up and walking into the other room with him. 'Of course you are, my sweet. You might want to have an afternoon nap, though.'

Jenny pulled out another couple of wet wipes and gave the Bumbo a cursory once-over. The banana gave up easily so she turned her attention to the more stubborn baked bean juice welded to the corner of the hob. Rubbing harder and harder, she imagined it was Lucy's face.

She'd show them she could still have a night out on the town *and* be able to look after a baby. It was three hours in a bar, for goodness' sake; not reporting from a war-torn country. She'd been doing it for years.

CHAPTER SEVENTEEN

When I told Mr Baby that I am concerned about our complete lack of a social life, he guffawed rudely and reminded me that I'd fallen asleep at twenty past nine last night.

Posh and Mr Posh already go out all the time; she even complains that it's too often. Since their 'post-birth bonding period', Sporty hasn't mentioned a romantic night out with Mr Sporty, and I assume that's because it would entail her actually putting Baby Sporty down. And who knows what goes on with Scary and the Secret Dad.

I've toyed with the idea of a girl's night out with the Spice Mums. But would we actually have anything to say to one another if the babies weren't there?...

From *The Undercover Mother*

✦

Choosing what to wear had been a mission. Antonia had come over to help her and had even loaned her a pair of sparkly shoes; Jenny was hoping they would distract people from her large backside. The only part of her outfit she was happy with was her bag; it was small and contained nothing but money, keys and mobile. If she could only shake off this feeling that she had forgotten something.

As the cab drew up outside Chequers, her butterflies got worse. This was madness. She had spent half her life in this place for the last five years. What was she worried about? She paid the cab driver, sucked in her stomach and walked inside.

'Jenny. You came.' Lucy made no effort to hide her disappointment, which helped to cheer Jenny a little. Lucy led the way to a small table at the back of the bar where three blonde women were sitting drinking cocktails. 'This is Mia, Tia and Pia.' *Okay, so those aren't their names, but they might as well be. They look like backing singers from the Barbie Band.* 'They're my "crew".' Lucy made inverted commas signs with her fingers.

Jenny didn't appreciate her mocking tone.

'It's so great to meet you!' said Tia. Or was that Mia? 'How is your baby? I think babies are so cute!' The others murmured agreement.

'Er, yes. He's great, thanks. He just turned four months.'

'It must be lovely being at home all week,' said Pia (Mia?) wistfully. 'I'd love not having to get up to an alarm clock every morning.'

'Yeah, would be good, wouldn't it?' Jenny was bored of this already. 'Unfortunately, though, babies are very similar to alarm clocks. Except you don't choose what time to set them and they don't have a snooze button.'

'Still, all that time to do what you want. You could start a hobby. Like…' Lucy waved her hand around, pretending to try to think of something. 'Like writing a blog.'

Jenny narrowed her eyes. She wasn't going to give Lucy the benefit of a scathing comment. Even if she could think of one. 'No time for hobbies. Babies take up a lot of time.'

'Really?' Lucy looked as if she didn't believe her. 'But doesn't it… sorry, I mean "he", just lie there most of the time?'

The other three women looked at Jenny expectantly. Suddenly, she had a yearning for the couch at home. 'Sorry. I just need to go to the toilet. I'll be right back.'

✦

The toilet door deadened the noise from the bar. When did they decide to make the music in this place so loud? Jenny checked her mobile for messages from Dan and sent an *Everything okay?* text. Being here felt wrong. Why had she come? Was she going to challenge Lucy to an arm wrestle for her job? Maybe she should just have a couple of drinks, show her face around a bit and then slink off early. Leave them wanting more.

On her way back from the toilet, she was accosted by Frank. Frank was the owner of Chequers and the campest straight man you could hope to meet. His eyes flicked her up and down her in the time it took most people to blink. 'Jenny! So fab to see you! I heard you were ill or something?'

Jenny kissed him on both cheeks. 'No, I just had a baby.'

'Oh.' His expression suggested illness would have been preferable. 'Well, you're here now. What can I get you? Mojito?'

'Thanks, Frank. But I need to start slowly. It's been a while. Maybe a white wine spritzer?'

Frank grimaced. 'This is not the sixth-form disco, sweetheart. I'll bring you something over. Are you sitting with the lovely Lucy?'

When Jenny got back to the 'lovely Lucy', she found the girls surrounded by a group of men. Her heart sank. She already felt like a maiden aunt at a wedding, and being forced to chat to lads on the pull was only going to make the night worse. Lucy wriggled out from the group and pulled Jenny to one side. At least three of the men watched her go.

'Mark has been asking after you. Wanted to know if you were coming back to *Flair*,' she shouted above the music.

Jenny was surprised he even cared. She'd filed his business card in the recycling bin as soon as she'd got back from the advertising event. 'Really? See a lot of him, do you?'

Lucy smirked. 'Depends what you mean by *seeing a lot*.' That was a mental picture Jenny could have lived without.

Lucy sipped her drink and looked out over the dance floor. 'I'm surprised you came tonight, actually. Eva warned me that you might cry off.'

Jenny was affronted. 'Did she? Why?'

Lucy shrugged. 'People change once they have babies. She said you wouldn't party like you used to.'

'That's ridiculous! She couldn't be more wrong. I couldn't wait to get out tonight,' Jenny shouted back, waving her fists either side of her head to symbolise her readiness to boogie. She felt an awakening rush of adrenalin. How dare Eva assume she'd changed? 'It's so good to be back doing what I love to do.' Just at that moment, Frank appeared carrying something creamy but deadly. She snatched it from him and took a huge gulp. 'Let's get this party started!'

◆

It wasn't long before she was praying for the night to be over. The dance floor was a tragedy. Cramming her feet into Antonia's six-inch heels had been a really bad idea. Her feet still hadn't gone back to their pre-pregnancy size and she would be walking like a newborn calf in the morning. She couldn't avoid her reflection in one of the many mirrors, either. When had she started dancing like her mother?

And why had she drunk those awful drinks? Tomorrow was going to be hard. Nappy changing with a hangover? Horrific. But she knew why she'd drunk them. Because she hadn't wanted to admit to Lucy that Eva had been right.

Still on the dance floor, Lucy was enjoying the attention of a good-looking man in a rather shiny suit, so, once she had briefly caught her eye, Jenny made the internationally recognised sign for a telephone call with her thumb and little finger, and slipped outside.

It took Dan seven rings to answer and, when he did, he sounded sleepy. 'Hello?'

'Hi, it's me. Just checking everything is okay.'

'Yes, fine. We were just dozing in front of *Storage Wars*.'

'Did he have his milk at eight o'clock?'

'Yep. Guzzled the lot.'

'Did you wind him?'

'Yes. He did a burp suitably loud for a boys' night.'

'And he's now asleep?'

'We both were until you called. Are you having a good time?'

'Yes, it's great,' she lied. 'So good to be out and about. But I can come home if you're feeling tired?'

'No, I'm fine. Now you've woken me up I might go and make something to eat.'

'Well, shall I come home and watch Henry so you can eat in peace? Or I could pick you up some takeaway?'

'I'm only going to have a sandwich. I can easily eat that, even if he wakes up.' Dan paused. 'Hang on, are you looking for an excuse to leave?'

'No! No, of course not. I can't wait to get back on the dance floor. I'll leave you to it. See you later.'

When she got back to the table, there were two psychedelic shots waiting for her. 'You're playing catch up – get those two down you!' shouted Lucy.

Jenny took one look at the bile green and electric blue liquids in front of her and made a decision. 'I'm so sorry. Dan just isn't coping and I could hear Henry screaming down the phone. I have to go.'

✦

Outside, Jenny had to fight her way through a sea of fake tan and sparkles, tottering girls with their arms threaded together and men punching each other on the shoulder and laughing. At least the queue at the taxi rank was short; most people weren't going home this side of midnight. Her feet ached, her head buzzed and she just wanted to be home. Home with Henry and Dan. Having a cuddle. And tea. She really wanted tea.

If her toes hadn't been so sore, she would have kicked herself. Why had she said she would come out with Lucy? There was probably a smug text on its way to Eva right now, saying Jenny was a lightweight and had gone home early. That she couldn't cut it any more.

Maybe Lucy was right.

Jenny was almost at the front of the taxi queue when she noticed a familiar, slim figure walking towards her, slightly unsteady on its feet. It took her a moment to recognise who it was because the figure was wearing a fitted black dress rather than her trademark floaty top and jeans. And because she was crying.

'Naomi? Is that you? Are you okay?'

Naomi looked up, gave a grimacing smile and then started to cry harder. 'No, I'm not okay. I've just had a huge row with John and left him in a bar down there. I tried to call Gail, but she turns her ringer off in the evening so that work can't disturb her time with Jake.' She started to rummage in her bag for a tissue. 'It was supposed to be a romantic night. It was supposed to be just us. It was awful. Just awful.' She started to sob again.

Jenny put an arm around her. 'Come with me. I can drop you home and you can tell me all about it.' They were at the front of the queue. Jenny gave the cab driver Naomi's address and nudged her inside.

'Why did we even bother going out tonight?' Naomi sobbed. 'We started rowing before we'd even left the house. His bloody interfering mother!'

'What happened? Did she change Daisy's clothes again?' Jenny could just imagine how that might have gone down.

'She's babysitting for us tonight, which—' Naomi held her hands up in front of her swaying body '—I am grateful for. She said we should have some time together as a couple. I was almost feeling guilty for the things I've said about her, and then she had to ruin it all by bringing about ten jars of baby food with her.'

'Right.' Jenny began to piece together why Naomi was so upset. 'And that was bad because…'

'Because we are not giving Daisy anything until she's six months old. And even then I won't be feeding her stupid pap from a jar. I don't CARE that she thinks Daisy is hungry. I couldn't give a CHUFF that she weaned John at four months. She needs to STOP STICKING HER BLOODY BIG FAT NOSE IN!'

Jenny had never seen Naomi this angry. 'Could you not just take the jars and throw them away when she's gone?'

'NO!' roared Naomi, loud enough for the cab driver to glance back at them in his rear-view mirror. 'That's what John says. Always trying to keep the peace. Never telling her to leave us alone to do it our way. If we don't tell her to stop, where is it going to end? I just know she's going to be one of those grandmothers who is always bringing sweets and junk food. Well, not for my baby, she isn't.'

Jenny had fond memories of her own grandmother's sweet tin, but she didn't think she should mention that. 'At least you got a romantic night out, though?' Naomi's reaction quickly told her that this redirection hadn't had the desired effect.

'Ha! Romantic night out? Just the two of us? That's what I thought, too.' She hiccupped loudly. 'Except when we got there, the place was full of John's bloody friends.'

'Oh. Did he know they were going to be there?'

'He says not, but I have my doubts. That silly bloody cow he went to bloody Peru with was there looking like a bloody catwalk model. John made a pretence of sitting somewhere on our own, but of course they wouldn't let us. And then off they went, stories from their younger days. What fun they all used to have. What a shame they hardly saw John any more. Blah, blah, bloody blah.' Jenny wondered if Naomi was breaking some record for the most bloodys in one breath. 'And they treat me like I'm the woman who bloody ruined everything.'

Jenny had often expressed concern that Dan never bothered to stay in touch with his friends, but she could see the up-side to it now. 'Maybe John didn't realise—'

'So I told him!' Naomi cut her off. 'I told him that I had nearly got an abortion when I found out I was pregnant and I asked him if he wished I had.'

Jenny was speechless. For the next few moments, she just focused on the raised eyebrows in the cab driver's rear-view mirror.

CHAPTER EIGHTEEN

There's a side effect to motherhood that no one tells you about: all the crying.

Not the baby. You.

Sure, you expect to get weepy and emotional when you're pregnant. It's the damn hormones. When the baby blues kicked in, I cried so much I'm surprised I wasn't treated for dehydration. However, that's not the crying I'm talking about. It's the other sort, the crying that creeps up on you when you're not expecting it.

At each stage of The Boy's development there seems to be fresh opportunities for my tear ducts to kick into overdrive. I cried when I found breastfeeding difficult (although, in my defence, part of that was actual physical pain), sobbed when Mr Baby had to go back to work, and wept when The Boy smiled for the first time. There's likely to be a full-on tsunami when he starts to walk or call me 'Mum'...

From The Undercover Mother

✦

The problem with health freaks is that they never have the hard stuff to hand when it's needed. There was only decaf coffee in Naomi's cupboards, but it would have to do. Over the rumble of the boiling kettle, Jenny heard the bathroom door bang open and got there just in time to hold Naomi's hair back from the toilet bowl as she threw up. A relationship-defining moment in most of her friendships: surprising it should happen with Naomi.

'I'm sorry. I'm so sorry,' Naomi sobbed between heaves. 'You must think I'm…'

'Shhh. Don't speak. You'll be all right in a minute.' Although tomorrow morning was going to be rough for both of them.

Naomi couldn't face coffee. Instead, she curled up on the sofa, holding a large glass of water with both hands. 'What did you say to John's mum?'

'I just told her you'd eaten some dodgy prawns.' It was very unlikely that Naomi's mother-in-law had believed Jenny's story, but at least she'd left without any fuss.

Naomi sipped her water. They were quiet for few moments and then she asked, 'Do you hate me? Now you know that I thought about… about ending the pregnancy.'

'Hate you? Of course not. It's none of my business.' Jenny wasn't naive: she knew other people who had faced this tough decision. But this was Naomi. 'Breast is best' Naomi. She even used washable baby wipes. She'd been so enthusiastic about everything at antenatal. Who could have guessed she hadn't been ecstatic to find herself pregnant?

'I want you to understand why. I want to tell you.'

And Jenny wanted to know. 'You don't need to explain yourself to me.'

Naomi sat up straight; she wasn't going to be put off. 'My head was all over the place. I'd had such a great time travelling and I just wanted to keep going. I only came home to work and get some money together.'

'What about John – were you not together?'

'We only met a few weeks before I came home. I liked him, and we'd been texting. He even hinted he might like to come with me if I went away again, but it was early days. Can you imagine how I felt? I was so frightened. It felt like the world was closing in on me. I didn't know if I *ever* wanted a baby, let alone right then. Do you know how it feels to be trapped like that?'

Did Jenny know? No, it was not something she had ever had to face. But that was much more through luck than judgement. What if she'd got pregnant when she'd been with Mark? It didn't bear thinking about.

'I understand, Naomi. Honestly, I do.'

Naomi took another large gulp of water. 'I thought I would just have to take a pill – like a strong morning-after pill – and that would be it. But I was too far gone. I'd been sick for a while and my period was late, but everything had gone out of kilter while I was travelling. It took a while before I realised.'

'So, you would have had to…'

Naomi grimaced. 'They called it a medical procedure. They talked me through the whole thing, what it would entail. Suddenly it all seemed real. What I was actually doing.' Tears started to drip from the end of her nose.

Naomi seemed almost relieved to be unburdening herself. Perhaps she hadn't told many people about this. Had she told anyone? Clearly, John hadn't known until tonight.

'My sister had a miscarriage just before I went away. It was awful. And when I was sitting in the waiting room, reading the pamphlets they gave me, I just kept thinking about my sister. How much she had cried and cried after her miscarriage. And now, when I think about Ruth…' Naomi covered her mouth with her hand.

Jenny had been thinking about Ruth, too. She put her hand on Naomi's arm. 'Were you on your own at the clinic?'

Naomi nodded.

'Did John even know that you were pregnant at that point?'

Naomi shook her head and her lip started to wobble again.

'So you had no idea how he was going to react?'

'How *anyone* was going to react. I hadn't told anyone.'

'Oh, Naomi. That must have been so hard.'

Naomi just nodded slowly. Jenny put her arms around her as she sobbed.

After a while, Naomi sat up and wiped her face. 'When they called my name, I couldn't do it. I couldn't even walk through the door. I got up, went home and told my parents.'

'And then John?'

Naomi nodded. 'And he was incredible. He made it sound like we could do it. We could have the baby and make a go of things together. So we did.' She paused. 'You know at the class, when Sally said we should sing or read to the babies? That they might recognise our voices when they were born?'

Jenny wasn't sure why they were talking about this. 'Yes, I remember.'

Naomi's voice dropped to a whisper. 'She would have heard. Daisy would have heard what I was doing. What I was… planning on doing.'

'Oh, Naomi.'

Naomi started to cry again. 'I'm not sure how I will ever make it up to her. Every time I look at Daisy I think… I think that…' She put her head back on Jenny's shoulder. 'You won't tell anyone, will you, Jenny? Please don't tell anyone.'

'Of course I won't.' The only person Jenny was due to see in the next few days was Ruth, and she certainly wouldn't be regaling *her* with Naomi's story.

Naomi the super-mother. It made a lot of sense now.

✦

Ruth was due at ten. Jenny would rather have met her at a café, which wouldn't involve tidying up, but Ruth had wanted to talk to her where no one else would be able to overhear them.

That morning, Henry had been an absolute angel, not waking up until almost seven o'clock. A full eight hours' sleep! Now he lay on a mat, kicking his feet at the slightly sinister-looking animals dangling from his play gym. The dirty plates from last night's dinner and the pile of laundry that needed to be sorted could wait. Time to open the laptop and work on the blog.

The disastrous night out with Lucy had confirmed it. Jenny didn't want her 'Girl About Town' job back any time soon – if ever. She had hated watching Lucy schmooze her way around that club, but she didn't want to be the one doing it in her place. It had been horrible. And exhausting.

However, Eva's non-committal attitude about whether the blog would transfer to the magazine was speaking volumes. 'Mildly funny' were the words she had used; words that were fairly damning in Eva's high-octane world. Jenny knew that there was something missing. It had been easy before, as someone always did something crazy or stupid: disappearing with the waiter at a new restaurant, or losing their shoes at a nightclub. It was more difficult to find something humorous when all you were doing was drinking tea and singing nursery rhymes.

She began to write in her notepad.

Gail was still not revealing anything about Joe. There had to be a good story there; some reason why they still hadn't met him, or even seen a photo. Dan's suggestion that 'he probably just isn't interested in us' didn't cut it. Even if Gail didn't want to introduce him to the whole group, surely one of them should have seen him by now?

Next, she wrote 'Naomi and John' with a big question mark. A Google search for 'Babies and your relationship' uncovered some startling stats. One study showed that a baby increased the risk of divorce by around 37 per cent – even higher if you had a baby within a year of meeting each other. A newly single mother might make for more exciting blog storylines, but Jenny was really hoping that Naomi and John would make it.

Lastly, she wrote Antonia's name down and drew two arrows to the words 'Man in café?' There had been nothing much to suggest there was anything less than innocent about her rendezvous, but

Jenny had a hunch that there was more to it than two friends meeting for a drink.

This just left Ruth. Jenny sighed and sat back in her chair. Ruth hadn't featured in *The Undercover Mother* so far; it hadn't felt right. But there were other women who this had happened to, other women who it was going to happen to. Could she somehow put Ruth's story in there in a way that was sensitive and helpful?

It wasn't worth thinking about until she had spoken to Ruth about it, though. It was one thing writing about Naomi's obsession with organic cotton without telling her; this was completely different. The question was, if she told Ruth about the blog, would she have to tell the others? Jenny looked at her watch. Ruth was due to visit in about half an hour: time to start scooping debris into cupboards and under the sofa.

✦

Ruth was right on time and carrying a large cake tin when Jenny opened the door. She waved the tin as she came in. 'I'm still baking.'

'Well, the cake we ate at your house was delicious.' Jenny took the tin from her. 'I'll make us a cup of tea to go with it. Go through to the lounge.' Jenny went into the kitchen to put the kettle on and find a pretty plate for the cake. When she carried it through to the lounge, she found Ruth sitting on the floor, holding Henry's hand, tears running down her face.

Ruth turned a wet face towards Jenny as she came in. 'Sorry, I'm sorry. I thought I would be okay.'

'Don't apologise. It was silly – we should have gone out on our own.'

'No, no.' Ruth shook her head. 'I've got to get used to it. It's just, you know, he's the same age and everything.'

Jenny put the cake plate down on the coffee table. 'Do you want to talk about it, or do you want me to make inane chatter about reality TV and the price of washing powder?'

Ruth gave a weak smile and then turned back to look at Henry, who still had a grip of steel on her finger. 'I told you we were trying again, didn't I?'

Jenny nodded. 'Yes. You told me and Naomi when we came to yours.'

'Well, neither of us could bear to go back into that monthly cycle of ovulation charts and disappointment, and the fertility people still won't touch us. So, we're just letting nature take her course and waiting to see what happens.' Ruth didn't seem very enthusiastic about this plan.

'But is that what *you* want?'

Ruth took a deep breath. She turned her head slowly and looked at Jenny, then looked back at Henry, who was kicking his feet at a dangling giraffe. 'I'm on the pill.'

Jenny was confused. 'But I thought you said…' As Ruth looked up at her, she grasped what she was trying to tell her. 'Oh. David doesn't know.'

Ruth shook her head. Guilt flashed across her face. Clearly, this was not something she had told anyone else. Her voice was just above a whisper. 'I'm scared.'

Jenny took her hand. 'Oh, Ruth, of course you are. But surely that kind of thing doesn't happen twice? Everything should be fine next time. That's what the doctors told you, didn't they?'

Ruth nodded, but her eyes were full as she looked at Jenny. 'It was so awful.'

Jenny struggled not to start crying herself. The thought of losing Henry was unbearable. Physically painful. 'I can't even begin to imagine what it was like. I am so sorry that you had to go through that.'

Ruth was gazing at Henry again. 'She was so beautiful, Jen. She looked just like David. She had a perfect little mouth and her eyes were closed so gently, like she was sleeping. She felt warm from being inside me and I just kept hoping. I couldn't understand why they couldn't do anything to revive her when she looked so perfect… We dressed her in a little white sleepsuit and just kept looking at her… I didn't want to leave. It didn't feel right, leaving her alone like that.' Her voice wavered and she paused. With her free hand, she brushed the tears away from her face.

Jenny squeezed the hand she was holding. What could she say? Nothing would help.

Ruth hadn't taken her eyes from Henry the whole time she was talking. 'My mum offered to go to the house and clear away the baby things before I went home, but I asked her not to. I wasn't ready to give them up yet… That beautiful pram, which took us weeks to choose… The crocheted blanket my sister made for her… The tiny vests and sleepsuits that I'd washed and folded so neatly in her drawers… For the first few days, I just sat in the nursery, touching everything, saying goodbye to it. It was like it wasn't meant to be, like I'd been playing a game about having a baby, and now I had to stop playing and go back to work.' She paused again and took a deep breath before looking at Jenny. 'And that's how I feel now. That it just wasn't meant to be.'

Jenny's heart hurt for her. 'Have you told David how you feel?'

Ruth shook her head. 'I don't think I can. That man was destined to be a dad. How can I take it away from him?'

Jenny knew she was right. But it was also obvious how much he loved his wife.

'How can I say to him that I don't want to try for another baby? It would break his heart.'

Jenny thought of the story Ruth had told her at the antenatal class, about the number of pregnancy tests she had taken in her excitement about having a baby. 'Are you *sure* that you don't want to try again?'

'No, I'm not sure. If a doctor could guarantee me a healthy baby, I'd walk over hot coals and cut glass to get to it. But no one can guarantee me that, can they? No one can promise that I won't have to feel again that my own body somehow killed my baby, for no reason that anyone can give me. That I won't have to go through labour again and still go home with nothing except a huge aching emptiness that never goes away. Have to watch my husband be terribly, terribly brave, and then listen to him sob in the next room when he thinks I'm asleep.' She paused again, then whispered, 'If it happened to us again, Jenny, I don't think we could survive it.'

Jenny couldn't bear to see the pain in Ruth's eyes. There had to be a way to help. 'You can't carry all this on your own. I know that David would understand. What about counselling? Have you had support from someone who has helped other people in your situation?'

'Yes, the hospital was very good. We both had bereavement counselling and it helped a bit, being able to talk about how we felt. But even they admitted that these feelings might never go away completely. I don't even *want* them to go away; I don't want to forget her.'

Jenny was adrift in uncharted territory. *Go with your gut.* 'Having another baby wouldn't mean you'd forget her. You wouldn't be replacing her.'

Ruth looked up with a face so haunted that it made Jenny's heart contract involuntarily. 'I have spent years wanting to be pregnant, and now it is the most terrifying thing I can imagine.'

✦

When Ruth had gone home, Jenny picked Henry up from his play mat and held him close. His warm, wriggly body felt solid and real in her arms. Putting her nose into the crease of his neck, she breathed in deeply. Right then, she couldn't care less about Lucy and her 'Girl About Town' column. How could a night out on the town meeting random strangers possibly compare with this?

However, it didn't look like *The Undercover Mother* was going to make it into print, either. Jenny had hoped that writing about Ruth's experiences might have taken the blog in a different direction and piqued Eva's interest. But after the conversation they'd just had, it would have been completely inappropriate to talk to Ruth about the blog. It all seemed so unimportant.

So where did that leave her? She didn't want to fight for her 'Girl About Town' job, and Eva didn't want her to write about being a mum. Maybe the time had come to see if someone else would?

Henry had dozed off on her shoulder. Holding him with one arm, she slipped carefully onto a seat at the dining table and opened her laptop.

Google search.

Mark McLinley.

CHAPTER NINETEEN

I love being a mum. I really do. But sometimes, it's a little... (come closer)... boring.

I can't mention this to the Spice Mums. Scary has to leave Baby Scary every day to go to work, so she would think me downright ungrateful if I moaned about my day at home. Sporty, meanwhile, is emphatic that being a mother is the best thing that ever happened to her and maintains that she enjoys every single minute. Can that really be true?

There are, of course, an awful lot of minutes in the day where I AM enjoying it. But there are others when the repetition of changing, feeding and getting to sleep makes me yearn for my previous life of boozy lunches and adult conversation. I wouldn't swap time with The Boy for anything, but I'd be lying if I told you I preferred a cheese sandwich in my kitchen to brie parcels at Mezzo...

From *The Undercover Mother*

✦

The restaurant was busy but quiet, apart from a low hum of conversation and the occasional chink of glasses. The maître d' was attentive in taking Jenny's coat and escorting her to the table where Mark was waiting. Ever the gentleman, Mark stood to kiss her on both cheeks, then pulled out a chair for her to sit. It felt like decades since she'd last done this.

'Great choice of restaurant.' She looked around her. 'It's a new one to me.'

Mark was in his element here. Looking like he'd just stepped out of the pages of *GQ*, he'd already attracted glances from two of the other tables. 'I thought you'd like it. You did always have a fondness for the finer things in life.' He winked.

Jenny was determined to keep all conversations strictly business. She already felt guilty. She had told Dan who she was meeting – had practically asked for his permission – but her husband wasn't a jealous man. 'If you think that's best, it's fine by me. Just order the most expensive thing on the menu.' But it wasn't Dan she felt guilty about.

'Thanks for seeing me so quickly. I know you must be pretty busy.'

Mark smiled. 'There's got to be some payback for you having put up with me for all that time.' He opened his expensive suit jacket and leaned forwards. 'Anyway, I'm hoping this conversation is going to be to our mutual benefit…?'

A waiter appeared by the side of the table and filled their water glasses. Mark picked up the wine list. 'Before we get down to business, what would you like to drink? Are you still a Chablis girl?'

What was it with all these references to their mutual past? Had this been a terrible mistake?

'Whatever you want to order will be fine. I'm on quite a tight schedule so I'd like to hear what you thought of *The Undercover Mother*.'

'We'll get to it, Jen. Let me order the wine first.' Mark took his time reading the wine list. Then he asked the wine waiter for his opinion, before settling on something whose long French name sounded expensive.

Finally, he turned his attention back to her. 'I must admit, I was a little surprised to get your call. I thought you were attached to *Flair* with an umbilical cord. Does Eva know you're meeting me?'

Jenny's conscience twanged. Of course Eva didn't know.

'I'm still on maternity leave. I only came to the advertisers' event to keep my hand in.'

Mark smirked. 'Good for you. Best not to burn your boats, eh?'

Jenny knew that Mark was an expert on not burning boats. Or rather, making sure he had a new bed-warmer lined up before he ousted the current one.

Despite herself, Jenny couldn't resist. 'So, how *is* Lucy?'

Mark chuckled. 'I don't know what you mean.'

If Mark and Lucy were in a relationship, Jenny knew he would have told Lucy to keep it secret in the interests of avoiding 'talk' that might get back to Eva about her journalists fraternising with a rival editor. She wasn't interested in the gory details.

'Have you read the pages I sent?'

Mark sighed a 'You're no fun any more' sigh. 'I did. Well done. You've made a boring topic almost entertaining.'

Jenny ignored the faint praise. There was too much at stake to annoy him. 'So, what do you think?'

Mark looked confused. 'What do you mean? I've just told you what I think. It's entertaining.'

It was Jenny's turn to sigh. Did he want her to beg? 'About running the column. *The Undercover Mother.* In your magazine.' Should she try sign language?

'*The Undercover Mother*? In my…?' Mark's frown of incomprehension smoothed away and a smile spread across his face. 'This is a joke, right? One of your jokes?'

Jenny felt her face grow hot. 'Not a joke, no. You told me to call you if I wanted to write the column for you instead of Eva. At the advertising event. You gave me your card.' She wished she hadn't recycled it – she could have pulled it out of her bag as proof. He had said that, hadn't he?

'I don't want to be rude here, Jen, but that is not what I said. A motherhood column? No. Not for *Suave*. Not at all. If Eva doesn't want it, I can't imagine why you thought that I would.'

Jenny didn't need to ask how he knew that Eva didn't want the column. *Damn Lucy.* She stiffened. 'So, why did you agree to see me?'

Mark sat back in his chair. 'Isn't it obvious? To discuss you writing a new column for me. Once you've got yourself back into shape, obviously. A staff writer position, with your own column, just like "Girl About Town". But bigger. Better. I was thinking along the lines of the "View from the Boys" column I wrote for *Flair*, but the other way around. You can help our testosterone-fuelled readers to get into the mind of a woman. We could call it "What Women Want".' He leaned forward conspiratorially. 'Don't you want to show Eva and Lucy what you can do?'

Jenny excused herself to go to the toilet. There, she splashed water onto her face to cool it down. Either the lunchtime wine or the embarrassment of having pitched a parenting column to her Lothario of an ex-boyfriend had given her an uncomfortable rosy glow. How had she been so stupid?

When she got back to the table, Mark had refilled her glass and was trying a different route of attack.

'You were made for this kind of life.' Mark swept his hand out to encompass the restaurant. 'What kind of social events will you go to as a parenting writer? Mothercare openings? Church fetes with "Bouncing Baby" competitions?' He laughed. 'Come on, Jen. Tell me you aren't missing all this—?'

She couldn't tell him that, because she was. She was missing meals in nice restaurants, and getting dressed up and drinking cocktails with ridiculous names. She was missing it all. Despite the awkwardness of being here with Mark, she loved the food, the service, the being somewhere new where not many people could get a table this side of Christmas. Mentally, she had already written a rave review about it being an 'ultimate date venue'. But she still wouldn't swap it for an evening on the sofa with Dan and Henry.

'It's great, but that's just not me any more. I want to do something new. Write about being a parent.'

Mark shook his head. 'You're lying.'

✦

After the chrome and white of the restaurant, Jenny's kitchen felt shabby and unstylish and cramped – even though Claire had cleaned it for her whilst she babysat Henry.

Jenny tried to see her sister's work as an act of kindness rather than judgement.

'How was your lunch? Have you signed a new contract?'

Jenny wasn't ready to admit what had happened. 'Not yet. We still need to discuss what the nature of the column will be. Where's Henry?'

'Upstairs in his cot, having a nap. What do you mean, "the nature of the column"? I thought you were going to write this "Undercover Mother" thing?'

Jenny was impressed that Claire remembered the name of the blog. She was also impressed that Henry was taking a nap in his own cot. How had Claire managed that?

'Possibly. Or maybe a wider subject. Like general women's stuff. Lifestyle. Social life. You know.'

Claire narrowed her eyes. 'You're going back to what you did before.'

Jenny wasn't in the mood to discuss it. She hadn't given Mark a definite 'no', because he'd made her feel so uncertain about everything. He'd been so dismissive of the blog... And she had really enjoyed being out in the real world again. Maybe she *could* do Mark's column and still be home enough for Henry. She needed time to think.

'I don't know what I'm going to do yet.'

Claire had never suffered from uncertainty in her life. She plucked her cashmere cardigan from the back of one of the kitchen chairs and slipped it on. 'Well, I think you're mad. Do you remember how often you were out when you were doing that job? Your husband is quite possibly the most patient man I know.'

Here we go again. 'You don't understand.'

Claire was pulling on her boots. 'You're right. I don't. You've finally got a wonderful life with a husband and a baby and you want to jeopardise it by—'

'My life has always been pretty wonderful, thank you very much.' It was amazing how much this line still rankled with Jenny. 'Just because you think a husband and baby is the pinnacle of success doesn't mean that it actually is. Do you know there are women out there who don't even *want* children? Can you imagine?'

Claire finished zipping up her boots and stood up. 'I know that you think my life is the height of boredom, Jennifer, but being a mum is the most fulfilling thing I have ever done. One day you are going to look back at all the things you have missed out on and wonder if the posh lunches were really worth it.'

Jenny was too angry to trust her mouth. How dare her sister reduce her writing career to 'posh lunches'?

Claire hadn't finished. 'And on that subject, you might have mentioned that Henry has started rolling over. I left him on his mat whilst I went to the toilet and he was almost at the door by the time I got back.'

Jenny froze. She had been trying for weeks now to get Henry to move. She should be pleased that he was doing it. So why did she feel tears pricking at the back of her eyes? *Do* not *cry.*

But Jenny's face gave her away and Claire realised what she had done. She softened her voice. 'Oh, Jen. I'm so sorry. Was this his first time? I honestly wouldn't have said anything if I'd known. It's awful when you miss out on any of the firsts.'

Her sister's sympathy made Jenny even more cross. This was ridiculous. Why did it matter that she hadn't seen his first roll? But somehow, it did.

'It doesn't matter. I'm sure I'll see it later.'

Claire started to say something, then stopped. She picked up their coffee cups and took them to the sink to wash them up.

Even this bugged Jenny. Why couldn't she just stick them in the dishwasher like a normal person?

'Actually, I was going to ask you for a favour.' Claire rinsed the cups and put them on the draining board. She didn't turn around. 'Can you help me write a CV?'

This was a surprise. 'A CV? What do you need a CV for?'

'A job, of course. It's been a while since I've applied for a job and you're good at writing, so I thought you could help.' Claire found a tea towel in the drawer and started to dry the cups.

Jenny was still confused. 'A job? For you?'

Claire opened a few cupboards before finding a home for the mugs. 'Yes, for me. What's so shocking? I did work before I had the children, you know.'

Jenny could barely remember her sister pre-parenthood. 'But why now?'

'Both children are at secondary school. I'm at home all day. There's no reason for me not to get a job.'

Jenny detected Steve, Claire's husband, in this. He'd spent the last decade or so openly questioning what his wife did all day.

Any joke about her leaving her children alone would only open the floodgates for another lecture, so Jenny kept to the facts. 'What are you applying for?'

'I don't know yet. Office work, I suppose. I can only work ten till two so that I can drop off and collect the children. And I need the school holidays off, of course.' She thought for a moment. 'And no weekend work. Other than that, I'm completely flexible.' She looked at Jenny so brightly that Jenny didn't have the heart to tell her she was living in cloud cuckoo land.

Jenny stifled a smile. 'Okay. Well, when you've found something which fits the bill, let me know and we'll knock up a CV.'

'Great. Thanks.' Henry started to cry upstairs. 'I'll go, and let you see to him.'

Jenny gave her sister a brief kiss on the cheek. 'Thanks for looking after him.'

Claire smiled. 'It was a pleasure. A real pleasure.' She paused in putting her coat on. 'You haven't even explored the idea of what it would be like to give up work, Jen. Have you tried a baby group?'

Jenny shook her head and started up the stairs. 'No, I've been too busy.' *Too busy putting it off.*

'Just try it,' Claire called after her. 'Speak to some of the mums there. Find out how they find it being at home with a baby. You might surprise yourself.'

CHAPTER TWENTY

This week I learned about Attachment Parenting, which seems to mean that parents are, like Sporty, almost always physically attached to their baby. There are also Authoritative Parents, who set clear rules and expect their child to follow them. My money is on Scary for that one – I'd like to see anyone brave enough to refuse her instructions. Posh, on the other hand, with her detached attitude, is more likely to be a Permissive Parent. According to parenting websites, these parents allow their child to do as they wish, only stepping in at the last moment – if, for example, the child is hanging off a window ledge or about to climb inside the cooker.

The list goes on. Snowplough Parenting (clearing anything potentially harmful out of their child's way – from friends who might upset them, to the wrong kind of sandwich on a play date); Helicopter Parenting (over-protective parents who constantly hover over their child); Outsourced Parenting (employing baby home-proofers, sleep consultants and, I kid you not, a thumb-sucking guru who will fly from Chicago – for rates starting at $4,300 – to cure your child of putting its fingers in its mouth) and Tiger Parenting (the new term for the competitive mother who can be identified by her hissing of, 'You will thank me for this one day,' as she drags her weeping child to piano practice for the fourth time that week.)

Now I am completely freaked out – which of these nutcases am I going to turn into?...

From *The Undercover Mother*

✦

Standing outside the church hall, Jenny could hear muffled cries, shouts and a clatter of crockery from inside. Taking a deep breath, she opened the door – to be confronted by a baby gate. Worse, a brand of baby gate she hadn't seen before.

She hoisted Henry onto her hip, pushing and squeezing anything on the gate that looked remotely like a button, quickly degenerating into shaking it in the hope that it would miraculously open. Thankfully, one of the other mothers rescued her, before dashing off in the wake of a chubby toddler.

The church hall was pretty bare, but the floor was covered in an array of coloured plastic. There were babies and small children *everywhere*. Usually, Jenny would have no problem walking up to complete strangers and starting a conversation – but that was when she had a glass of wine in her hand. What was the form here? 'Get a grip,' she mumbled under her breath, and strode purposefully towards a large play mat.

Laying Henry next to a collection of small toys, watching as he kicked his legs and gurgled, she marvelled at how much she loved him. Maybe letting the column go wouldn't be such a huge price to pay to get to spend more time with him.

Her conversation with Ruth earlier that morning had brought it home, loud and clear, how lucky she was.

'I need to talk to someone and you're the only one who knows what's going on,' Ruth blurted, as soon as Jenny had answered the phone.

If Ruth came over, Jenny had thought, that would give her an excuse for missing the baby group again. 'Of course. Do you want to come here for a coffee?'

'No. Sorry. It's not that I don't want to, but I haven't really felt like going out anywhere this week.' Ruth took a deep breath. 'It's David. He has been talking about starting fertility treatment again.

He's not pushing – he says he will wait as long as I need to, but he wants me to know that he's ready when I am.'

That was a surprise. 'I thought he was happy with the "let nature take its course" approach for a while?'

'Well, he was. But he said nature doesn't seem to want to play ball.'

Jenny paused before phrasing her next question. 'Is nature still not being given a chance?'

'If you mean am I still on the pill, then yes.' Ruth took a deep breath. Her voice dropped to a whisper. 'I can't stand deceiving him, Jenny. I've even thought about just leaving him and giving him the chance to meet someone else.'

Jenny's heart beat faster. This was really serious. 'That's crazy, Ruth! Why are you thinking like that?'

'Because it's my fault, Jenny.' Ruth's voice was so soft, Jenny had had to push her mobile into her ear to hear her. 'I'm the one who can't fall pregnant without help. I'm the one who can't hold on to a baby once I am pregnant. Whose body managed to actually…' She trailed off and Jenny heard a stifled sob on the other end of the line. 'If David meets someone else, he could have a baby without all this trouble.'

Jenny's heart was breaking for her. 'But he doesn't want a baby with anyone else, Ruth. He wants you. You do know that, don't you?'

Ruth was crying openly. 'I do. I do. And I don't know if I could actually leave him, it's just… your brain… it goes round and round and… I'm sorry, you don't want me going on about all this.'

'Ruth. I'm your friend. Of course I want to talk to you about this. I am here any time. But I do think you need to speak to David, too.'

'I just can't. I can't. But I don't know what to do. I am terrified of coming off the pill. What if I get pregnant? What then? How long will it last?'

Jenny had wished with all her heart that she had been able to answer Ruth's questions. What was she supposed to say?

She was interrupted from thinking about Ruth now by the sight of a poncho-wearing woman waving at her from across the room. Before Jenny could wave back, a dark-haired woman wearing a more conventional jeans and shirt combo dived down beside her, plonking a little girl with dark curls beside Henry.

'Saved you, just in time.'

'Sorry?'

'Serena – super mother. She was just about to swoop over and welcome you.'

Jenny glanced over at the poncho lady, who, having seen Jenny being welcomed by this other mother, had resumed her conversation with the woman beside her. 'Oh, does she run the group?'

'Thinks she does. I'm Fiona, by the way.'

'Jenny. It's my first time.'

'I guessed as much from the way you walked across the room as if the ground was covered in landmines.'

Jenny hadn't realised her fear had been so apparent. 'First time I've attempted a baby group, actually.' She didn't explain that she was only there because her big sister had made her come. So she could say that she'd taken Henry somewhere other than Costa.

Fiona nodded sagely. 'Then let me introduce you to the natives. Serena, you just almost met. Earth mother extraordinaire. She spent so long with her baby wrapped to her chest, I began to question whether it was real. Self-proclaimed authority on breastfeeding, skin-to-skin and co-sleeping and, if it wasn't for her stomach-churning description of how she ate her own placenta, I would believe that she was still attached to her child by the umbilical cord.'

Serena sounded like she'd make the perfect friend for Naomi.

'They,' Fiona continued, nodding towards a group on the far side, 'are the stay-at-home mums. On the surface, they have a life to be envied: lunches out, no alarm in the morning and no guilt about leaving their child in childcare. However, get one on her own and the truth comes out.' She counted off on her fingers. 'The relentlessness, the husband who doesn't understand, the frustration of being labelled "just a mum".'

Jenny looked at them intently. What would it be like to never go to work again? These women looked perfectly happy and calm. Maybe Claire had a point about her fulfilling life.

'Over there, you have the nannies and childminders. The mothers of those children are currently trying to ignore the constant nagging guilt they feel about being at work all day – the level of guilt being proportional to whether they were forced to go back to work full-time or whether they chose to.'

Jenny followed Fiona's nod with her eyes. Maybe getting paid to sing nursery rhymes and shake rattles made it easier.

She turned her attention back to Fiona. 'So, which group do you belong to?'

Fiona tucked her dark fringe behind her ear with her thumb. Her curls matched her daughter's. 'Ah, well, I'm part-time.'

'Really?' If Jenny was only writing interviews and reviews, part-time might be an option for her, too. Dan had tentatively suggested that part-time might be a good compromise. But 'compromise' wasn't a word Jenny was hugely comfortable with. It sounded so half-hearted. 'That must be good?'

'Yeah. Sadly, it sounds better than it is. When I'm at work I have to catch up with what I missed on my two days off, so I end up taking piles of work home which I never actually do, because when I am at home I'm with Violet—' she gestured at the curly haired toddler, who was playing happily with a plastic teapot and cups '—and I have to spend all day at baby groups, like this one.'

Jenny was also finding it increasingly difficult to write whilst she was at home with Henry. During the day it was impossible to concentrate because he wanted her attention, and when he went to bed at night she was far too exhausted. She had started to use the

Dictaphone app on her phone so that she could speak her thoughts aloud when they came to her, but the combination of the speech recognition software and Henry's garbled interruptions had made for some interesting typos.

'But why would you want to spend your day off here?'

'It's the guilt. You need to make up for the time you leave them by filling the day with *quality* activity.' Fiona smiled ruefully. 'Just wait and see.'

It wasn't what Jenny wanted to hear. Surely this Fiona was exaggerating?

The whole time they had been talking, Fiona's daughter had been making tea for herself, a rubber frog and a chewed-up teddy bear. Considering she only looked to be around two, she had put together a very nice picnic for the three of them. 'Your daughter looks very happy playing by herself.' The way to get any mother smiling was to praise her child.

Fiona glanced at her daughter. 'Yes, she's very independent. I think it's important, don't you?'

Jenny wasn't sure whether she did or not, so she mumbled an incoherent response which Fiona took for agreement.

This was obviously another topic close to Fiona's heart. 'I have a friend who complains that her daughter is clingy, but at the same time she's constantly picking the child up. Doesn't leave her alone for a moment. What does she expect?'

Jenny, who had just been about to pull Henry onto her lap, froze mid-air and pretended that she was just stretching her arms.

'Clearly it's the mothers who are the needy ones – let the child breathe, for goodness' sake. Oh, here you go, here's the queen of them.'

Jenny turned to see Serena smiling benignly at Henry. 'And who is this handsome little man?'

'This is Henry, and I'm Jenny.'

'Serena. And this is my little one, Storm. So nice to see new faces. I trust that Fiona isn't scaring you off?'

Jenny opened her mouth but Fiona answered first. 'I thought I'd leave that to you, Serena.'

Serena spoke to Jenny with a mock-confidential air. 'Fiona and I have very different ideas about raising children. I believe in attachment parenting.' She stopped there, as if Jenny should know what that was. Jenny was reluctant to admit that she didn't. She would google it when she got home.

'Whereas I think that children need a routine and a bit of time alone,' said Fiona.

'Now, Fiona, you know that…'

And that was it: the two of them quickly became embroiled in an in-depth parenting discussion which Jenny didn't understand, much less want to be a part of.

Jenny wanted to kill Claire. Admittedly, she had found this group herself, but it had been Claire who had forced her to come. These women were insane. Full-time, part-time, attachment, independent. What did it all mean? If being a stay-at-home mum meant more of this, she would be running back to work.

But how much work could she do without missing out on Henry's babyhood? Last week, she'd missed the rolling over. Next it might be crawling. Or walking. Even if she could persuade Eva, or Mark, that she could write part-time, it didn't sound like that was a solution, either. She felt hot and clammy, and it wasn't just the overheated room.

Gently pulling Henry onto her lap, she stood up slowly and began to back away until she was in reaching distance of the exit. Just before the doorway, she turned and was confronted by her nemesis: the damn baby gate.

Then, like an angel sent from the gods of JoJo Maman Bébé, Antonia appeared at the door, slipped a finger under the gate and flicked it open.

Without stopping to ask what she was doing there, Jenny swooped down on her, hissing, 'Go, go, go! Save yourself! We don't have much time!'

CHAPTER TWENTY-ONE

Pretty much as soon as you give birth, you are supposed to encourage your child to be as independent as possible. From a few days old, they are supposed to fall asleep on their own without being so much as rocked, for fear that they will use you as a 'prop' to fall asleep. When you wean them, you aren't supposed to actually feed them any more because they have to feed themselves: with a spoon, with their hands, or even by putting their face in the bowl and snuffling away like a truffle pig, if necessary. I am pretty sure that current wisdom would ideally have you packing them off to live alone at nine years old, having no further need for a parent in their independent life.

It's not that I am at the other extreme: I won't be sticking my boob through the school gates or climbing into bed with The Boy and his first girlfriend, but I've only just given birth to him; surely I am allowed to look after him for a while?...

From *The Undercover Mother*

✦

Jenny had never been so glad to see a slice of lemon drizzle.

After escaping from the church hall, she and Antonia had relocated to a nearby coffee shop. Henry and Jessica were asleep in their prams and there were no other children nearby to interrupt the quiet hum of conversation and the occasional clink of a cake fork. Jenny began to breathe again.

Antonia slid a tray bearing vintage crockery onto their table. 'Here you are, darling. That should make you feel better. If I'd known you were planning on visiting that place, I would have warned you. It's a hothouse for competitive parenting. You should have heard the discussion they had the other week about nurseries. Montessori this and organic menus that.' Antonia shuddered. 'It can be exhausting just listening to them.'

It had been worse than exhausting. Fiona had left Jenny feeling rather depressed. She recounted their conversation to Antonia.

'Then she said part-time work is even worse. She feels a failure at both.'

Antonia grimaced. 'Sounds to me like she's trying to be Superwoman. She's like Gail and Naomi rolled together. How tedious for you.'

Oddly, Jenny felt defensive. 'I don't think it's that. I think she just likes her job. I mean, if you enjoy what you do, it must be pretty hard to just stop, mustn't it?' If her dinner with Mark had taught her anything, it had made her realise how much she missed her own job. A draughty church hall and a weak cup of tea were no replacement for white tablecloths and a cold glass of white wine.

Antonia was nonplussed. 'So, why doesn't she just get a childminder and go back to work full-time?'

Maybe Antonia, who hadn't worked even before she had Jessica, was the wrong audience for this conversation. Still, Jenny tried.

'Because maybe her job takes up a lot of time. And maybe she feels guilty about leaving her baby.' And maybe she has the kind of job which involves a lot of socialising and she would never get to see her child, or her husband, because her job had the tendency to take over her life. Jenny pushed down the lump in her throat with another forkful of cake.

Antonia looked bored. 'She should just make up her mind as to what she wants then, rather than moaning about it to complete strangers.'

'She wasn't moaning exactly. She was just… talking. Trying to figure out how you can… you know… do both. Be with your baby, go to work, see your friends, kiss your husband occasionally.'

Antonia snorted derisively. 'That sounds exhausting. There aren't enough hours in the day for all that, darling. Sounds to me as if your new friend has a serious case of FOMO.'

Jenny gave up trying to explain to Antonia that it was more than just a Fear Of Missing Out. 'Maybe.'

Antonia stirred her coffee and then scooped the foam from the top with almost medical precision. 'I don't suppose there were any men there today, were there?'

On the surface, the question seemed idle, but there was something about the way Antonia carefully avoided Jenny's eye as she asked it that piqued Jenny's interest. 'No, I don't think there were any at all. Why, do any dads go normally?'

Antonia put her spoon down and picked up her cup. Her expression had closed down again. She clearly wasn't going to share why she had asked about the men. 'From time to time, but not often. Put off by all that undiluted oestrogen, I should think.'

Jenny could well believe it. Dan would rather have his eyes gouged out with a baby spoon than set foot in a place like that. Mind you, she'd been quite surprised to find Antonia there, too. The Cath Kidston tablecloths and bone china plates of this coffee shop seemed a much more appropriate habitat for her.

'I must admit, I never pictured you as the baby group type, either.'

Antonia tucked a rare stray hair behind her ear. 'Oh, I'm not. I've only been a few times and I only stay if there's someone worth talking to.'

Jenny marvelled at how perfect Antonia looked. Even though she was wearing a long-sleeved top on a really warm day, she looked cool and classy. Meticulous make-up, crisp clothes and perfectly painted fingernails gave off an aura of elegance and style. Self-consciously,

Jenny put a hand over the milk stain down the front of her own top and shuffled her legs further under the table to camouflage her crumpled trousers.

'Well, it was a nice surprise to see you. It feels like ages since we were at your house.'

'Yes, it has been a while since I've seen any of you. I did speak to Naomi last week. Jess had a really bunged-up nose and I thought she might know something herbal I could use. She told me about her drunken episode and her conversation with you. About the fact that she's thinking of leaving. Do you think she and John are really in trouble?'

Antonia was picking absently at the cake in front of her as she spoke. Jenny had already hoovered up half of her lemon drizzle and it was taking all her willpower to not eat any more until Antonia had caught up a little. At the rate at which Antonia was picking at her coffee cake, crumb by crumb, this was never going to happen. Quite possibly, this was why Antonia had fared so much better at clothes shopping than Jenny had.

'I haven't seen her since, but I don't think she's actually going to leave him, do you? Surely it's all just a case of too much, too soon. They were only together for a short while before Daisy came. It'll settle down.' Jenny wasn't sure if she believed this or just hoped it was true.

'Maybe, maybe not.' Antonia shrugged. 'Responsibility can do funny things to a man. Sometimes good. Sometimes not so good.'

'John seems pretty steady. And they were clearly very in love with each other when they were at the classes. I'm surprised he didn't set the small of her back on fire, he was rubbing it so frequently.'

Antonia laughed. 'Gosh, yes. And do you remember the way she looked at him every time he asked a question?' She mimicked Naomi's puppy dog expression and then stuck her fingers down her throat.

Jenny felt a twinge of guilt. 'There you go. They must love each other. I'm sure they'll be fine.'

Antonia raised an eyebrow. 'Well, I hope you're right. But we're both old enough to know that appearances aren't everything.'

Jenny gave up on her own appearance of self-restraint and had another mouthful of cake. 'By the way, the man you saw Gail with at Geoff's work do wasn't Joe. It was her boss. You were right.'

Antonia nodded. 'I told you so. He didn't look like her boyfriend at all.'

Something occurred to Jenny, and she said it aloud before she'd even thought it through. 'Unless her boss *is* Joe?' How had she not thought of this before?

Antonia wasn't buying it. 'Goodness, I doubt it very much. I told you, he was about thirty years older than her.'

Jenny wasn't ready to give up on her theory yet. 'Des O'Connor and David Jason… they both had babies in their seventies. It would make a lot of sense as to why she won't tell us anything about him or show us a picture. Maybe he's married! Can't you get Geoff to do a bit of digging around?'

Antonia sat up straighter and her mood seemed to change. 'Sorry. Not his style.' She picked up a sachet of sweetener and tapped it on the table. 'Anyway, I can't stay too much longer, I'm afraid. I've only brought Jessica out for a short while, as my mother is coming to visit today.'

She seemed agitated. Jenny felt colour rise in her cheeks. Did Antonia think she was being too nosy about Gail? But she'd been the one gossiping about Naomi and John… so why was she upset?

'Is everything okay?'

Antonia lifted her cup to her lips and blew on the coffee to cool it. If Jenny hadn't known what a confident person Antonia was, she would have sworn she was composing herself.

'I'm fine, absolutely fine. It's my mother's visit this afternoon. Always puts me on edge.' She glanced at her watch. 'Actually, darling, I know this is terribly rude but I must shoot off and get the house straight before she comes. I just need to go to the Ladies'.

Would you mind watching Jess for me so that I don't have to take the pram in there?'

Jenny watched Antonia walk quickly towards the toilet, carrying her expensive handbag under her arm. Her 'FOMO' comments had struck a chord. Maybe Jenny also needed to accept that she couldn't have everything. Going over to Mark to write a rival column to 'Girl About Town' would give her back a social life, but it would be at the cost of time with Henry. Staying at home with Henry would mean she didn't miss anything he did, but she couldn't imagine her life without writing. How was she supposed to choose?

Antonia had left her mobile on the table and it buzzed now with an incoming text message. The vibration moved it across the table and Jenny put out her hand to stop it from falling off the edge. That's why she couldn't help but see the message which flashed up on the screen from 'Mum'.

Got your message about rearranging. Completely understand.
I'll see you tomorrow instead x

Jenny replaced the phone on the table. When Antonia came back, she picked it up, glanced at the message and then dropped it into her bag.

'We should arrange to meet up soon, darling. Shall I text you some dates?'

Jenny felt more than slightly snubbed. Either Antonia didn't want to be with her, or she had something, or someone, more interesting to see. Either way, Jenny wasn't going to suggest they met up alone again.

'Actually, Naomi mentioned something called soft play.' She glanced at Antonia. 'I'll ask her to call them and book us a place or whatever you have to do.' Jenny hadn't fancied the sound of the soft play place, but it couldn't be as bad as the baby group had been. And even if she was only motivated by guilt, she needed to find something she could go to with Henry. She'd call Naomi as soon as Antonia left.

CHAPTER TWENTY-TWO

At five months old, The Boy is done with lying in his pram while I drink coffee and eat cake. Far more interesting for him to give me palpitations as he makes a lunge for anything hot, sharp or small enough to choke on. Despite my bad experience at the baby group, I have reconciled myself to the need to find somewhere with distractions. For him, not me.

Sporty has tried everything: rhyme time, sensory play, massage... Baby Sporty has more social engagements that the queen. At some point, I decided to give in to the mum guilt and go to one of these places with her.

That is how I first discovered that hell on Earth exists – and it's inflatable...

From The Undercover Mother

✦

Small people were swarming everywhere: appearing from tunnels, whooshing down slides and falling all over each other in pits of brightly coloured plastic balls. The air was permeated with a smell of feet, sweat and baked beans, and the noise level approached that of a death metal concert. Picking her way across the floor, Jenny could see her own horror mirrored in the faces of Antonia and Gail. Where was Naomi leading them? Naomi stopped and indicated a sorry-looking set of chairs. Apparently, here.

Gail started to take off her changing bag and then seemed to think better of it: Orla Kiely wasn't used to plastic tables. 'What in the name of sanity is this place?'

Naomi put both hands on her baby-sling-wrapped hips. 'We need somewhere the babies can play and we can talk to one another, rather than trying to keep them amused in a restaurant.'

Antonia lifted the hem of her Michael Kors maxi dress and peered at the floor. 'I'd heard of these places. But I had no idea it would be so terribly awful.'

Naomi stuck her chin out. 'Well, you all asked me to choose somewhere to meet and I thought we should try something different.'

Naomi was getting upset and she had enough to deal with. Jenny put a hand on her shoulder. 'It was a good idea, Naomi. Look, we can get lunch here, too.'

The others followed her pointing finger with their eyes to a white Formica counter in front of a display cabinet full of brightly coloured drink cartons. Leaning on the counter was a bored-looking young woman, staring vacantly out into the room. From the doorway beside her, another girl appeared and called out, 'Twenny-free!' whereupon a harried-looking mother in the corner put up her hand and was rewarded with two plates of sausages and beans. At least that explained the smell.

Sensing that her lunch tangent had not been a wise one, Jenny suggested that they sit. Antonia was horrified when Naomi explained she would have to leave her expensive shoes on the floor where anyone could take them. She did her best to secrete them in her tiny handbag.

That tiny bag was the object of Jenny's envy. 'How do you manage with such a small bag? My bag is big enough for a weekend break and I still can't fit everything in.'

Antonia shrugged. 'I leave most of the stuff in the car unless I need it. I can't bear the "bag lady" look. No offence, darling.'

'None taken.' Jenny had an overriding urge to snap the heel off one of Antonia's protruding shoes. She still hadn't forgiven her for lying about her mother's visit.

'See! This is good!' beamed Naomi. 'Look how much the babies are enjoying themselves.'

They all had to admit that the children did seem very happy, rolling around in the small padded area for under twos, throwing balls onto the ground and then laughing at them.

With everyone relaxed, Jenny thought it was a good time to start doing some digging. 'How is everyone getting on?'

Antonia was still trying to poke her shoes further down into her bag. 'We've been interviewing for a nanny. Geoff suggested it a while ago and I'm beginning to think it might have its merits.'

Gail looked surprised. 'Are you going to get a job?'

Antonia shook her head. Gail hid her face by bending over to pick up Jake, who had flopped over onto his stomach and wasn't enjoying it. Her face was probably a picture. Not a friendly one.

Naomi frowned. 'I'm not sure I would be able to let someone else look after Daisy. I'm not judging you, though.' *Course you're bloody not.*

Jenny was still annoyed with Antonia, but she wasn't going to let the others make her feel guilty. 'Think of the benefits. You could just pop out to the shops on your own. Have a lie-in whenever you needed it. Sit and drink a cup of coffee whilst it's still hot. Hold on, I want a nanny, too!' Jenny pretended to stamp her feet.

Antonia smiled. 'That's what I thought. It'll give me a little bit of freedom. I'm not getting some flighty young thing. We've hopefully found someone, and she comes with a lot of experience.'

Gail crossed her legs and folded her arms. 'Be careful who you choose. Husbands often have affairs with the nanny.'

Antonia's smile was cold. 'I think you have to pay them extra for that, darling.'

'You'll have time to read a book. Have a long, hot shower every morning. Maybe even a bath!' Jenny tried to wrestle the tone to a lighter level.

Naomi was far less enthusiastic. 'I can see the benefits but I just don't think I would trust someone else whilst they are so small.

Oh, hang on.' She jumped up and went to rescue Daisy, who had rolled her way into a pile of foam animals and didn't seem to be able to find her way out.

Antonia followed her with her eyes. 'This is the shape of things to come. Soon we'll all be jumping up every two minutes, now they've started to move around.'

'You'll be all right, the nanny can jump up for you.' Gail smiled sweetly, as if she was joking. She clearly wasn't.

Antonia stuck out her chin. 'You don't think the nanny is a good idea, then?'

'Who am I to judge?' Gail held her hands out at the side, palms upward. 'I have my mother providing my childcare. I'm hardly a model for the stay-at-home mother.'

'But you clearly don't approve.'

'It's about choice, isn't it? I have little choice about whether I leave Jake or give up my job. You have a choice whether you want to be with your daughter all the time or not. No one else can make your choices for you, can they?'

'Is anyone feeling brave enough to risk a coffee?' Jenny needed to keep them all on speaking terms: no talk meant no blog ideas. 'I'm dying for a caffeine hit... can you watch Henry for me?'

Naomi reappeared with a wriggling Daisy under one arm. 'Would you get a peppermint tea for me? I just need to change Daisy's nappy. Can you pass me my changing bag? Thanks.'

'I'll come with you.' Gail stood up, flicking imaginary lint from her smart trousers. 'I'm sure Jake needs a change, too. I'll have a black coffee, thanks.'

✦

Jenny made it back to Antonia, and placed the tray of drinks on the table nearest to where they had perched. 'I wouldn't get your hopes up about the coffee. We're not in Starbucks any more,

Toto.' She glanced in the direction that the other two had taken. 'Everything okay?'

Antonia was tight-lipped and merely nodded. She took a mug from the tray, but just stared at its contents.

'Don't worry about the others. I'm sure they didn't mean to sound so judgemental.' Jenny wasn't so sure about that, but it seemed the right thing to say.

Antonia looked up. Her eyes were glittery. 'I know what they think. They think I don't want to look after my own daughter.'

'No! Of course they don't.' *Or maybe they do.*

Antonia went back to staring at the murky coffee. Then she put the mug back on the tray. 'I just want to get it right, Jen. I just want to have everything done properly. Jess was premature. I know the midwife said three weeks doesn't make any difference but I want to make sure she's okay. And Geoff is no help at all. Everything is on me.' Her voice cracked. She paused to compose herself. 'I just want a little professional help. Is that so terrible?'

'It's not terrible at all. Not at all.' Isn't that what all new mums wanted – someone on hand who knew what the hell they were doing? 'But don't be so hard on yourself, Antonia. We're all in the same boat. None of us got the manual.'

Antonia smiled. She ran a finger under her eyes. Jenny could have told her that her make-up was still perfect. Time to change the subject. 'I'm looking forward to our night out with the husbands. Is Geoff still keeping it free?'

Jenny had been pleased with her brainwave: a night out with the husbands might give her a new angle. She hadn't broken the news to Dan yet.

'He is. I've written it into every diary he has so he can't make another arrangement.' Antonia got up and shook her dress gently. She leaned down to pick up Jessica. 'Speaking of which, I think I'm going to go. We've got a dinner tonight with some of Geoff's clients and I could do with trying to get some rest this afternoon.'

'But you haven't even drunk your coffee.'

Antonia peered at the mugs on the table. 'It doesn't look up to much, does it? I'll get a drink when I get home. I really should go. Can you say goodbye to the others for me?'

'Of course.' Jenny watched Antonia walk to the door with Jessica on her hip, putting on her large sunglasses before opening the door to go out.

✦

'Where's Antonia?' Naomi was the first to return with a still-wriggling Daisy under her arm.

Jenny knew that Naomi would take this personally. 'She genuinely had to go. Something about a business dinner to prepare for.'

'She hated it here, didn't she?' Naomi's face was a mixture of defiance and deflation.

'No, no, it wasn't that, really. She had to go. She said to thank you for arranging today,' Jenny lied.

'Sometimes I wonder if she really wants to be with us all,' Naomi sniffed. 'She can be quite superior at times… or maybe that's just with me.'

Jenny didn't want a rift developing in the group. It was difficult enough keeping Gail and Antonia in the same room. 'No, I know what you mean, but I think that's just her way.'

Gail marched over. 'Those baby change facilities are disgusting. I have never smelt such a stench in my life. Excuse me.' She stopped a young girl who was half-heartedly wiping tea around a table near them. 'The bin in your baby change room needs emptying immediately.'

The girl continued wiping. 'I'll let them know. I'm not on bins today.'

Gail shuddered. 'I need a shower after being in there for five minutes. You'd think a place aimed at children would have good facilities for changing nappies. It's disgusting.'

'Henry is going to need a change soon. Maybe I'll just go home and do it there.' Jenny was grateful for an excuse to go. Another day gone with no material. Although she could probably knock up a post about this place. A whole new inflatable world she hadn't known existed.

'Good idea. Thanks for the drink. I'll have that and then go myself,' said Gail. She put Jake back into the baby area, picked up a mug, peered into it and then put it down again. 'Where's Antonia?'

'Gone.' The expression on Naomi's face implied that the two of them had been discussing Antonia in the baby change room.

Jenny was irritated by their knowing looks. 'She had to get ready for a business dinner,' she told Gail, firmly.

'Of course, the perfect wife needs to do her duty.'

There was venom in Gail's tone. Surely it wasn't just about the nanny thing? 'That's a bit harsh.'

Gail held her hands up. 'Sorry, I take it back.' She turned to Naomi. 'At least John doesn't make you attend dinner parties with his work colleagues.'

'Even that would be better than spending time with his friends and family.' Naomi sighed as she scooped up Daisy. Obviously, things had not improved between them.

'Have you talked to him about it?' asked Jenny.

Naomi shook her head. 'Not properly. But I will. I'm going back to stay with my parents in a couple of weeks. I'll see how that goes. Then I'll talk to him.'

From the look on Gail's face, Naomi had obviously been talking to her about it. And Jenny wasn't sure that Gail was the best person to talk to about men.

'Well, we'll all have a nice night out with our men next week, anyway,' said Jenny, brightly. 'Even Ruth and David are coming!'

'Yes, I've been meaning to talk to you about that.' Gail had her head inside her changing bag, rearranging the contents. 'I'm not sure I can make it.'

Jenny's heart sank. 'No. You can't back out. We are so looking forward to finally meeting Joe.'

'He might be working.'

'Not again!' said Naomi. 'What were you just telling me about putting my foot down? We want to meet him. Tell him to come later on if he has to.'

'We'll see.'

CHAPTER TWENTY-THREE

Pre-baby, I boasted that my social life would not really change after the small addition to our family. Knowing nods from friends who already had children only made me more adamant that I would be out at least one evening each weekend, and possibly a couple of nights in the week, too.

Extreme exhaustion has put paid to that so far. But, a couple of weeks ago, I made it out and have now realised there's another reason that parents of young children are not often seen out past 10 p.m. Hangovers and babies do not mix.

One of the key issues is that small babies cannot move themselves to where you are languishing on the sofa trying to half-sleep the pain and nausea away. Therefore, when they cry for attention, you have to haul your backside over to them, even when you feel as if you're on a moving ship. Rocking them in your arms is also a struggle when your head is thumping harder than the drummer in a marching band. And don't even get me started on nappy changes. It's not a proud moment to be dry heaving in the direction of your own child's bottom…

From *The Undercover Mother*

✦

'Why, oh, why do you organise these things, wife?' Dan groaned and lay back on the bed, his hands over his face.

'Because if I don't, no one else will.'

He was always like this about going out. Henry's birth had given him even more excuses to not leave the house. Tonight, he was coming.

Dan splayed his fingers to look at her. 'Maybe because they don't actually want to meet up with a bunch of random people when the only thing they have in common is that they managed to pop out a baby at around the same time?'

'It will be nice.' Jenny was firm. 'Stop moaning.' Dan hadn't guessed that she was hoping to get some material from the husbands and she wasn't about to enlighten him, because he might sabotage her efforts.

She had sent Mark an email to tell him that she wasn't interested in writing the column he'd suggested. Email, because she hadn't trusted herself not to buckle if he'd had the opportunity to persuade her otherwise. This made it even more urgent for her to get some good information. If the girls weren't going to spill anything juicy, maybe their drunk husbands would.

'It will be nice for you men to get a chance to talk to one another.'

Dan took his hands away from his face and laughed. 'What do you think we're going to talk about? Which of us has changed the biggest nappy? The merits of a three-wheel over a four-wheel pram? Or maybe, "Changing bags: practicality over aesthetics?"'

'Stop being sarcastic. You need to be nice to me this evening because they all think we're a lovely couple.' She threw a pillow at him. 'You need to pretend to be interested in them.'

'I'm interested in you.' He pulled Jenny on top of him and rolled her over on the bed.

'Stop it!' She was laughing. 'I have only just managed to make my hair look halfway presentable and my parents will be here to babysit in a minute.'

'I only need a minute…'

✦

Ruth and David were already at the restaurant when they arrived.

'I'm so glad you came.' Jenny had been worried that Ruth would pull out at the last minute. She wanted Ruth there. Sitting at home brooding was no good for anyone.

'David said we had to come.' Ruth smiled.

'And I'm such a ruthless tyrant she could do nothing but agree.' David held out his hand to Dan. 'Hello, mate, couldn't get out of it, then?'

'Tried my best, but apparently there was a three-line whip on this one. Drink?'

'I'll come with you.' David looked at Ruth and Jenny, wagging his finger at them. 'You two play nice.'

Ruth smacked his arm as he left. 'Shall we find a seat? Strangely, I feel nervous.'

'It's because you haven't seen everyone for a while. It'll be fine once the night gets going.'

Ruth lowered her voice. 'I have to tell you this quickly before everyone else gets here. Don't react.' She glanced over to David and Dan and turned her back to them. 'I've stopped taking the pill.'

Jenny quickly turned her back to the men too, so that they couldn't see her face. 'That's fantastic,' she whispered. 'Did you talk to David?'

Ruth shook her head. 'No, he doesn't know I was ever taking it.' She took a deep breath. 'Nothing has happened yet and I'm still terrified, but "Feel the fear and do it anyway", eh?'

Jenny squeezed her hand. 'I'm very proud of you.'

A young waiter materialised and showed them to a table. 'Are we sitting next to our partners or opposite them?' asked Ruth. 'Hang on, there are only eight places – who isn't coming. Is it Gail?'

Jenny nodded. 'Joe couldn't make it and she said she would feel like a spare part. I told her not to be ridiculous, but she was adamant.' She had tried everything to cajole Gail, but to no avail. It was the final straw. Jenny was going to find out about Joe one way or another. Even if she had to stalk her.

'That's a shame.' Ruth paused. 'Oh, here are Geoff and Antonia now.' Ruth smiled and waved. Antonia came straight over and Geoff joined the other men at the bar.

'How lovely to see you, darling,' Antonia said to Ruth. 'How are you? I'm really sorry about…'

Ruth cut her off. 'I know. Thanks. I'd rather we just ignored that huge subject tonight.'

'Of course, of course, whatever you want,' said Antonia. 'My husband is driving this evening so I intend to get very drunk. Will either of you be joining me?'

'Well, we're getting a taxi home, but I only got Dan here on the promise that I would do the early morning stint with Henry tomorrow.' The morning after Jenny's night out with Lucy was still a painful memory. No amount of Chablis was worth that. 'Are our husbands going to join us, or are they staying there?' She motioned to Dan and he gave her a mock salute.

As the three men strolled over, Naomi and John arrived. 'Blimey, she scrubs up well,' whispered Dan to Jenny. She could see by the looks on the other men's faces that they thought the same.

Jenny had to admit that Naomi looked very good. She hoped for John's sake that he had been suitably complimentary.

'Is that a wine list?' asked Geoff. 'What are we ordering?'

'That's what we were just deciding,' said Antonia.

'I think we should have a couple of bottles of champagne,' said Geoff. 'It is, after all, the first time we've all been out together since the last antenatal class, and weren't they an absolute hoot?'

'We're not all here,' said Antonia, pointedly.

'Well, almost all. I'm buying,' Geoff continued, plucking the wine list from Antonia's hands and beckoning the waiter over. 'No, no, it's fine.' He held up his hand as the other men tried to argue. 'I'll expense it – I'm due a few treats after the amount of time I've spent with clients this week.'

'It's true,' said Antonia. 'Let him buy it.'

'How's the nanny working out?' Naomi asked Antonia.

'You have a nanny?' Ruth looked over the top of her menu. 'Are you going to work?'

Antonia shook her head. 'She just started and she is absolutely amazing. She knows so much, and Jessica behaves like a perfect baby for her.'

'I still don't think I'd like it, to be honest,' said Naomi. 'I like being the one that looks after Daisy and does everything that she needs. I like being there for her.'

'I'm still there most of the time,' said Antonia.

Geoff took his eyes off his menu and looked at her. 'Really? Because every time I call the house, you seem to have just gone out.'

Really? Where was Antonia going? Jenny stuck up for her all the same. 'You have no idea what it's like being at home all day – we *need* to go out for our sanity.'

'Just ignore him. I do.' Antonia waved her hand. 'When are you going back to work at your magazine?'

Jenny sighed. 'Next month. I can't believe it's come around so quickly. I should be going in to speak to my boss about it, but I've been putting it off. There may not be a column for me when I go back.' No one from *Flair* had called her, either. That was ominous.

'So, what else could you do? Oh, I know!' Naomi closed her menu and wriggled in her seat enthusiastically. 'Why don't you try one of the baby magazines? Think of all the things we've been through in the last couple of months. There must be tons of things you could write about.'

Jenny felt her face freeze. She didn't dare make eye contact with Dan. Would tonight be a good time to tell them about the blog? There was a friendly vibe around the table. Everyone would have had a glass of wine…

'As long as you don't write about us, darling.' Antonia pulled a face. 'Exposing our inadequacies to the world.'

'Crikey, no!' agreed Naomi.

Jenny laughed weakly. 'As if I would.' Dan kicked her under the table. She kicked him back.

'Oh, I don't know.' Geoff raised an eyebrow at Antonia. 'I'd quite like to find out what you ladies get up to during the day.'

Just then, the waiter arrived at the table with the champagne and a couple of ice buckets. He took their food order.

'Let's have a toast,' said Naomi. 'Who wants to make it?'

'Geoff bought the champagne,' said David. 'It should be him.'

Antonia cut in. 'No. I'll do it.'

Everyone raised their glass and looked at her.

'Here's to friendship.'

✦

After David and Ruth had dropped them home, Jenny's parents had left and Dan had fallen into bed and was snoring, Jenny sat and watched Henry asleep in his cot. There was something soothing about his little chest rising and falling with his breath.

The evening had been a success, apart from Gail's no-show, and she was still thinking about Antonia's toast. She had called them *friends*. Would she feel the same if she knew that Jenny was writing about her? Probably not.

This wasn't the only thing troubling her. Although Jenny had picked up a couple of ideas that evening which might be useful for the blog, she had nothing that was likely to make Eva jump up from behind her desk shouting, 'Stop the press!' And if she couldn't make the blog good enough, she didn't have a Plan B.

And, on top of all that, she'd returned home to a voicemail message from her sister, insisting that she meet her for lunch on Monday.

Maybe she should just crawl into the cot next to Henry and refuse to ever come out again.

CHAPTER TWENTY-FOUR

Surprisingly, after an afternoon spent cooking, blending and decanting butternut squash, carrot and apple into tiny plastic pots, I felt a strange sense of accomplishment. I should have taken longer to enjoy the moment: I didn't feel anywhere near as fulfilled in the next few days, as The Boy spat the damn stuff back out again.

Last week, I tried distraction. I was quite excited as I thought I'd found a winning technique: putting the radio on and dancing around to Dexy's Midnight Runners whilst shovelling the food in. Unfortunately, I soon discovered that during my world-famous double spin in 'Come on Eileen', he was surreptitiously spitting the food into his lap.

The other mums aren't much help. Posh has her nanny firmly ensconced to deal with the weaning when Baby Posh is ready, and Scary's mum has done it all before. Sporty has tried to convert me to her plans for baby-led weaning. But Henry picks up the carrot sticks, looks me directly in the eye and then drops them over the side of the high chair...

From *The Undercover Mother*

✦

In the past, a 'bad night' had usually meant embarrassing drunken antics or getting stuck listening to a terrible covers band. Now it meant walking up and down the hallway with a screaming child.

This morning, Henry was spreadeagled on his play mat. It was all very well for him to sleep *now*. Why not last night, when she had jiggled, walked, cuddled, put him down, picked him up? Sung? Soothed? Begged? It was tempting to pinch him awake and cry loudly into his ear – see how he liked it.

At least with him asleep, eating would be logistically easier. Jenny had tried to cancel on Claire – dealing with her sister was difficult at the best of times, let alone when she was extra tired and emotional. But Claire had been insistent.

And, over lunch, she was full of cheer. 'Isn't this nice, being able to meet up in the week? Just think, if you decide to work part-time, we'll be able to do this all the time.'

That did not sound an attractive prospect.

'I don't even know whether I'll have a job to go back to.' She might as well tell Claire and get the 'I told you so' out of the way. 'I've turned down Mark's offer. I'm not going to work for him.'

Claire didn't skip a beat. 'Well, I must say I'm glad. I never liked him.'

Jenny was grateful for her sister's solidarity. She'd only met Mark a couple of times – family get-togethers were never his thing – but she'd never approved of his lack of 'settling-down' qualities. Dan, on the other hand, had been greeted by Jenny's family as if he were the answer to their prayers.

'So, what will you do instead?'

Jenny shrugged. 'Maybe I'll do as you said. Give it up. Stay at home with Henry. Pick up a bit of freelance work to pay the bills.'

She was so exhausted this morning that she had begun to think this might be the best thing. She was tired of trying to do everything. Right now she wanted to take it all: nappies, writing, weaning, meetings, rhyme time, research, friends, family – even Henry – and run like the wind in the opposite direction. She had had enough.

Claire shook her head. 'That's never going to work.'

'Pardon?' Jenny was tired, but surely she wasn't hearing things? 'Why not?'

'Because you love your job. You'd miss it too much.'

Trying to think through the fog in her brain was beginning to give Jenny a headache. 'But I thought you told me that raising a child was the best job in the world?'

'It is.' Claire refilled their water glasses. 'For me. Not for you.'

Jenny prickled. 'You don't think I can do it?'

Claire sighed. 'I can't say anything right, can I? Of course you can do it. But you don't want to. That's the difference. I wanted to. I wanted to be at home looking after them and making my home nice and taking them to baby groups.'

Jenny gulped down the huge lump that was threatening in her throat. 'Are you saying that I don't love Henry enough?'

On some level, Jenny knew that she was overreacting because she was so tired. But she had tried really, really hard to do everything with Henry that everyone else was doing. Why couldn't Claire see that?

'Jenny, please. All I'm trying to say is that there is no right or wrong. I chose one way but it's not the only way. And there are some… downsides… whatever choice you make.'

Jenny narrowed her eyes. 'What are you talking about?'

Claire put down her knife and fork. 'I can't get a job.'

'Well, that's because you were asking for ridiculously restricted hours.' Fatigue-induced irritability made it difficult for Jenny to be sympathetic.

'I worked out pretty early on that those hours were going to be impossible to find. One recruitment agent actually laughed at me.'

Jenny suppressed a smile.

'So I stopped looking for those hours and just asked what they had generally.'

'And?'

'Nothing. Or almost nothing. It appears that I am not actually qualified to do anything which uses my brain. It doesn't matter what I did before, the fourteen-year gap in my CV is as unbridgeable as the Grand Canyon.'

Jenny felt guilty about the smile. 'You haven't been looking very long. You just need to keep at it.'

Claire shook her head. 'I even tried my old company. But there's no one there who remembers me, and the HR person I spoke to – who sounded about twelve – just spoke in clichés about the business having *moved on* since I was there. Apparently, I don't have the *skill sets* needed.' She took a gulp of her water. 'What the hell is a "skill set", anyway? I used to type and answer the phone.' She stabbed at a piece of broccoli. 'That's why I think you're right.'

That woke Jenny up. 'Right about what?'

'About keeping your job going. Not giving it up altogether. At least you'll have something on your CV when no one needs you any more or wants you to… to…'

Claire burst into tears.

✦

In the next twenty minutes, it all came out. How the kids had needed her less and less since they'd started secondary school. How long and boring her days had become. Although it had been her husband who had suggested she look for a job, Claire had been a little bit excited about it.

'I thought I'd be able to find something interesting. I wasn't looking to be a brain surgeon. Doctor's receptionist or sales assistant would have been nice. But it turns out that no one wants to employ someone whose CV reads like Mrs Beeton's diary.' Claire dabbed at her eyes with a napkin.

'I'm sure something will come up.' Jenny squeezed Claire's hand encouragingly.

Henry woke up in his usual subtle way: eyes open, mouth open. Jenny looked at her watch. It was his lunchtime. She had been so close to finishing a hot meal.

'Let me feed him,' said Claire. 'You eat your lunch.'

Jenny watched in awe as her sister spooned the orange mush into Henry's open mouth. Where was the spitting? The grizzling? The pulling at his tongue as if he were being poisoned?

'You're so good at that.'

Claire shrugged. 'I've done it enough times.' She picked up a corner of Henry's bib and expertly wiped a smear from the corner of his mouth. 'I miss it, actually.'

It was so obvious, Jenny wondered why she hadn't thought of it earlier. 'Have you thought about working with children?'

Claire paused with the spoon midway to Henry's mouth. He actually reached out to try and grab it. *She has mystical powers.*

'Do you know, I hadn't even thought of it. What about all the qualifications?'

'You've got time to do them now the kids are more independent.' Jenny handed Claire a yoghurt. 'I'll google it if you like. Find out what you need.'

When she'd found her mobile in her bag, Jenny saw she had a *Call me* text from Eva. It was so rare to get a message from her that Jenny called back straight away.

'She's just gone into a meeting,' Maureen told her when she answered. 'But I know she wants to see you pretty urgently. When can you come in?'

Jenny tried not to get her hopes up, but her imagination ran wild. Maybe Eva had had an epiphany about the blog. Jenny had been getting a lot of comments in the previous few weeks – Eva might finally be taking it seriously. There was no way she would ask to see Jenny urgently just to tell her that she was letting her go; she was far too busy for that. And Lucy was doing so well on 'Girl About Town' that she wouldn't be asking her back for that, either. What else could it be but that she had decided to give her a shot at *The Undercover Mother* column, and was ready for her to start immediately?

'How about tomorrow?'

CHAPTER TWENTY-FIVE

I spent a lot of time selecting a beautiful baby journal with lots of lined pages for writing touching and amusing anecdotes about The Boy's first year – I am a writer, after all.

The pre-birth bit is complete – including trivial details of the contents of my hospital bag and my completely fabricated craving for chocolate eclairs. After his birth? Not so much.

Posh has created a dated photobook, while Sporty has written so much in her baby diary that she had to buy a second one. I hoped that Scary's lack of sentimentality would mean that she had performed as poorly in the baby journal department as I had, but it turns out her mum has made her a beautiful scrapbook of the first few months. Maybe I can get away with just printing a few of these blogs?...

From *The Undercover Mother*

✦

There had to be a way to tell the other mums about *The Undercover Mother*. Jenny just needed to work out how to phrase it.

'*Can you believe we've all been friends now for over six months? Hey, I know what I meant to say – I have been writing about you all online without telling you and now my editor is going to put it in a magazine!*'

No. Too flippant.

'*I have been offered a column writing about motherhood and I'd love to feature you all. You've all been so fantastic these last few months... new mothers everywhere could learn so much from you!*'

Too sycophantic. And a lie.

'*I really need this to keep hold of my career.*'

Too pathetic.

'Shouldn't you be getting ready for your meeting with Eva?' Dan appeared in the doorway.

'What are you doing up? I was going to let you have a lie in.' Jenny raised her head from where she was lying on the sofa with Henry, watching some inane baby programme. They'd been up since 5.30 a.m. and she was doing her best to tune out the beaming weirdos on the TV and doze off.

'I thought you'd need some time to get ready. I know it takes longer these days.' Shifting random toys and baby gear out of his path with his foot, Dan scooped Henry from Jenny's arms, avoiding the kick she gave him. She glanced down at her washed-out maternity pyjamas, stained dressing gown and chunky bed socks. He had a point.

'So, when the column goes into the magazine, will you tell the others that you've been writing about them?'

Jenny grimaced. 'I haven't made my mind up. Maybe they won't realise it's about them?' She looked at him hopefully. 'Do you think I *have* to tell them?'

Dan shrugged his shoulders and settled down next to her on the sofa. 'You haven't used their real names, so probably not. But they'll definitely recognise themselves, so you might wake up next to the severed head of Sophie the Teething Giraffe.'

Jenny closed her eyes, then opened them and pushed herself upright. 'I'd better get in the shower.'

Getting dressed for work put her in a different frame of mind. This was the digital age. Everyone put their whole lives online nowadays. And it wasn't as if she had written anything hugely controversial about the other mums. She hadn't even used their names.

But she hadn't told them what she was doing.

She pulled a brush through her hair. Okay, then. She just needed to tell them and get it over with. Worst-case scenario, they would be angry, stop speaking to her and that would be the end of it. It wasn't as if they were really friends, anyway.

So why did that make her feel sad?

She was getting ahead of herself, anyway. Eva hadn't confirmed that she wanted the column at all. In fact, after Naomi's suggestion, Jenny had been researching baby magazines. Quite a few of them could benefit from a column which gave a healthy dose of reality. But Eva had been the one to ask for this meeting. Dared she hope that this was a good sign?

✦

Normally, the office was a buzz of activity at this time of the morning. Today, it was almost empty. Jenny was both disappointed and relieved: disappointed by the lack of her old buddies but relieved not to see Lucy sitting at her desk.

Eva looked really happy to see her. She even came out from behind her desk and gave Jenny a hug, before kissing her on both cheeks.

'Jen! I'm so pleased you've come in. It's been too long. You're looking fabulous. Sit! Sit!' She indicated a chair and sat back down. 'How is that wonderful little boy of yours?'

Eva was never this gushing and complimentary. Jenny began to get a horrible sinking feeling. Was she trying to soften some kind of blow?

But Eva had a big surprise.

'I have a proposition for you.'

Jenny felt a wave of relief. Even the thought of touting herself around to other editors had been exhausting. She loved this magazine. She loved working for Eva. She loved everything and everybody. This was going to work out.

'*The Undercover Mother*? You want it?'

But the shake of Eva's head was emphatic. 'God, no! I'll admit the blog reads pretty well, but it's still not for us. I know—' she held up her hand to prevent Jenny from interrupting '—that a lot of our readers are mothers themselves. But they buy our magazine to escape the humdrum, not to be reminded of it.'

Jenny bristled but kept quiet. So, what *was* Eva proposing?

Eva began to shift paper around on her desk, looking uncharacteristically wrong-footed. She coughed a couple of times and replaced two pens into a chrome pen pot. Then she looked up again and took a breath. 'Actually, I was hoping you might like your old job back.'

Now Jenny was confused. 'My old job? "Girl About Town"? But what about Lucy?' Eva had extolled Lucy's virtues on more than one occasion. *She's enthusiastic. She's hardworking. She meets her deadlines.* Plus, Jenny had read enough of the columns to grudgingly recognise that the woman could write. How had she fallen from grace so suddenly?

Eva picked up one of the pens from the pot and tapped it on the desk. 'Lucy's gone. She works for Mark McLinley now.'

'Oh.' So, Jenny's writing talents weren't so unique after all. All that smooth talking over lunch about Jenny being the writer he wanted. Turned out, he just needed a willing female. No change there, then. He really was a prick. She forced a smile. 'She might well live to regret that move.'

Eva raised an eyebrow. 'Indeed. I had heard that he offered the job somewhere else first.' She paused to make her point, then leaned forwards so her elbows were resting on her desk, hands clasped together. 'So, how about it? Can you start back next week?'

'Next week?' Jenny stopped smiling.

Eva nodded. 'Lucy offered to work her notice but I told her she could go – we don't want her saving her best pieces for him whilst we're paying her wages. We have enough to cobble something together in the short term, but there's no one else on staff who is ready to make the step up. That's why I need you.'

Jenny's heart began to beat quickly. This was the last thing she'd expected. She'd been devastated to lose 'Girl About Town': she'd loved it. But could she still do it? She needed time to think.

'I have to admit, I'm surprised.'

'I don't see why.' Eva shrugged. 'You're the obvious choice. Plus, I remember you telling me that I was wrong to give Lucy your job when you were only going to be gone a few months.' She put her head on one side. 'Don't tell me you've *changed*.'

Jenny's mind raced. She was out of the habit of thinking on her feet. Nowadays it took her at least five minutes to choose which biscuit she wanted to dip into her tea. This was too big a decision to rush, but she didn't want Eva to think she wasn't grateful. She needed to say yes without saying yes. She took a deep breath.

'I've got an idea.'

✦

It would be a gross exaggeration to say that Eva was keen on Jenny's plan. She'd sold it to her as 'Girl About Town: On Tour' – a whole weekend in Brighton which would give her enough material for two, maybe even three, issues of the magazine. At the worst, she'd argued, if she decided not to take the job afterwards, Eva would get another few weeks' breathing space to find someone else. At best, Jenny would agree to take her old job back. Either way, Eva would benefit.

It hadn't been the weekend away itself that Eva was dubious about, as they had done specials like this before: Jenny had visited Edinburgh, Cardiff and Manchester in the last two years. No, Eva's sticking point was that Jenny wanted to take the other mums away with her this time, and she wanted the magazine to foot the bill for all of them. After a bit of negotiation they'd agreed *Flair* would pay for travel and other costs, on the proviso that the five of them found somewhere to stay themselves, which seemed fair to Jenny.

A weekend away for the five of them – no babies, no husbands and a shedload of alcohol – might reap a rich reward of the revelations which Jenny knew were bubbling beneath the surface. When she returned from Brighton, she would give Eva the 'Girl About Town' columns she had promised, but she would also present her with an *Undercover Mother* column that would blow her away.

Now all she had to do was persuade the other mums to come with her.

CHAPTER TWENTY-SIX

Before I settled down and had a baby, I used to get annoyed by the constant questions of nosy relatives and friends: 'When are you going to settle down/get married/buy a house/have a baby?'

It turns out that, when you have done all the above, the questions just take a different direction: 'Is he sleeping through the night? Can he pick up small objects? Have you weaned him yet? Has he said his first word? Turned over? Crawled? Walked?' It's relentless. And, much as I try to ignore them, it's difficult not to herald the arrival of a first tooth for one of the other babies with a rummage around The Boy's mouth to check whether his are threatening to make an appearance.

I tried to have a conversation with Sporty about the pressure I'm feeling, but she got all hippy on me: 'I just want her to be happy.' Well, of course I want The Boy to be happy, too. But how happy could he be if he got to eighteen with no teeth?...

From *The Undercover Mother*

✦

Jenny was up at 6 a.m. with Henry, trying to tidy the house one-handed whilst balancing him on her hip. Dan had tried his very best to get out of being present for the get-together. For the previous week, he had been muttering that he might need to work that weekend, but Jenny had been unrelenting: all the other dads were going to come, and she was pretty sure that she had even managed to persuade Gail to bring Joe.

Which made it even more irritating when Antonia turned up without Geoff.

'Geoff had to work,' was all Antonia said on the matter, in a tone which suggested that she had said a great deal more to *him* but to no avail. Jessica had been left at home with the nanny, and Antonia looked stunning in a tailored navy-blue dress with matching shoes. Maybe this was not her only social engagement of the day.

'How come he gets out of it and I don't?' whispered Dan, on his way to take Antonia's coat to their bedroom.

'Because it's your bloody house!'

'Because you're my bloody wife, more like,' he grumbled as he walked up the stairs.

'And don't you hide up there!' she hissed at his back.

Naomi and John arrived next; Jenny could have kissed John for coming. She scanned them both as they came in: they seemed happy enough. John helped Naomi with her coat and gave it to Dan (who mimed hanging himself to John – Jenny would need to talk to him about that later) and then placed his hand on the small of her back as they walked into the lounge. That looked positive.

'Your lounge is lovely,' said Naomi.

'Thanks.' Her Earth Mother proclamations aside, Jenny was really beginning to warm to Naomi.

She had just got a drink for everyone when the doorbell rang again. This was the moment she had really been looking forward to, and she could feel the others tense, too. Well, the women anyway: John and Dan had already taken refuge in the kitchen. 'That must be Gail!' she said. 'Are we ready to finally meet Joe?'

'Very ready,' said Antonia, sarcastically. Jenny was too excited to pay much attention to her tone.

She couldn't explain why she was so intrigued to finally meet Joe. As Dan had rightly pointed out, she didn't know the husbands of the girls she worked with and she had known them a lot longer than she'd known Gail. It was the mystery, she supposed.

Dan got to the door before she did and opened it – to find only Gail and Jake. Gail noticed Jenny glance over her shoulder. 'Just the two of us, I'm afraid.'

'The mystery continues,' Dan whispered at Jenny on his way back to the kitchen, as she followed Gail into the lounge.

'Hello! Oh – no Joe?' Naomi sounded disappointed to see Gail walk in alone, carrying a sleeping Jake in his car seat. You could say what you liked about that girl, Jenny thought, but she wasn't afraid to ask the hot questions.

Antonia smiled smugly, as if she'd been expecting this. 'Let me guess, tied up at work?'

Jenny jumped in quickly. 'Is he unwell?'

Gail shook her head. 'No. He's fine. We just broke up.'

There was a moment of silence and then a clamour of voices: 'I'm so sorry!' 'Are you okay?' 'What happened?'

Antonia stayed silent and drank her wine.

Gail didn't look remotely heartbroken. 'These things happen.' She slipped off a black jacket and exchanged it for a glass of wine from Dan, who scuttled straight back to the safety of the kitchen.

'And we haven't even seen him,' said Naomi, as Gail sat down next to her. It felt a bit insensitive for Naomi to say that out loud, even if it was pretty much exactly what Jenny was thinking.

'And now we won't,' chipped in Antonia.

'No.' Gail stared at her. 'You won't.'

Well, there went any chance of Gail opening up and telling them the gory details. But now, Jenny had a more urgent agenda. 'Perhaps I might have something to take your mind off Joe for a while.' She smiled hopefully at all three of them. 'What do you think about a girls' weekend in Brighton on expenses?'

They all looked surprised. 'Have you just thought of that?' asked Gail.

'Not exactly,' said Jenny. 'The thing is, I've been offered my old job back, writing "Girl About Town" again.'

'Your single girl column? That's great!' Naomi patted Jenny's leg. 'You must be really pleased.'

'Yes, it is great. But I don't know whether to take it. They need me to start almost immediately and I'm still not sure about going back to work yet.'

'Why are you unsure, darling?' asked Antonia. 'I thought you loved it?'

'I do. I did. It's just I'm not sure how I'll fit it around Henry. I used to do pretty unsociable hours. Anyway, to help me make up my mind, I've suggested to my editor that I write a guest column about a girls' weekend in Brighton. I'll see how I get on with that and go from there. What do you think? Are you happy to be my temporary crew for the weekend?' She crossed her fingers behind her back.

'Yeah! That would be great fun,' said Naomi. 'I love the seaside. Daisy loves the beach, too.'

'Ah.' Jenny had assumed they would know it didn't include the babies. 'I meant just us. It's only one night. Come on, Naomi. You deserve a night off.'

'Count me in.' Antonia raised her wine glass. 'The nanny can do an overnight.'

Jenny looked at Naomi. 'Please?'

Naomi looked uncertain. 'I'll have to talk to John about it, and I will need to express my milk while I'm away, but… it would be nice to have a night off.'

'Great.' Jenny was relieved. 'I've spoken to Ruth already and she said she'll come. She'll be here soon.' She glanced at her watch and then turned to Gail. 'What about you?'

'Why not?' Gail scrolled through the calendar on her mobile. 'The next few weekends I'm pretty free.'

'Free and single, apparently,' murmured Antonia.

Jenny glanced at Gail. She needed to keep the peace until she had them on the train to Brighton. Thankfully, John appeared to distract them.

'Sorry to interrupt. Henry has woken up so I thought I'd come and get Daisy to play with him.' He took her from Naomi's lap, pecking Naomi on the cheek as he did so.

After he'd left the room, Antonia turned her attention to Naomi. 'You and John seem okay—?'

'Do we?' Naomi shrugged. 'It's a bit more complicated than it looks.' She glanced at Gail.

'Really?' asked Jenny. 'In what way?' What had Naomi told Gail that she wasn't sharing with the rest of them?

For once, Naomi wasn't forthcoming with information. 'It's too soon to say anything. When I know for sure, I'll tell you all. I promise.'

Antonia was more interested in the weekend away. 'What have you got planned for us in Brighton then, darling?'

'Whatever you fancy doing, really. I'll look into hotels and restaurants. We need to go as soon as possible. I need enough time to write the article and submit it to my boss.' In fact, it was going to be *articles*. Plural. But no need to tell them about that yet.

There was a flurry of diaries and mobiles until finally they worked out a date that they could all commit to. Jenny's mobile rang. It was Ruth.

'I'm not going to make it.'

'Oh, no, everyone was looking forward to seeing you. Are you okay?' Jenny left the others discussing what clothes they would need to pack and walked into the hallway, pulling the door closed behind her.

'Not really. I got my period this morning.'

'Oh, Ruth. I'm sorry.'

'It's okay. I wasn't expecting things to happen immediately. Or at all.' Ruth laughed hollowly. 'I just don't feel up to an afternoon with babies.'

'I understand. Of course you don't. We'll catch up soon, anyway. And I have a date for you for our weekend trip to Brighton. A month from today. The other three are up for it, too. It'll just be babes, booze and no babies. It'll do us all good.'

'I'm not sure, Jen. I think I'll put a downer on the weekend for you all. What if I'm feeling like this? I'm not much fun at the moment.'

'You won't put a downer on it. Look, let's book it and if you feel like you don't want to come when we get to it, you can pull out. If you do come, I think we should be in for some interesting conversations. There have been a few developments today already.'

Before she returned to the living room, Jenny popped into the kitchen and wrote the date for the Brighton weekend on the calendar. Dan and John were sitting at the kitchen table, each with a baby.

'Get used to that, boys. One month today and you'll be fending for yourselves.'

Which meant she had one month, one weekend and one humdinger of an 'Undercover Mother' article. This had to work.

CHAPTER TWENTY-SEVEN

Packing to go away has been trickier than I anticipated. The clothes I bought with Posh have been dressed up and down to within an inch of their lives over the last four months, and I am NOT buying anything else when I will be two dress sizes smaller soon. Yes, I will.

I've also looked longingly at my pre-birth bikinis, but I don't think the good people of Brighton are ready to see me in a two-piece. I don't want people running out of their houses with brooms and hoses to keep me wet until they can throw me back in.

It's also the first time in over six months that I've packed a bag which doesn't contain nappies or baby wipes. You'd think that would make me happy, wouldn't you?...

From *The Undercover Mother*

✦

Clothes had been chosen, the bag was packed and Jenny was ready to go. She just needed to leave the house. To leave Henry.

'Are you sure you're going to be okay? I can still cancel if you don't want me to leave you on your own overnight.' This was harder than she'd thought it would be.

'Nice try, coward. We're looking forward to a boys-only night, aren't we, Henry?' Dan picked up the remote control and changed the programme to *Ice Road Truckers*.

Jenny still didn't move. 'Thanks for letting me go this weekend. For looking after Henry, I mean.'

'You do realise he's fifty per cent mine, don't you? I'm not sure you should be praising me for looking after my own son.'

Jenny studied Dan closely. 'You will remember to feed him, won't you?'

'Stop worrying about us and worry about how you're going to stop Gail and Antonia from killing each other before you even get there.'

He had a fair point. The two of them barely managed to avoid sniping at each other on a two-hour play date; a whole weekend in each other's company might well end in one of them pushing the other into the English Channel.

When Gail had found out that they would be staying in a house that belonged to one of Antonia's friends, she had tried to pull out altogether.

'Why can't we just stay in a hotel?' she had asked over the phone.

'Because Antonia's friend offered and this will be free,' explained Jenny. 'Plus, it will be nicer to have a bit of space to hang out in all together, rather than be in separate rooms. Apparently the house is huge.'

'I bet it is. Another Yummy Mummy palace. It'll be all Cath Kidston and Le Creuset.'

In the end, Gail had given in. But not before making Jenny promise on Henry's life that she would not have to share a room with Antonia.

'They've hardly seen each other lately, so maybe they'll be all right,' Jenny said to Dan now. She wasn't as confident as she sounded, but she was more worried that Ruth might be regretting saying that she would come. She had been rather bullied into it. 'Have you spoken to David recently? Did he say that Ruth was still okay about coming?'

'Yeah, I think so. I spoke to him last week once I found out that you'd kindly arranged for the men to spend this afternoon at Geoff's place. Thanks for that, by the way.'

Jenny held up her hands. She had been as surprised as Dan when Antonia had suggested it. 'He invited you all, not me. And don't forget to ask the questions I gave you whilst you're there. It might make for a good blog – "The Father's View".'

Dan looked at her levelly. 'Don't use me as your mole. Now, go and meet your friends. We've got ice trucks to watch.'

Jenny stayed where she was. 'Don't forget his dinners. It's not like when he was a baby and you could just give him milk. You have to feed him proper food now.'

'Oh, so that's what the tiny space-age pots in the fridge labelled "breakfast", "lunch" and "dinner" are. I thought we were expecting an astronaut to come and stay. That's rather disappointing.'

'And don't forget his nap.'

'Jen, I have looked after him before. Anyway, it'll be good practice for me. If you go back to your column, we'll be on our own most Friday and Saturday nights.'

Her stomach did its recently familiar lurch. And not with excitement.

✦

The house was in a private mews set just back from the main seaside road. Looking like something from a Jane Austen novel, it had three floors, plus a basement with its own front door. Jenny envisaged herself wearing a long dress, taking a turn around the drawing room.

'It was so kind of your friend to let us stay here, Antonia. How do you know her?'

'We're old school friends. She's away all summer and said I'm welcome to use the house whilst she's away.' Antonia's high-heeled shoes clicked as she walked up the steps to the glossy black front door and unlocked it. 'She lets the basement out as a holiday let, but we're staying in the main house.' Antonia pushed open the front door. 'There are three double bedrooms to choose from. I'll take the one at the top, which is my friend's room. The rest of you can fight it out as to who's sharing with whom.'

✦

Naomi emptied her rucksack onto the bed in the room she was sharing with Jenny. Jenny would have preferred to share with Ruth, but if she was going to find out what Naomi was keeping secret – what it was about her relationship with John that was 'more complicated' than it looked – then she needed to get her on her own.

'Antonia was quick to bags a room to herself,' Naomi said.

Whenever there was a disagreement between Gail and Antonia, Naomi seemed to side with Gail. There were a lot of knowing looks exchanged between them. Jenny was getting a little bored with keeping the peace. 'Well, it is her friend's house. Maybe her friend asked her to stay in her room alone?'

'Maybe. Or maybe she's too good to share with one of us.' Naomi picked up a framed photograph that was on the dressing table. 'What a fabulous house, though. It must be great to live here all the time. I love the sea. It reminds me of happier times.'

Naomi had an irritating tendency towards the dramatic. Jenny had to remind herself that Naomi's life was a little difficult right now. *Be kind.* 'Things still not good? Does John know that you're thinking about moving back with your parents?'

Naomi took a deep breath. 'There's been a bit of a development.'

'Oh? Good or bad?'

'I'm not sure I have the answer to that.' Naomi turned to look around the room. 'Where do you think we should put our clothes?' She reached into her rucksack to pull out her last few things.

Was she seriously dragging this out? Was she leaving John or not? 'Naomi. Stop for a minute. What do you mean?'

Naomi sighed, sat down on the bed and looked at Jenny. 'I'm pregnant.'

Now, that was a surprise.

Jenny sank down onto the opposite bed. 'What?'

'Yep. Took a test the day before we came to your house. It was an accident. I still don't think it's really sunk in.'

Jenny was amazed that John and Naomi had the energy to have sex often enough to get pregnant by accident. Again. This girl's fertility was a medical marvel. 'Does John know?'

Naomi shook her head. 'No. I think he knows that something is up because he's been super attentive lately. But I want to decide what I'm going to do first.' She got up from the bed, opened a drawer in the bedside cabinet and scooted her clothes inside. 'That's me done. I'm going to head downstairs, are you coming?' She walked over to the door and reached for the handle.

Jenny was still reeling. 'Don't you want to talk about this?'

Naomi shook her head. 'No. I really don't. This weekend I don't even want to think about it. Please don't say anything to the others either, will you? Well, Gail knows, but she knows I don't want to talk about it.' She opened the door. 'I'll see you downstairs in a minute.'

Jenny certainly hadn't been expecting that news. And what did Naomi mean about deciding what she was going to do?

One thing Jenny hoped fervently was that Naomi meant what she said about not telling the others. This was the last thing Ruth needed to hear right now.

✦

'This settee feels like heaven! You must come and sit here.' Naomi was strewn across the couch, talking to Gail in the opposite chair, as Jenny joined them. 'This woman – Amanda, is it? I want her life.'

'I wonder what she's like.' Gail picked up a picture of the owner of the house and her happy-looking children from one of the side tables. 'She looks around our age, yours and mine, I mean, Jenny. Although she had her children a lot younger.'

'Sometimes I wish I had.' Jenny sat next to Naomi. 'I'm absolutely knackered. Maybe this would have been a lot easier if I were a few years younger like you, Naomi. Or more. What's the optimum age for your body to have children – sixteen or something?' She made a mental note to speak to some younger mums for the blog, and see if they did have more energy. And then remembered that she might not be writing it any more.

'Bloody hell, I couldn't have had children at sixteen,' said Gail. 'I could barely decide what colour eyeshadow to wear at that age. And Stephen Harris was definitely not father material.'

'Who was Stephen Harris?' Naomi sat up.

'My boyfriend then. Although he was seventeen and drove a moped. Very cool.' Gail nodded her head at the memory. 'I can't quite imagine him changing a nappy, though.'

Jenny smiled. 'People from our past grew up too, you know. He won't still be seventeen, this Stephen Harris. He could be married with a whole army of little Harris juniors.'

Gail shuddered at the thought. 'I wonder if they all pick their nose and wipe it under the seat of their moped.'

Ruth joined them. 'I'd love to meet the woman that owns this house.' She perched on the arm of the sofa beside Naomi.

'That's funny, we were just saying that,' said Jenny.

'She's got certificates up in the bathroom, mostly awarded to her kids by the look of them – cycling proficiency, swimming and horse riding, that sort of thing. Then she's got a couple for herself – pole dancing and burlesque.'

'I've done that for an article,' said Jenny. 'It's good fun.'

'It must be great, getting to try new things for free,' said Naomi. 'Have you started gathering material for your "Girl About Town" article? I'm so excited that we're all going to be in it. I've never been in print before!'

All three of them were looking at her expectantly.

Jenny took a deep breath.

Antonia entered, waving a bottle of wine. 'Anyone for a drink?'

Jenny breathed out. 'I'll get the glasses.'

Ruth followed Jenny to the kitchen, found a long glass and filled it with water. 'Only a very small wine for me, thanks. If I don't pace myself, you're going to be tucking me up in bed by eight thirty.'

'How are you feeling generally?'

'Up and down.' Ruth lowered her voice to barely a whisper. 'Nothing has happened yet. Not that I expected it to, but, you know. This time we know what we're facing. Each month you do the stupid test and you get your hopes up.'

Jenny squeezed her arm. 'It'll happen Ruth, I just know it will.'

'What's the hold up with the glasses?' called Antonia.

◆

Everyone had a glass in their hand. All five of them in the same room for the first time since the babies had been born and, after the monumental effort it had taken to get them all there, Jenny hoped it was going to be worth it. This had to work.

'Well done for organising us, darling.' Antonia patted Jenny's knee. 'It'll be nice to have some uninterrupted conversations.'

'I'm not sure I remember how to have a proper conversation.' Naomi tucked her knees into her linen top, her bare feet poking out at the bottom.

When they first met, there'd been Antenatal Sally and her fabulous ice breakers. But Jenny wasn't about to suggest they balance halfway up the wall whilst pretending to time a contraction. And with Ruth there, their talk mustn't wander to the children. 'Why don't we go out for a few hours?'

'That sounds like a good plan. I'd love a walk along the beach,' said Naomi.

'I'd like to do some shopping,' said Ruth. 'It's David's birthday in a couple of weeks and I might find something a bit quirky down here.'

Gail nodded at her. 'Good idea. I'll tag along.'

'I'm not sure I can be bothered to trawl around the shops.' Jenny wanted to keep them talking, not shopping. She needed a game plan.

'Me, neither, darling. We can follow them down there and then go and find a coffee shop if you want?' suggested Antonia.

Perfect. Antonia's turn.

CHAPTER TWENTY-EIGHT

My lounge regularly looks as if someone has eaten the entire contents of the Toys R Us catalogue and thrown up everywhere. Rattles, coloured balls, baby gyms. It was impossible to stop people from buying brightly coloured plastic monstrosities for The Boy, and it wasn't long before I gave up my 'wooden toys only' mantra and joined in myself.

Sporty almost had a stand-up row with her in-laws on the subject – she only wants toys made from organic materials, from 'ethically responsible' suppliers. Whilst I applaud her moral stance, you need to remortgage your house to afford some of that stuff.

Hopefully I can find him something in one of the hip and trendy baby shops in Brighton. Guilt gifting? Me?...

From *The Undercover Mother*

✦

The Lanes were busy that Saturday. There were couples looking in the windows of the antique jewellery shops with their rows and rows of sparkling, and not so sparkling, gems. Jenny loved her own engagement ring, although it was rather dwarfed by the rock on Antonia's finger.

'That's a gorgeous ring.' Jenny motioned towards Antonia's hand.

'Yes, it is rather.' Antonia wasn't particularly enthusiastic. 'It's not my real engagement ring. We got engaged at university. Once Geoff started to earn good money, he wanted me to have something bigger.'

'Lucky you.'

'Mmmm.' Antonia looked down at her ring finger. 'I think I prefer the original.'

They emerged from The Lanes into a more modern part of town and stopped at the first coffee shop they saw. It was quite busy, and Jenny went to find a table whilst Antonia queued for coffee and cake. Once she was seated at a corner table, Jenny checked her messages. Dan had sent a photo of Henry eating chips with a message, *What mummy doesn't know...* She felt a pang. Was this how she'd feel when she was back at work? She slipped her mobile back into her bag as Antonia arrived at the table.

'I didn't know which cake you'd want, so I got a couple of options.' Antonia was holding a tray laden with two huge slices of cake and coffee cups the size of cereal bowls.

'Wonderful. I like anything under the heading "cake", to be honest.' Jenny helped Antonia transfer the cups and plates to the table.

'Apparently there's a speed-dating event here later. The young man behind the counter was wondering if we'd be interested. Sounds terribly funny.'

Jenny pulled a face. 'I've ticked that box already, thanks – I did it for the magazine.' She picked up a fork and started on the chocolate cake, which was nearest to her.

'Really?' Antonia leant forward. 'What was it like?'

'Great fun, actually. I went with a friend and every time the bell rang and I turned to meet my next date I could see my friend behind him either giving me a thumbs-up or pretending to cut her throat.' It had been a source of much hilarity. All the women at the event had seemed perfectly nice, but the men had been all kinds of crazy. 'Full of character' is how Jenny's nan would have described them.

'I do wonder sometimes what it would have been like to have dated more. Maybe I've watched too much *Sex and the City*, but it looks like terrific fun.'

'Geoff wasn't your first boyfriend, surely?' Jenny was shocked at the thought.

'Gosh, no, but dating at university is less, "Would you like to go for dinner?" and more, "Do you fancy a pint and a snog?" I wish I could have dated as a grown-up. Had dinner in fancy restaurants, making small talk about art and culture.' Antonia smiled wryly at Jenny, shaking her head. 'Am I living in a fantasy land?'

'Completely. Maybe it's different if you live in New York and look like Sarah Jessica Parker, but my experience was rather different. I once had a date with a man who had just left a religious cult and wanted some "experiences" before deciding whether to go back in. Then there was the fitness freak who didn't talk about anything except weights and running and, oh yes, the one that called me to say he was five minutes away and then didn't turn up at all. Absolutely no one worth wasting a pair of designer shoes on.'

'They all sound ghastly. I'm almost feeling better about settling down young.' Antonia stirred her coffee slowly. 'Mind you, I'm going to advise Jessica to shop around a bit more than I did. Even if she does have to date a few disasters along the way.'

Jenny shrugged. 'There were some good ones, too. But, I must admit, I was rather relieved to meet Dan and not have to put myself out there any more. It's exhausting.'

Antonia nodded. 'Why do you think we women all have this inbuilt desire to find one person to spend our lives with? Men don't seem to have the same feeling at all. Geoff's got several friends over forty who have no intentions whatsoever of settling down yet.'

Jenny shrugged again. 'I guess there must be something biological about it. We hit thirty and then that clock starts ticking loudly in our ears. By the time I met Dan, I had the equivalent of Big Ben chiming in my brain.' She had been so fed up with commitment-phobes like Mark McLinley that, when she first met Dan, she had told him brazenly that she was looking for a potential husband

and father for her future children. When he had calmly asked her if he could just finish his pint first, she'd known he was a keeper.

Antonia didn't look convinced. 'That's what I've heard, but, to be honest, I don't think that ever happened to me. It just seemed to be about the right time to have a baby. We'd been together a long time. We had a nice home.' She counted out her first two points on her fingers and then made pretend quotation marks in the air. 'And "everyone else was doing it".' She took a sweetener sachet from the pot on the table and started to tap it on the table. 'Actually, I think Geoff was keener than I was – keep the little woman happy, give her a baby to look after.'

Jenny was about to go in for a forkful of Victoria sponge but she paused. This was the opening she had been waiting for. 'And *are* you happy?'

'Why wouldn't I be happy?' Antonia changed her tone and looked a little defensive. Jenny knew that she needed to tread carefully. Before today, she hadn't even seen Antonia with messy hair, and now she was trying to get her to open up about her marriage.

'I don't know.' Jenny paused; she needed to phrase this tactfully. 'It's just, when I met you after that church hall baby group, I got the feeling that you were expecting to see someone there. A man.'

Antonia looked confused. 'What do you mean?'

It was now or never. Jenny took a deep breath. 'And when we went out shopping for my new clothes, I saw you having a coffee with a young man.'

Understanding slowly dawned in Antonia's eyes. 'Are you asking me if I'm having an affair?' She looked as if Jenny had slapped her. *Bad move.* She shouldn't have asked so directly. She should have waited until they had had a lot of alcohol. There would have been more chance of Antonia speaking freely and, if she hadn't, Jenny could have blamed her question on being drunk.

Then a smile slowly spread across Antonia's face, until it reached her eyes. 'You *do* think I'm having an affair, don't you?' She sat back in her chair and seemed to be enjoying the thought of it. 'You actually think that I am seeing someone else?'

Either Antonia was a fantastic actress, or Jenny had somehow got her wires completely crossed. 'No, no, I wasn't saying that exactly,' she stuttered. 'I just wondered…' She trailed off, at a loss for what to say. This wasn't the reaction she had expected at all.

Antonia was laughing now: big, shoulder-shuddering laughs. 'Oh, Jenny, darling. Your journalism skills must be on maternity leave, too. Me having an affair!' She wiped her eyes and gradually stopped laughing. 'I wish you had told me this sooner. Have you been thinking this all that time?' She started to laugh again and then composed herself. 'You're right, I'm not as happy as I should be. There are some things that need to change. But I am working on it.' She nodded, thoughtfully. 'In fact, I think they are about to change very, very soon.' She picked up a fork and took an uncharacteristically large piece of cake. Then she glanced at her watch and started to gather her things together. 'Goodness, look at the time. I've just realised that no one will be able to get back into the house. I'm the only one with a key. Maybe I should get back there now, in case anyone has returned early.' She picked up her sunglasses from the table and put them onto her head like an Alice band. 'We'll pick this conversation up later, sweetie, I promise. I'll see you later.'

She patted Jenny's hand and then left, starting to laugh to herself again. She obviously wasn't expecting Jenny to follow her back to the house.

Almost in a daze, Jenny wandered around some gift shops. She was completely stumped by their conversation. Had she read it completely wrong? Maybe Antonia wasn't having an affair, but she *had* admitted to being unhappy. So, what *was* going on? Why had she found it so funny?

Her phone beeped: it was Gail, saying that she and Ruth were about to head back. She sent a return message to ask where they were. She would meet them so they could walk home together.

✦

Gail stood up and waved at her from a small table in the corner. Jenny squeezed her way past a large group of Pimm's-wielding girls who were dressed in fewer clothes than she wore to bed.

'You found us, then.'

'Through the miracle that is GPS.' Jenny waved her mobile. 'Where's Ruth?'

'In the toilet. I'm glad you're here. We had a tricky moment.'

Jenny could tell her a thing or two about tricky moments today. 'Why? What happened?'

Gail tipped up her glass and drank the last of her drink. 'We inadvertently wandered into a baby shop.'

Jenny grimaced. 'Oh. Was she upset?'

'She was okay. It just prompted her to ask me why I have never asked her anything about what happened.' Jenny waited for Gail to continue. 'And I just said that I didn't know what to say. I mean, of course it was terrible for her. Why would it have helped for me to ask inane questions?' Not for the first time, Gail's business-like approach to life seemed slightly cold to Jenny. 'Then I tried to change the subject by mentioning that I'd heard she was trying for another baby. Then she seemed even more upset. *That's* why I don't start these conversations with people.'

Jenny sighed. 'I assume Naomi told you about Ruth trying again? She shouldn't have, but that's not your fault.' Jenny knew why Gail's comment would have upset Ruth. It must be bad enough looking at that negative pregnancy test, without having everyone else knowing about it. She hoped again that Naomi would keep her own pregnancy news to herself. Although this was Naomi. She was about as discreet as a half-page advert in *The Times*.

Gail's phone pinged with a message. 'It's Naomi. She's still at the beach. Shall we go and collect her?'

CHAPTER TWENTY-NINE

Why do some parents always feel the need to tell you that, whatever the age of your baby, you are at the 'easy stage'? 'Are you finding feeding difficult?' they say. 'Wait until you wean them and you have to spend half your life making vats of puréed root vegetables.' 'Are you worried about them picking up germs by crawling around everywhere? Wait until they're running away from you in a busy shopping centre.' 'Tired because your baby isn't sleeping? Wait until they're teenagers and you're lying awake all night waiting for them to come home.' Seriously, parenthood seems like an catalogue of woe to some people.

Although the other mums think that Posh has it easy with her nanny and her cleaner, I think she is actually struggling a bit. The thing is, babies are rather disruptive creatures and her life seemed pretty perfectly scheduled beforehand. The advantage to being as disorganised as me is that no one expected me to be on time even before I had The Boy. Now they are just grateful when I turn up at all...

From *The Undercover Mother*

✦

The beach was busy; it was a sunny day and it was crowded with families, groups of teenagers and elderly couples. People always seemed happy on a beach. Apart from small children being roughly towel-dried by their mothers, that was.

Naomi certainly seemed at home on the beach. She was sitting with her toes in the water, chatting to another woman. As Jenny, Ruth and Gail drew near, the two of them looked up.

'Oh, you must be the other mums!' Naomi's new friend looked at them appraisingly, making Jenny wonder what Naomi had been telling her. 'I'm Gemma.'

Gemma seemed more like Antonia's kind of person than Naomi's, with her expensive-looking clothes and pair of designer sunglasses pushing back a sleek mane of hair. She was drinking San Pellegrino from a plastic wine glass.

'Gemma lives around here,' said Naomi. 'Lucky woman.'

'Well, in Shoreham actually, which is pretty close but not as expensive.' Gemma was still scrutinising them. 'It's nice and… Timothy! Not too far!'

Jenny jumped and looked in the direction of Gemma's yell to where a small boy wearing armbands was making a bid for a Channel crossing. She couldn't quite believe that one day Henry would be as big as that. She had only just got her head around the idea that she had a baby; the thought that he would soon turn into a toddler and then into an actual boy was beyond her powers of imagination.

'Naomi tells me that all your babies have just turned six months.' Gemma turned back to them, keeping one eye trained on her mini-Olympian. 'I'm sure it all seems very easy right now. Just wait until they're running around like this one – you'll have to have eyes in the back of your head.'

'Is your little boy okay out there on his own?' Jenny was slightly concerned for his safety. He seemed intent on getting as near to the water as he could. Although, after only a few minutes in his mother's company, she could understand why.

'Oh, yes.' Gemma squinted up at Jenny. 'Jenny, right? Naomi mentioned that you're a bit of a worrier sometimes.' She put her head on one side. 'You'd enjoy it all a lot more if you just relaxed, you know.'

Jenny shot Naomi a look which, if it didn't kill, would definitely leave a gaping wound. *Relax?* Like sitting there sipping your drink even when it looked like your child might be making an attempt to get to France? Naomi had the grace to look embarrassed.

Ruth was gazing out at the horizon. 'I love the beach. I grew up on the coast. When I was young, I used to sit for hours looking out to sea, sorting out whatever teenage angst was going around in my head.'

'Hear, hear. I'm trying to persuade Naomi to follow her heart and move here, nearer the sea,' said Gemma.

Naomi hadn't mentioned a desire to move to the coast before. Jenny frowned. Plus, John worked with his father; he wouldn't be able to relocate here very easily. Naomi wasn't still planning on leaving him, now that she was pregnant, was she? Although she hadn't told John she was pregnant yet. She would, though, surely?

'It would be fantastic,' gushed Naomi. 'I'd love to bring up Daisy near the sea. We'd be here every day.' She glanced at Gail and looked away. 'Maybe I should start to consider it.'

'I'll give you my mobile number just in case!' Gemma was enthusiastic. 'I know all the best nurseries and schools.'

'Have you got older children, too?' Jenny looked around. Where were they?

Gemma nodded. 'Yes, I've got three boys. The other two are at home with their dad. Eighteen months between the first two and then less than a year between the second and the youngest.'

Less than a year? *Blimey.* Less than a year? That meant that the second one must have been less than three months old when she fell pregnant again. She must have been having sex whilst she was still on the maternity ward. Gail pulled an open-mouthed face at Jenny behind Gemma's back, and Jenny tried not to smile.

'It's the best way to do it,' Gemma spoke with authority. 'Get the baby stage out of the way all at the same time.'

'Really?' Naomi asked, eagerly. 'You think it's good to have them close together? I've wondered whether a small or large age gap is better.'

'Definitely a small age gap.' Gemma had the usual assurance of the know-it-alls who can't understand that anyone else could have a perfectly nice life doing things slightly differently from them. Jenny's life had been plagued with people like this. The 'My Life Is Perfect – You Need To Do The Same' evangelists. It wasn't only their arrogance that bugged her, it was their incomprehension about how their comments made you feel. When she had been single, she had had to put up with them on a regular basis. Being nudged by everyone at family celebrations. *When are you going to find a nice young man and settle down? You're not getting any younger, you know!* This was even worse, though, with Ruth standing beside her, having to listen to this woman describe planning, conceiving and birthing a baby in less time than it took most people to decide to change their hair colour.

Gail caught Jenny's eye again and winked. She put her head on one side in exactly the same way Gemma had done. 'Is that why you're having trouble getting up to help your son? Three pregnancies in three years, left you a bit...' Gail motioned towards her nether regions, giving a very good impression of caring concern.

Jenny didn't know where to look, but she was pleased to see Ruth also trying to conceal a smile.

Gemma seemed oblivious to Gail's sarcasm. 'No, no, I had no problems with any of my pregnancies or births. It's all about a positive mental attitude, I think.' *Surprise, surprise, she's one of* those. Jenny felt the hairs rise on the back of her neck. Next, she would be announcing how some women make 'a lot of fuss' about childbirth. And then Jenny would be forced to push her under the next big wave.

Enough was enough: she couldn't listen to this Gemma woman any more. 'We really should be going soon, ladies. Antonia will be waiting for us back at the house.'

'Good idea,' agreed Gail. 'There's a bottle of wine in the fridge which is shouting my name.' She put her hands either side of her mouth as a funnel, and changed her voice. '*Gail! Drink me now!*'

Gemma raised her head and turned to Gail with acute interest. 'Gail? Are you the one who doesn't have a—?'

Naomi jumped up, hurriedly. 'Yes, yes, you're right, we should go. It was great to meet you, Gemma. You've given me lots to think about.'

What exactly *had* Naomi been thinking?

'I might try and get a quick nap,' said Ruth, as they walked off the beach. 'I'm sure that wine must have been double strength. I only had half a glass.'

'We'll allow you an hour and then we want you back.' Jenny waved a finger at her. She was as keen as Gail to get the vino flowing. Some drunkenness would either generate a little fun for her 'Girl About Town: On Tour' feature, or would loosen their tongues enough to give her the big scoop for *The Undercover Mother* that might make Eva change her mind. Tonight had to be the night.

CHAPTER THIRTY

My kitchen has been taken over by plastic pots with escapologist lids. We even have a whole cupboard dedicated to them now. I've tried to limit the problem: regular culls where any pot or lid without a perfectly matched partner is shown the door. But somehow they continue to breed, gremlin-like, in the darkness of the cupboard under the sink.

It's not just the pots. There are baby spoons, beakers, plastic bibs. There was a time when I wouldn't even allow a mismatched mug into the cupboard. Now Mr Baby and I can sometimes be found eating our dinner from a Peppa Pig plate.

Dinner this weekend with the Spice Mums will be a much more refined affair. I am hoping that the wine will be flowing and the stories will follow…

From *The Undercover Mother*

✦

Although the afternoon was almost over, the angle of the sun meant that the terrace behind the house was light and warm. Arranged around a wooden table were four chairs and a long bench, all with navy and white striped seat cushions and a few floral scatter cushions.

Antonia was sitting alone at one end of the table, speaking intently into her mobile. Jenny walked onto the terrace slowly, to give her a chance to finish her call.

'That will be great. See you then.' Antonia closed her phone case and put it down.

Jenny sat down next to her and placed five glasses on the table. The dark green foliage that surrounded them made this area feel very secluded and private. The perfect place for a quiet conversation. 'Wine?' she asked. Then Gail and Ruth came out of their room, laughing about something, and joined them in the garden. *Dammit.*

Gail looked very relaxed. 'This garden is a lovely little sun trap, isn't it?'

'I can't remember the last time I just sat still in the sun like this,' sighed Ruth. 'Just a very small one for me, please,' she said, as Jenny waved the bottle in her direction. She held out two glasses and passed one of them to Gail once they were filled. 'Well, don't we all scrub up well?'

'It seems to take me a lot longer to get ready these days.' Jenny started on her wine. 'I was looking at some younger photos of myself the other day and noticed that my hair is definitely thinner than it was – and I'm definitely fatter. If only it was the other way around.'

Gail nodded. 'The hair thing is very annoying. I've got these strange tufts all over the place where it's starting to grow back. That's why I had it all cropped. I couldn't bear it.'

Jenny looked at Gail's new hairstyle enviously. It was rather severe, but it suited her. If Jenny had cut her hair like that she would have looked like an extra from *Full Metal Jacket*.

Naomi wandered out onto the patio, still brushing her hair. 'More wine? I never knew you were all such alcoholics.' She slipped onto the bench next to Ruth. What had looked like a plain navy dress crumpled on Naomi's bed was something special now it was clinging to all the right places on her body. If John wasn't making her happy, he'd better buck his ideas up, thought Jenny. *There'll be plenty of men out there tonight who would like to.*

'Let's look at our itineraries.' Antonia picked up a piece of paper from the table and rustled it importantly. The others retrieved theirs from their bags and did the same.

'Okay. Okay. Very funny.' Jenny poked her tongue out at them. She'd emailed details of the restaurant and other venues hoping it would make it less likely that they'd drop out.

Antonia peered at her copy. 'This restaurant you've booked sounds nice.'

'I hope so – I'm feeling the pressure of being the organiser now. I don't actually know Brighton that well, so I got some recommendations from people at the magazine.' Jenny took a large gulp of wine. She really hoped she'd got it right. The last thing she wanted was people going home early tonight. 'I've got us on the guest lists at a couple of decent clubs that we could go to after dinner if you want to dance, but I've also got the names of a few bars if you'd prefer that. I'll mention that I'm writing a feature for *Flair* and we might even get some free drinks.'

'Either sounds good to me.' Antonia raised her glass. 'Here's to you, Jen, darling. Thanks for organising us.' The others echoed her sentiments and Jenny smiled and pretended to bow. Maybe it was the wine, but she felt an unexpected rush of warmth towards them all.

'I just hope you enjoy it.' Jenny held up crossed fingers. 'Last time I was here was my hen weekend.'

'Has everyone else been to Brighton before?' Gail looked around at each of them. 'I haven't been here for about ten years. I'm looking forward to exploring the nightlife.'

'Me, too,' said Naomi. 'It's ages since I've had a proper night out. Plus, we must make sure we're fun and interesting so that Jenny can write about us in her "Girl About Town" column. What do we need to do, Jen?'

'Nothing out of the ordinary. I'll mostly be writing about the venues,' Jenny could feel a blush beginning in her cheeks and took a swig of wine to disguise it. 'If something funny happens, I might include it.'

'Do you think we'll get chatted up tonight?' In a fitted black dress and four-inch heels, Antonia probably had a good chance of turning a few heads. 'Or are we too old for that? It might be fun to have a little flirt.'

But meeting men was not part of Jenny's plan. They would just get in the way. 'Count me out. Flirting requires a lot more energy than I've got. I don't think I could even muster up a bat of my eyelashes.'

'The part I always found exhausting about flirting was having to pretend to be interested in whatever the guy was saying,' said Ruth. '"Really? You think a Mercedes outclasses a BMW? That's absolutely fascinating!"'

Antonia raised an eyebrow. 'I think you've all forgotten how exciting it can be to have a new man interested in you.'

Gail looked at her sharply. 'You sound as if you've had recent experience.'

Antonia sat back in her chair and dangled her glass between her thumb and forefinger. 'I just think it would be fun to play at being footloose and fancy free for a night.'

'I think *you've* forgotten how hideous it is to be in a nightclub at 2 a.m. watching the last-ditch desperados frantically looking for someone.' Jenny shuddered. 'It's not for me.'

Antonia picked up the bottle of wine and started to refill everyone's glass. Naomi seemed to have emptied hers, even though she shouldn't be drinking.

'Let's have one last drink and then head off for dinner,' said Antonia. 'Then maybe we can have a look at some of these desperados for ourselves.'

◆

The restaurant was perfect. The floor was dark wood, the chairs were dark brown leather and a low-hung chandelier dimly lit each table. Jenny had requested a circular table – a square would have been awkward for five – and all was as she'd hoped. *Thank goodness.*

'This looks great. Well done, darling.' Antonia squeezed Jenny's arm and the others murmured agreement. A waiter came to meet them, took their coats and then showed them to their table.

'What a great menu.' Ruth flicked through the leather-bound volume she'd been given by the waiter. 'I'm definitely off my diet tonight.' She peered over as the next table's food was being delivered. 'I reckon I could eat about three of those plates. Oh, why do I love food so much?'

Naomi shook her head. 'I don't know why you worry – it's not as if you're overweight.'

'That's very kind of you, my dear, but the belt buckle holes do not lie.' Ruth pulled a face. 'I think I actually prefer food to sex.'

'God, don't we all.' Antonia looked up from the wine list.

'How can you say that?' Naomi was indignant. 'I've hardly ever seen you eat anything.'

'So, what does that tell you?' Antonia said in a husky voice. They all laughed.

Maybe Jenny wasn't the only one whose romantic life had taken a back seat. 'We've barely had sex since the baby. I'm just so knackered all the time. Getting up at 3 a.m. night after night is killing me.'

'I'm exhausted, too,' said Naomi, ruefully, 'but John is an every-night kind of man. Sometimes I think I might fall asleep halfway through. No, seriously,' she said, as the others started to laugh.

'When Dan and I first met we couldn't get enough of each other, either. I blame these babies and their constant neediness.'

'It's not just having a baby that does it.' Ruth looked down into her glass, then up at the others.

Jenny could have kicked herself for letting the conversation lapse into baby talk, but before she could change the topic, the waiter arrived to take their order. She had purposefully chosen a restaurant with good vegetarian options for Naomi, and a good wine list for Antonia. Everyone should be happy.

After they'd ordered, Antonia tried to lighten the conversation. 'Let's get serious with the girl talk. Anal sex, ladies. Yes or no?' They all chorused 'No' except Gail, who looked exaggeratedly coy over the top of her glass. This made them all laugh, even Ruth.

'Really?' Naomi looked rather shocked. 'It's not for me. John did suggest it once but I really couldn't be arsed.' It took her a few seconds of everyone laughing to realise what she had said and join in the laughter herself.

'Me, neither,' said Ruth. 'I feel the same way about anal sex as I do about bungee jumping – I've heard people say it's amazing, but that doesn't mean I ever want to try it.'

'You're obviously more a woman of the world than the rest of us,' Jenny said to Gail. 'Anything exciting you want to share with us?' *Please?*

Gail tried to look innocent. 'Not me, I'm a good Catholic girl.' She laughed and let the mock pious expression drop. 'I've had a few experiences in my time. When I was eighteen, I told my mum I was on a gap year and followed an amateur rock band around Europe. Now, *that* was a pretty wild time.'

After Gail's tales of seedy hotels and equally seedy wannabe rock stars, Naomi told them about a group-therapy session at a yoga retreat which sounded like it had been a borderline orgy, and Jenny told a long, funny anecdote about the time she'd dated a devoutly religious man who would take his cross from around his neck every time they had sex and then leave almost immediately to go to confession. 'So much for you good Catholics,' she teased Gail.

'What's the point of life if you don't live it to the full? Have some fun and then move on. That's what men do.' Gail raised her glass as she spoke.

'Not all men are like that,' said Ruth. Jenny knew she was thinking about David. He hadn't had much fun in the last year. Good men stayed.

Antonia took a large gulp of her wine and stared into the glass. 'A lot are, though.'

Antonia agreeing with Gail was a surprise. Where was this going?

'And as long as they're getting what they want out of a relationship, they'll say and do whatever's required to keep it ticking along.'

Jenny and Ruth exchanged glances.

Antonia looked up. 'Geoff's having an affair.'

There was an instant hush around the table. With unfortunate timing, the waiter delivered their meals and it took a couple of minutes for everyone to get the correct plate. When the waiter left, everyone picked up their forks and started to eat.

No wonder Antonia had acted so strangely with Jenny in the café earlier. It was *Geoff* who was having the affair. Clearly, it was impossible for them to go back to talking about losing your bra in Budapest after that announcement, but did Antonia want to talk about it any further?

The silence was painful. And Antonia had brought it up, after all. Jenny took the bull by the horns. 'Are you sure, Antonia?'

Antonia drank more wine. 'As sure as finding the nanny's knickers in your bed when you return from a weekend at your mother's.'

'The nanny?' Gail looked shocked. 'The nanny?' she repeated, in disbelief.

Jenny felt the same. How had she got it so wrong? She felt terrible for suggesting to Antonia that it had been her who had been playing away from home.

Antonia stared at her glass again. 'Not just the nanny, though. This isn't the first time it's happened. He's not particularly discreet.' She smiled weakly. 'I guess when you've been found out before and your wife does nothing, then you no longer need to bother covering your tracks.' Antonia tried her best to look world-weary and nonchalant, but she was clearly neither. 'I know for sure of at least three others. One of them was a friend of mine.'

Gail's eyes were bright and fierce. 'How the hell can you put up with that? I would want to kill him. I damn sure wouldn't still be married to him. He'd have been out of that door after the very first time. Why are you putting up with it?'

Although Gail's outburst was unsettling, Jenny agreed with her.

Antonia shrugged, then tried to make a joke. 'Don't worry, I get my revenge by spending as much of his money as I can. This dinner is on me. How is that spinach cannelloni, Naomi?'

How could she be so matter of fact? If Dan was having an affair, Jenny would be a wreck. But she followed Antonia's lead and talked about her dinner. Naomi and Ruth did the same. Everyone was awkward. They couldn't talk about babies. They couldn't talk about husbands. Or sex. Antonia wasn't even eating anything, and Gail continued to stare at her as if she'd never seen her before. By the time the waiter collected their plates and brought dessert menus, the conversation had dropped to the subject of their favourite book, and who would play them in a movie of their life. Safe subjects. No use to *The Undercover Mother*.

'I never know what to order for dessert.' Naomi ran her finger down the options. 'Everything sounds so nice and then I always end up ordering cheesecake.'

'Why don't you go for the trio of desserts, then?' suggested Ruth. 'One of them is a tiny cheesecake but then you get to try two other things, too – crème brûlée and chocolate ganache.'

'That sounds like something they put on your face at a health spa.' Jenny needed to get the evening back on track, and quickly. *Just keep talking.*

'Oh, let's do that next time,' sighed Naomi. 'Have a weekend at a health spa.' Ruth and Antonia agreed; Gail continued to sip her wine. Silently. Why wasn't she joining in?

'I did think about that this time, but I wasn't sure I knew you all well enough yet to get my wobbly bits out in front of you.'

'Honestly, I don't know why you all worry so much about weight and size! You are what you are and if you don't like it, you just need to do some exercise, not cut back on food,' said Naomi. Ruth and Jenny glanced at each other: *Give her another few years.*

'What are you going to have for dessert?' Jenny asked Gail, trying to bring her back into the conversation. Gail was now staring at the menu, her face dark and forbidding.

'I'm not sure.' She was tight-lipped and not taking her eyes from the choices in front of her, although she didn't appear to be reading them. 'I might not bother with dessert, actually. I'm going to the bathroom.' Without looking at the others, she got up from the table and stalked towards the toilets.

The others looked at each other uncomfortably. 'What's wrong with her?' Naomi asked Jenny.

Jenny shrugged. 'Bad memories, maybe?'

'Or good ones?' Antonia suggested. Jenny didn't understand what she meant, but the atmosphere around the table was already too uncomfortable to question her further. She just wanted to change the subject before the whole night went down the pan.

'Right, are we having dessert or shall we pay the bill?'

'Let's pay the bill and go.' Antonia motioned to the waiter for their bill. 'Time for a change of scene.'

Gail reappeared as they were getting their coats. Jenny muttered to Ruth, 'And to think I was worried that you would be the one to feel uncomfortable.'

Ruth's eyes were wide. 'I can't believe what I'm hearing. What else are we going to find out?'

CHAPTER THIRTY-ONE

On the first few dates with your future husband, you might discuss whether you have the same taste in films or whether he likes Chinese food as much as you. You probably don't consider how good he'll be at sponging baby sick off the sofa and whether he'll be able to recall every verse of 'You Are My Sunshine' as he walks up and down the hall carrying a screaming infant at 2 a.m.

Not every dad is up to the task. Mr Sporty is a little wet for me, but no one can argue that he isn't a good dad. According to Posh, Mr Posh is only on his own with Baby Posh when she goes to the toilet, and he wouldn't know one end of a tube of Sudocrem from the other. As for Mr Scary... WE STILL DON'T KNOW!...

From *The Undercover Mother*

✦

Leaving the restaurant, Jenny checked her mobile. A text from Dan: Henry was asleep.

Grateful for an excuse to avoid the strained small-talk after Antonia's revelation, and eager to see what had happened on the boys' night in, she hung back a little from the others and called him.

'How was it?'

'Fabulous,' said Dan. 'We painted each other's toenails, watched a brom-com and ate Ryvita covered in a variety of toppings.'

'Very amusing.' Jenny kept an eye on the others. Antonia and Ruth seemed to be chatting quite amiably now. Gail was striding ahead whilst Naomi tried to keep up with her. 'Did the afternoon at Geoff's go well? Was it better than you expected?'

It had been quite a surprise to Jenny when Geoff had invited the men over. But she'd been almost as surprised when she'd found out Antonia had been the one behind it. At the time, Antonia had winked and said, 'That way he won't be able to slink out and leave Jess with the nanny.' Now Jenny was wondering if there had been another reason.

She could almost hear Dan shrug at the other end. 'It was fine. A little dull but fine.'

As usual, she was going to have to pull the information out of him. 'Did you get any gossip for me?'

Dan groaned. 'Oh, no, I knew I should have recorded the whole thing. Is it not bad enough that you forced me to go and spend half a day with three men I barely know, but now you want me to give you a full summary of the afternoon's proceedings?'

Jenny was surprised he would even ask; of course that was what she was expecting. 'Was the nanny there?'

Dan sounded surprised. 'Emily? Yes, Geoff wanted the poor girl to watch all the babies whilst we cracked open a few bottles, but we managed to persuade him that we needed to stay sober to take them home. She seemed like a nice girl.'

Jenny bristled; she wasn't the jealous type ordinarily, but this one was clearly a man-eater. 'How nice?'

'What do you mean, "How nice"? Just normal nice.'

Jenny didn't rate her husband's assessment. What kind of 'nice girl' would sleep with someone's husband? And one who had a young baby. 'Did you notice anything about her behaviour towards Geoff?'

'Did I notice *what*? Oh, I see, has Antonia told you to ask? She doesn't seem the jealous type. No. I didn't notice anything. To be honest, we hardly saw her. She was looking after the babies whilst we drank tea, listened to Geoff and tried to gauge how early we could leave without getting into trouble with our wives.'

Jenny realised it was pointless expecting Dan to have picked up on any kind of non-verbal communication between the two of them. Geoff could have had the nanny pinned up against the kitchen cupboards and Dan would have assumed they were looking for the teabags. The man didn't have a suspicious bone in his body.

She tried a different tack. 'What about the others? How did John seem?'

'Fine. A little bit nervous about looking after Daisy on his own. I think Naomi has quite strong ideas about how she likes things done. He had strict instructions about what the baby was and wasn't allowed to eat, and he'd been told, on pain of death, not to take her to his mother. Obviously, I'm lucky to have a wife who just lets me do my own thing, follow my own instincts...'

'He didn't mention anything about Naomi, then?' Jenny interrupted.

'Not to me, no. Although, he and David were out in the kitchen talking for quite a while, which was joyous for me as I was left on my own with Geoff.'

'You don't like Geoff?' It surprised Jenny that Dan would have formed an opinion about him. He was usually ambivalent about most people – she could imagine him describing Saddam Hussein as, 'All right, I suppose'.

'He's all right, I suppose. Just likes talking about himself rather a lot. I tried to ask him about the work they'd had done on the house, but he didn't seem to know much about it.'

Jenny smiled at the thought of her DIY-loving husband assuming that Geoff would have had anything to do with the practical side of his house renovations. 'And what were John and David talking about?'

'Unfortunately, my spy equipment is on the blink so I wasn't able to follow their conversation from the other room. However, when I went out to get another drink, they did seem to be in the middle of a deep and meaningful so I didn't hang around.'

Interested and irritated in equal measure – how could he not have 'overheard' what they were saying?! – Jenny realised this was a fruitless line of questioning. She would have to prise more details out of him tomorrow when she got home. 'Anyway, how's my boy doing?'

'I'm fine, thank you, and Henry is fast asleep in bed after half a packet of rusks and a large mug of cocoa.'

'I'm not going to ask if that is a joke or not, as I don't want the answer. I'm having a nice time, thank you,' she prompted.

'Oh, good. Just so I know, what is the current situation? Are we still planning on arranged marriages between our children, or are they preparing to send your body parts back to me in individual envelopes?'

Jenny laughed. 'Jury is still out on that one.' She was tempted to give him an update on Naomi and Antonia, but he probably wouldn't want to know. His complete lack of interest in other people's lives never failed to astound her.

'Okay, I'll wait for the verdict with bated breath. So, have I given you everything you need now, officer? Can I go to bed, as your son is likely to be waking me up at 5.30 a.m. tomorrow?'

'You are excused. I need to get back to the others, anyway.' They were standing outside a busy-looking bar, waiting for her to catch up. 'Dan?'

'Yes?'

'Could you see yourself ever having an affair?'

Dan pretended to mull it over. 'Would I ever have an affair? Hmmm. Does this include the romantic liaison I have been attempting to initiate with the girl behind the counter at Screwfix?'

Jenny laughed. 'No. That one's allowed, as I know that you're only after her discount card.'

'In that case, no thanks on the affair. Your particular insane, irrational womanhood is more than enough for me. If I ever leave you, it will be for a quiet bedsit, not another woman.'

She knew he was telling the truth. Any envy she had felt for Antonia's lifestyle was long gone after the news of Geoff's affair. Jenny knew she had a good one. 'Dan?' she said again.

'Yes?'

'I love you.'

'I love you, too. We'll see you tomorrow.'

Putting her mobile back into her jacket pocket, she sped up to join the others as they entered the bar. The night was marching on and she still hadn't got the answers to any of her questions, plus now she had Geoff's affair to think about – would she include that in the column? And why was Gail so annoyed about it? Had it hit a nerve about the mysterious Joe? Maybe Gail thought her announcement that they had split had ended any speculation. But not for Jenny, it hadn't. She hoped, in Gail's current mood, it would only need a little prodding to provoke her to reveal all.

CHAPTER THIRTY-TWO

My 'real-life' friends are losing patience with me. I've turned down multiple nights out because I'm too damn tired and, even on the phone, I cut them off mid-conversation because The Boy has woken up or is gagging on a teething toy he's trying to push down his throat.

I don't even have anything of interest to say. They'll tell me something hilarious that happened at work or about a hot date they have lined up; all I have in exchange is that day's episode of Loose Women or the difficulty I've had in finding an effective teething gel.

But where does that leave me? I'm running out of interest in hearing about Sporty's view on cranial osteopathy for babies or Posh's latest purchase from JoJo Maman Bébé. When we go away for the weekend, we need topics of conversation that don't revolve around the babies. And there is only one thing to help with that. A lot of alcohol...

From *The Undercover Mother*

✦

The bar was busy, but not as heaving as some of those they'd passed, so they decided to take a chance. By the time they'd made their way in, Jenny was dying to go to the toilet. Leaving the others to hunt for a table, she went in search of the Ladies'.

After the noise of the bar, the ladies' toilet was surprisingly quiet. As always, Jenny went straight into the first cubicle because she had read an article once which said that the first cubicle in a public toilet was the one that was least used and therefore most likely to be clean. Obviously, this assumed that enough people to cancel out the law of averages hadn't read the same article. Hovering over the toilet so that her bottom didn't touch the seat, she read the peeling STD poster on the back of the cubicle door. She'd got as far as 'gonorrhoea' when she heard the door open and Gail called, 'Jenny, are you in here?'

'Yes, won't be long.' She flushed the toilet, then tore off another three squares of toilet paper and stuffed them into her handbag. She wasn't going to get caught out later when people starting peeing after every drink and the bar staff were too busy to replenish the stocks. 'All yours.'

She washed her hands thoroughly, following the instructions she had learnt from the posters in the maternity ward toilets. She had got as far as: 'Wet Hands, Use Soap, Lather', when she realised Gail was staring at her in the mirror. She looked Gail's reflection in the eye, pausing for whatever it was that she obviously wanted to say.

'It's me.'

Of course it was her. How drunk was she? 'What is you?'

Gail looked intently at Jenny's reflection. She took a deep breath. 'I am the woman, sorry, *one* of the women, involved with Geoff.' She paused and waited for a reaction, but the penny still wasn't dropping anywhere near Jenny's wine-addled brain. Gail repeated herself. 'I have been having an affair with Antonia's husband.'

Jenny stopped mid-rinse and continued to stare at Gail in the mirror. She still wasn't completely sure she had understood her correctly. 'You're having an affair with Antonia's husband?' Gail nodded. 'This Antonia?' Jenny gestured vaguely towards the toilet door. 'The Antonia you have known for months? Been for coffee with? Swapped birth stories with?'

'Yes. Yes.' Gail sounded irritated. 'The same Antonia who just told us that her husband is shagging their nanny. Which, incidentally, was a nice way for me to find out.'

'A nice way for you to…' Jenny trailed off in disbelief. She must have bumped her head and woken up in the middle of a daytime soap opera. 'You have to be kidding me, Gail. This has got to be some weird joke of yours.' She realised she was still staring at Gail's reflection and turned around to face her. 'There is no way a normal woman has an affair with a married man – a father – and then goes for a play date with his wife and baby daughter.'

Gail continued to look at her calmly. Jenny had always prided herself on her ability to read people and situations. She always saw the twist coming in a book or film. But this? This she had not seen coming at all. 'You're not joking, are you?' She searched Gail's face for a smirk, still sure she must be making this up. There wasn't one. 'Why the hell are you telling me this?'

Gail looked at herself in the mirror. She smoothed down the one hair that was out of place and adjusted her collar. 'Because I'm going to tell her. I would like your advice. You know her better than I do.'

Jenny stared at Gail as if she were speaking in a strange accent. She shook her head once in an effort to take everything in. Then she started to shake it again, more slowly this time.

'Oh, no, I don't want anything to do with this. How do I know her better? We all met on exactly the same day.'

'I met Geoff a long time before that.'

Jenny could almost feel the cogs of her brain turning. 'What do you mean, you met…' Realisation hit. 'He's not… tell me he's not the… Gail, is he?'

'Jake's father?' Gail nodded. 'Yes, he is.'

'And Joe?'

'Is Geoff.'

Jenny's hands went to her face. She couldn't believe how calmly Gail was telling her such explosive information. Indignant on Antonia's behalf, she began to feel quite angry. 'What were you thinking, Gail? A married man?'

Gail shrugged. 'The firm Geoff works for is a client of ours. I had to work closely with him on an investment portfolio and we got to know each other. At that point, his marriage was on the brink of separation. He and his wife – Antonia – met young and drifted apart. I worked long hours in those days, and it didn't bother me that we couldn't see each other often. Then I fell pregnant.'

'And?'

'And he told me he was leaving her. He promised.'

'But?'

'But then, as if by magic, Antonia discovered she was pregnant, too.'

Jenny shook her head slowly. This was a lot to take in. 'And how did you end up at the same antenatal class?'

'My secretary. She can find out anything. Geoff started to get very vague about when he was going to leave Antonia. She was unwell. Or unstable. Or they had a family event. My secretary called his for a "chat" and she said he'd been moaning about having to attend an antenatal class. She even found out when and where. The look on his face when I walked through the door was worth the effort.'

Jenny felt a little sick. Gail was so clinically calm, so unrepentant. How could she be telling her all of this without hanging her head in shame? 'Why would you want to do that?'

Gail frowned. 'Why? Think about it, Jenny. If your baby's father was attending an antenatal group with another woman, wouldn't you want to be there?'

'But the other woman was – is – his *wife*,' Jenny whispered in disbelief. Her mind whirred; the pieces fell into place: the contempt with which Gail treated Antonia and the fact they'd never, ever, met Joe. How had she not seen this? She looked at Gail in amazement; she was obviously very good at keeping secrets. And lying.

'But it's over? You told us that you'd broken up with Joe… Geoff… Jake's dad.'

Gail took a lipstick from her bag and looked in the mirror as she applied it. When she'd finished, she clicked it shut and turned back to Jenny.

'I made that up. It was easier than finding excuses all the time.' Gail sighed. 'I wasn't intending to meet up with you all after the class. Geoff warned me not to, said I would ruin his chance of an easy, quick divorce, that he couldn't leave her until after the baby was born and Antonia had everything under control. To start with, I kept in touch with you to find out what was going on. But then...'

'Then we became your friends.' Jenny was fully aware of the irony of this conversation. Hadn't she done the same thing? Without the extra-marital sex part.

'Before I met Antonia, she was just Geoff's cold and unloving wife. Now...'

Jenny almost nodded. She had also dismissed Antonia as a trophy wife when they'd first met. Her clothes, her manicures, her designer sunglasses. But, in the last few months, Jenny had seen another side to Antonia. There was much more to her than posh lunches and spa days. She was funny and generous. And she definitely didn't deserve this.

'Don't you think she has a right to know, Jen? I thought you'd be marching me out there immediately to own up.'

A fair point. If Dan had been having an affair with one of them, Jenny would definitely want to know. Friends were supposed to be honest with each other. She squashed down her own guilty feelings. There was a time and a place for honesty. And it wasn't tonight.

'But why *now*, Gail? Why this weekend?'

For the first time, Gail looked embarrassed. 'Until Antonia's announcement about the nanny's knickers, I thought Geoff and I had something special. I thought he had an unhappy marriage and had just happened to fall in love with me. I was frustrated that we weren't together yet, but I thought that was a sign that he was a decent, caring man. Turns out I was wrong on all counts.'

There was clearly another side to Gail, too. A stupid one. 'You really thought he was going to leave his wife one day? Gail, that's such a cliché.'

Gail stiffened and her eyes flashed. She started to tap her nails onto her folded arms. She opened her mouth to speak and then closed it again.

Jenny softened her tone. 'I'm sorry. I know tonight's revelation must make you feel awful, but Antonia has done nothing wrong. Why make *her* suffer?'

Her eyes glittering, Gail uncrossed her arms and tucked her hair behind her ears. 'I meant what I said – don't you think she has a right to know?'

Jenny imagined that the last thing Antonia needed was for Gail to reveal all in front of everyone. This was supposed to be a relaxing weekend. She put a hand on Gail's arm and lowered her voice.

'She already knows that he's had at least four affairs. Knowing that one of them was you, and about Jake, will only make it more painful for her – and it doesn't sound like it would change anything. Please think about this.'

Gail shook her head slowly and her lips tightened into a fine line. After a pause, she raised her head, resolutely. 'I don't think I can keep quiet any longer. She has a right to know. And I have a right to tell her. I'm not leaving this weekend without doing it.'

CHAPTER THIRTY-THREE

Hopefully a few glasses of wine will loosen tongues and I can find out what makes these women tick because, although we've known each other for months, I don't feel like I truly know them.

Weirdly, I know the important stuff. I've heard their fears, seen their boobs and we've talked about our vaginas, our toilet habits and how often we have sex with our husbands.

But I don't know the frothy stuff, the funny stuff, the 'Guess what I did when I was sixteen' stuff. And, if we are going to become proper, 'real-life' friends, that's the kind of information I need to know…

From *The Undercover Mother*

✦

Music thumped from large speakers at one end of the bar. Laughter and shouted conversations surrounded Jenny as she weaved her way through the crowd. Gail pointed in the direction of a table in one corner, where Ruth and Antonia were deep in conversation. Naomi was nowhere to be seen.

Antonia looked up and waved at them. 'We used to have two friends that looked like you.'

'Yes, sorry, there was a… er… a queue.' Jenny could barely look at her. 'Does anyone want another drink?' She was certainly in need of another. A large one.

'Naomi has just gone up to the bar,' said Ruth. 'If you catch her, she can add your drinks to the order.'

Gail put a hand on Jenny's arm. 'I'll go. Vodka and tonic?'

'Yes, please.' Jenny sat down again and tried to shake off her stupor. Geoff, Antonia's husband, was the father of Gail's child. She had wanted revelations, but this one was off the scale. Now it wasn't just Naomi she was worried about; she had to keep Gail quiet, too. Gail and Antonia must be kept apart; if they weren't alone, Gail couldn't tell her. All Jenny had to do was keep the conversation light and away from any topics which might veer into dangerous territory. *Act normal, act normal.* 'Have we missed anything?'

'Nothing much. Naomi has been queuing at the bar and Ruth's giving me a bit of impromptu life coaching.' As Ruth protested, Antonia patted her hand. 'Just joking, darling.'

'Tell me to mind my own business,' said Jenny, 'but why don't you just leave him?'

Antonia shrugged. 'What would I do? Honestly, Jenny, what would I do? I have never worked in my life – I married Geoff straight out of university and basically supported his career from that point on. I've entertained his colleagues, accompanied him on trips, shopped for gifts for his business contacts, but I've never had a real job. Quite frankly, I find the prospect of having to get one terrifying. I'm not—' she raised her finger to stop Ruth from interrupting her—'playing the society wife, afraid to chip a manicured fingernail. I mean that I am actually terrified.'

'But you have a degree,' Ruth insisted.

Antonia pulled a face. 'In Art History. I'm not sure that qualifies you for a great deal. Anyway, it's not just the job. It's everything. Looking after Jess, living on my own. I'm just used to the way things are.'

Naomi and Gail arrived with the drinks and a tray of shots.

Gail held up her hands. 'I couldn't stop her.' They pulled over two more seats and sat down.

'The barman gave them to us for free.' Naomi giggled. 'I've already drunk mine.'

Already drunk hers? By Jenny's reckoning, Naomi had had three glasses of wine and now this vile-looking concoction. If she was pregnant, she should not be drinking like that.

Ruth shook her head. 'I'll just be sick if I drink that.'

Antonia sniffed at her glass and then sipped at it. Jenny took one and downed it, grimacing at its sweet potency. Then she had Ruth's, too. She needed it.

Naomi leaned forward eagerly. 'I've had a great idea. Let's play a game of Truth.'

Half an hour ago, Jenny would have relished this. What better way to get what she needed. Now, she wasn't so sure. 'Aren't we all a bit old for that?'

Naomi wasn't listening. 'How many pennies have we got between us?'

Everyone looked into their purses and managed to produce a small pile of coins.

'Okay, take five each. This is what you have to do.' Naomi took a deep breath. 'Each person has to say something that they have never done before, such as, erm, such as, "*I have never been on a hot air balloon*." Then anyone who *has* been on a hot air balloon has to put one of her pennies into the middle. The winner is the person that is still left with pennies when everyone else has lost theirs.'

Jenny tried again to protest, but Antonia and Ruth were already sorting pennies into equal piles. There seemed an inevitability to this. Would they be so keen to take part if they knew what they might find out?

'Okay, who wants to go first?' This party animal was a new side to Naomi. Maybe breastfeeding had sucked the life out of her up until now. She was like a wind-up toy, newly released. 'Ruth?'

'Oh, er, okay.' Ruth thought for a moment. 'I have never... had anal sex!'

'Hey, that's cheating! I only told you that tonight – you can't use it against me!' Gail cried.

'No, that's the game!' Naomi fidgeted in her chair like a small child. 'We can use anything we know already – that's why it's fun. Come on. Money in the pot!' Gail dropped a penny onto the beer mat in the middle of the table. 'You can go next if you like?'

A wicked grin emerged on Gail's face. 'I have never had to have a tampon surgically removed.' She looked triumphantly at Jenny.

'You cow – I told you that in strictest confidence,' protested Jenny, as she plopped a penny onto the mat. It had come out during a phone conversation, discussing periods and whether they'd restarted. Motherhood gave rise to some scintillating subjects.

'Ouch.' Antonia grimaced.

'It's not as bad as it sounds. I was only fourteen and the string broke. My doctor had to get it out with forceps.'

'Ouch again.' Antonia crossed her legs. 'Thank God I didn't have to go through any of that business with Jess.'

'Jenny, your turn.' Naomi was enjoying her role of playmaker.

'Well, even though I'd love to get my own back on Gail, I'm afraid I don't have any more inside info.' Jenny faltered as she realised what a huge lie she had just told. 'I'm going to have to take a stab in the dark. I have never slept with someone on a first date.'

All four women looked at each other guiltily and then, one by one, they put a penny in the middle. Jenny put her hands to her mouth in mock shock.

'I doubt very much any of our one-night stands were much to write home about.' Ruth pulled a being-sick face. 'Mine was a waiter in Majorca.'

Antonia raised her glass. 'A spotty history student during freshers' week.'

Naomi giggled and brought hers up to join Antonia's. 'My brother's best friend on a Scouts' camping trip.'

Gail downed her drink and slammed her glass down on the table. 'A slimy lawyer two months ago!'

Everyone collapsed into laughter. Either the wine and shots were starting to have an effect, or Jenny was feeling another glow of warmth towards these women. Maybe this game was a good idea after all. They should keep it going.

'Whose turn is it next? Antonia?'

Antonia rolled her glass between her hands as she thought about it. 'This is more difficult than you think.'

'Is that because there's very little you haven't done?' asked Ruth, cheekily.

Antonia laughed. 'Okay, I'll have to do a boring one. I have never lied to my parents.'

'What, never?' Naomi was incredulous. 'I might as well put all my money in on that one.'

'I don't believe you,' scoffed Gail. 'I'm really close to my mum and even I've told a few white lies over the years. What about when you were a teenager? Never got drunk and then got a friend to call your parents with an excuse?'

'Nope.' Antonia shook her head. 'I have never lied to them.'

Gail wouldn't let it go. 'Not telling them things, that counts as a lie. Have you told them about Geoff's shenanigans?'

Jenny sucked in air. *Please don't do this.*

Antonia didn't falter. 'Yes, as a matter of fact, I have.'

'What?' Gail was incredulous again. 'You've told them and they haven't told you to get the hell out of there?'

Antonia sipped her drink. 'I told my mother. She… understood.'

The table went quiet and Jenny frantically tried to think of something to say: a funny question to ask or a story to tell. Not only because she didn't like the silence, but because she didn't want Gail to find a window for her own revelation.

Then Naomi took a deep breath and shared one of her own. 'Well, I haven't told my parents that I'm pregnant again and that I'm devastated about it.'

If the table was quiet before, it was in a vacuum of silence now. No one seemed to know what the appropriate response should be. Jenny focused on not looking anywhere near Ruth. She had been so preoccupied with Gail that she had forgotten to worry about Naomi. Why hadn't she kept her mouth shut? What was Ruth thinking?

Ruth was the first to react. She became very red in the face and levelled a steely gaze in Naomi's direction. 'You're pregnant again already? Was it planned?'

Naomi looked uncomfortable. 'No. Not planned.'

Ruth picked up her glass and took a long drink.

Naomi sat up straight, fiddling with the neckline of her dress as if it was too tight for her. 'I'm sorry. I don't know why that came out. Just forget I said anything.'

Jenny knew that this wasn't the first time Naomi had faced an unplanned pregnancy and she also knew how unhappy she was. But she couldn't let on that she knew about it; Ruth might feel it had been purposely hidden from her. Jenny put a hand on Naomi's arm. 'I'm sure this has been a big shock for you, Naomi. It must be hard to get your head around it.'

'Maybe you're just worried that your body won't cope with a pregnancy so soon after giving birth.' Gail was also trying to help Naomi dig herself out; they all felt the weight of Ruth's unrelenting stare.

'It isn't a physical issue,' Naomi explained reluctantly. 'I'm just not sure how I'm going to cope with two small children. I'm not sure that I even want another…'

Before she could say any more, Ruth stood up, threw the rest of her drink over Naomi, and walked out of the bar.

✦

'Should I go after her?' Jenny tried to help Naomi absorb some of the drink on her dress with the cheap bar napkins. Naomi was crying and Antonia was patting her on the back gently.

'No, I think we just leave her to her own thoughts for a while,' said Gail.

'I'm sorry. I'm so sorry,' sobbed Naomi.

'Ssshh,' soothed Jenny. 'You have no reason to apologise to us. Although maybe your timing could have been a little better.' She looked pointedly at Gail.

Antonia continued the patting. 'Does John know yet?'

Naomi shook her head. 'I haven't had a period the whole time I've been breastfeeding. The only reason I took a test was because I felt really sick for days.'

'Have you thought about what you want to do?' asked Antonia. 'You've been drinking an awful lot tonight, darling.'

'Actually, I haven't.' Naomi looked at her sheepishly. 'That's why I've been offering to get the drinks. Apart from a glass of wine at the house, most of which I tipped on the garden, and a small glass with dinner, I have been on tonic water.' She started to cry again. 'Ruth must hate me.'

'No, no.' Jenny took her hand. If Ruth did hate Naomi, it would have been understandable, but hatred wasn't Ruth's style. 'She's just angry at the situation. It must be hard for her to hear that someone can get pregnant by accident when it's been so difficult for her. To be honest, it must be difficult being around all of us, full stop.'

Jenny wanted to kick herself. Getting them all together this weekend had been a mistake. A selfish mistake. This wasn't about a stupid blog any more. She just wanted to go home.

Gail went to the bar to get Naomi a glass of water. When she came back and Naomi seemed a little more composed, she asked if anyone wanted another drink, but no one was in the mood.

'Shall we just head back, darlings?' Antonia started to slip on her jacket.

'Hang on. Maybe we should stay, just a little longer.' Gail nodded over Jenny's shoulder. 'There's a rather attractive-looking man making his way over here.'

Jenny turned in the direction of Gail's nod and looked the attractive man straight in the eye. *Oh, no!*

'Hi, Jen!' he said.

CHAPTER THIRTY-FOUR

Of course, the Spice Mums also don't really know me, either.

Due to my love affair with Google, they seem to view me as well informed and in control. Whereas my 'real-life' friends are constantly amazed that I have managed to even keep The Boy alive.

It's because they don't know anything about me pre-baby. They don't know how many crap boyfriends I had to go through before I met Mr Baby. That I could down a whole pint of cider and then recite the alphabet backwards. That I only joined the antenatal class so that I could get the lowdown on the hitherto unrevealed side of being a parent.

Which leads me to something else rather important that they don't know anything about...

From *The Undercover Mother*

✦

Given the state of Brian, he clearly wasn't there on a photography assignment for *Flair*. He beamed at Jenny, whilst also looking over her shoulder at the other three; Lucy must have run out of friends to set him up with and he was about to start on hers. Unsteady on his feet, it took him a moment or two to make it over to them, while Jenny tried in vain to head him off before the others had a chance to speak to him. What was *he* doing here?

'Well, this is a nice surprise, seeing you.' He had the faintest slur to his voice. Brian was a regular drinker so, if he was drunk, he must have had quite a bit. 'I didn't think you were back out in social circulation yet.'

Jenny glanced around her quickly, looking for an escape route. There was no way she wanted him talking to the others. If he worked out who they were, her cover would be well and truly blown. She could push him towards the bar but it was packed three-deep with people. Maybe she could take up smoking and jostle him outside onto the pavement? She searched for a group of sleazy-looking men who would likely be his friends. Why weren't they looking for him? 'I'm not, it's just a night away from…' She tried to move him away from the girls, or at least give him a look which signified *Say nothing*. But who was she kidding? Most men didn't do non-verbal signals sober, let alone drunk. When she used that look on Dan he always said, 'Are you okay? Have you got something in your eye?'

'Jenny's trying to say that we've all got a night off from our babies,' interrupted Naomi. She seemed to have got over her upset pretty quickly and was smiling flirtatiously at Brian. Gail was also giving Jenny an 'introduce us now' look. He did scrub up well, although right then he was looking more than a little worse for wear.

'Babies?' A light went on behind his slightly sozzled eyes. 'Oh, it's *you*!' He started pointing at them with delight. *Bugger*.

Antonia looked bemused. 'Who does this deranged man think we are? And who the devil is he?'

'Just one of the photographers from the magazine. I don't know him all that well,' Jenny said behind the back of her hand. 'He's not the sort of person I'd want to introduce you to. I'll get rid of him.' Grabbing hold of his arm, she leaned in and raised her voice. 'Brian, come with me to the bar. Let me buy you a drink.'

Brian was still pointing, moving his finger across the three of them as if he were deciding which one to pick. 'You're the Spice Mums!' he hooted, clearly enjoying himself. Alcohol had a lot to answer for.

Jenny felt the colour drain from her face. *Shit. Shit. Shit.* This was not the way it was supposed to be. If she ever did tell them, it was going to be nonchalantly. She would make it sound like a good thing. *Yes, I have been writing about you on a public blog for the last few months and I would like to carry on doing so in a magazine. Fun, eh?* But with the recent news of an unplanned pregnancy, Geoff's affair with the nanny and Gail's imminent announcement, this probably wasn't the best time to reveal that Jenny had been publishing their private conversations on the world wide web.

Antonia continued to stare at him with distaste. 'What the hell is he talking about?'

Jenny's finger was midway to her temple where she was about to rotate it and suggest that Brian was slightly unhinged – *'All those flashbulbs, messes with the grey matter'* – when she realised that it was pointless. She'd always known she would have to tell them sometime. She might as well get it over with. With any luck, sandwiching her announcement between Naomi's and Gail's might mean it got forgotten, anyway. *Maybe. Or maybe not.*

She sighed and faced them. 'I have something I have been meaning to tell you all.'

Brian definitely wasn't getting the vibe. 'You HAVE to be Posh!' He beamed at Antonia. He waved his hand up and down. 'The accent, the clothes. Got to be.' He looked at Naomi, then Gail, then back to Naomi, before settling on Gail. 'Scary. Definitely.'

Gail no longer looked interested in being introduced. Looking at Jenny, she said: 'I think you'd better speak quickly before Laddo here gets a swift kick somewhere soft.'

This didn't perturb Brian at all. 'See! Scary! I was right!' he crowed, before peering at Naomi. 'Which means you must be—'

'Brian! Stop! For the love of… just stop!' Jenny put her hands on his shoulders and turned him around to face a small group of men who had finally materialised and seemed to know him. 'The boys need you back now. I'll see you soon.' As he tottered back to his friends, she turned to face the girls. 'Maybe we should sit down.'

✦

'So, let me get this straight,' Gail spoke slowly. 'You've been meeting up with us, letting us feel that we can trust you, and then writing about all our private conversations.' She tapped her fingernails on the side of the fresh glass of wine that Jenny had bought.

'No, no,' said Jenny, hurriedly. 'Not the private ones, just the stuff we talk about when we're together as a group. General stuff. And no one knows who you are – I've given you all pseudonyms to protect your identities.'

'Yes, we heard,' said Antonia, dryly. 'The Spice Mums. How nice.'

'I just used the names. It seemed to… fit.' Jenny mumbled the last part and looked down. When she raised her eyes, they met Gail's angry-looking ones.

'And I'm scary, am I?'

Jenny almost squeaked. 'No, not scary, just…' She flailed around for an appropriate word. 'Firm?'

Gail harrumphed and crossed her arms.

'I think I've found it.' Naomi was thumbing her mobile phone screen. She read aloud from one of the earlier posts. '*As her baby feeds more often than a giant panda, Sporty's milk ducts must be working twenty-four-hour shifts….*' She looked up at Jenny. 'Is that me?' She sounded hurt.

'I know it sounds bad.' Jenny winced. 'But I had to make it funny. It needed to be entertaining and humorous. Because I needed to get as many readers as possible, I changed things a bit, exaggerated things you did or said. Made them sound more outlandish. You've got to understand, this is my job.'

'That's what Jeremy Kyle probably says to the contestants on that awful programme, right before he makes them look like human freaks in front of the entire nation.' Gail still looked annoyed.

'Are you even legally allowed to do this without our permission?' Antonia asked. Jenny swallowed. Surely Antonia wouldn't try to sue her? Dan had warned her about writing about a lawyer's wife.

'There's a disclaimer, and I haven't used any real names. It's not even really about *you*. You just give me ideas for topics.' This wasn't going well.

Naomi read aloud from her screen. '*At Posh's house the other day, we were looking at each other's babies, trying to see who they looked like.*' She looked up, accusingly. 'That actually happened.'

Antonia looked a little bit sick. 'What *exactly* did you write about that?'

Naomi passed her mobile over. 'It's all here. Read it for yourself.'

As Antonia read, Gail took over the interrogation. 'So, all this time, you've been merely grooming us? I know we haven't been friends long but, really, you felt no loyalty at all?'

Jenny was a gnat's winkle away from asking Gail how she had the audacity to talk about loyalty, but instead she took a deep breath and started again. 'That's the point I've been trying to make. At the beginning, I only joined the group for material for a column, but now—' she looked at them '—now I have begun to be fond of you all. I was going to tell you all about it this weekend. I was just waiting for the right time.'

Antonia waved Naomi's mobile at Gail. 'Do you want to take a look?' Gail took it and flicked quickly through the screen. 'To be honest, it's not that bad.'

'That's what I've been trying to tell y—'

Antonia held up a finger and cut Jenny off. 'That's not to say I don't think you should have told us.'

'I agree.' Gail passed the mobile back to Naomi. 'But there's nothing incriminating in there.' She looked levelly at Jenny. 'And I'm assuming there won't be.'

Jenny shook her head vehemently, not wanting to be cut off again if she opened her mouth.

'But I sound like a nutcase!' said Naomi. 'It sounds like you hate me, Jenny.'

'No, no! I admit, your character is hugely exaggerated – I actually based a lot of it on another mum I met.' She prayed silently that Naomi wouldn't ask her who. 'Sporty is actually nothing like you now.' In a lot of ways, that was true. Naomi didn't irritate her half as often these days. Not now Jenny knew her better.

Gail sighed. 'I think I'm done. Shall we just go back? We still need to find Ruth.'

'Yes,' said Antonia. 'I think I've had enough revelations for one evening, too.'

Whilst sighing with relief that she hadn't been tarred and feathered, Antonia's words struck a new fear into Jenny. In terms of revelations, Antonia was unknowingly heading for a rather gigantic one.

CHAPTER THIRTY-FIVE

The Boy managed to crawl a short distance last week. This was in response to a huge amount of encouragement, enthusiastic hand-clapping and, okay, I'll admit it, the dangling of a chocolate bar in front of his face. Since then, he seems to be completely over the concept of moving altogether.

It won't surprise you that Baby Sporty has been crawling for well over a month. If there was a baby triathlon (rolling, crawling, walking?) that child would win it. It's hardly surprising when you look at her genes: as well as joining a Buggy Bootcamp group about a week after giving birth, Sporty wears a frickin' Fitbit to the play centres so that she can measure how many padded ladders she's climbed and slides she's slid down.

It's going to be interesting when we spend the weekend without the babies in tow. If she wants to start powerwalking everywhere, I might just find myself a nice wine bar and watch her through the window…

From *The Undercover Mother*

✦

The streets were much busier on the walk home than when they'd arrived: the bars belching people out into the streets and the nightclubs eating them up again. Young, attractive men and women called from the foyers of the neon-lit fronts, inviting people in. Jenny couldn't help but notice that their invitations were a lot more earnest for the young girls behind them than they were for the four of them.

They made their way out to the seafront and started to leave the noise behind. The last ten minutes had been spent listening to Naomi spill her feelings about John, the prospect of another baby, and her life in general.

'Well, you know my opinion – I don't think you should stay in a situation when you're unhappy.' Gail was her usual frank self. 'You only get one chance at life. You need to decide what is going to be best for you, Naomi.'

'I don't recall her actually asking for your opinion,' said Antonia, stiffly, 'and it's not as easy as that. They have a child together.' She turned to Naomi. 'You need to think what it will be like bringing up Daisy on your own, Naomi. I know that I couldn't do it.'

'What, even with a full team of staff?' murmured Gail. Jenny dug her in the side. She understood where Gail's bitterness was coming from, but was hoping to avoid her dishing the dirt until they were back on home soil and Jenny could have nothing to do with it. Thankfully, Antonia didn't seem to have heard Gail over the noise of a stag party going past, and Naomi's sniffing.

'John is a really nice man. He has been wonderful about everything. And I *do* love him.' Naomi blew her nose noisily. 'I can't go on like this, but I really don't want to do anything to hurt him. Or his family.'

'You're not raising a child with his family,' warned Gail. 'This is about you and him, and sometimes being in love with someone is not enough. Anyway, how do you know he doesn't feel the same way? He might be trying to do the right thing as much as you are. Would he have asked you to move in with him if you hadn't been about to have a baby?'

Naomi started to cry again. Jenny put an arm around her, giving Gail a warning look. 'We can see that he loves you, Naomi. Look how supportive he was at the classes. Everyone could see how much he cared.'

Naomi wiped her eyes. 'But maybe Gail is right. Maybe he's just looking after me for Daisy's sake.'

Antonia signalled her boredom with a huge sigh. 'You're going to need to talk to him, darling. You need to tell him how you feel. I'm sure it will all work itself out. Tell him to get his mother to keep her beak out and you will be as right as rain.' Gail made a scoffing noise. This time, Antonia did hear her. 'Sorry, Gail. Did you have something you wanted to add?'

Gail shrugged her shoulders. 'Just seems ironic, you of all people advising someone to meet a problem head-on, and get it resolved.'

Antonia's eyebrows seemed to go even higher. 'Maybe not as ironic as the single mother giving relationship advice.'

Gail looked as if she might explode. Naomi took a sharp intake of breath. Jenny changed the subject. 'I think we need to try Ruth's number again… I'm really getting worried about her. Gail, could you call her, please?'

Gail punched the front of her phone screen like she was programming a virtual voodoo doll – and the death stare she'd given Antonia made it clear who she was imagining it to be. She held the phone to her ear for a few seconds. 'Still no answer. It's going directly to voicemail.'

'It's all my fault.' Naomi started to grizzle again. 'I'm dreading facing Ruth.'

Everything was coming to a head. Jenny picked up the pace. All she wanted to do was confirm that Ruth was safely back at the house and then get to bed.

✦

When they got back to the house, however, and Gail had checked the bedroom she was sharing with Ruth, she reported that, no, she was not back yet. Naomi went straight to bed after the others promised her that they would wake her if Ruth didn't return soon. Jenny was relieved to get rid of her. There were only so many times you could say, 'There, there,' before it started to get on your wick.

Exhausted, she sank down into one of the comfortable armchairs and checked her mobile again.

'I'm going to send Ruth another text. I know the phone reception is patchy down here, but she must have got one of them.' She felt bad being irritated with Ruth, but she really wanted to go to bed herself. Ruth's reaction to Naomi had surprised her. Of course, Jenny had expected her to be upset at the ease with which Naomi managed to fall pregnant when she wasn't even happy about it, but throwing a glass of wine over her was rather over the top. She tapped her foot as she typed, *Are you okay?* for the fifth time.

The only person who didn't seem concerned at all was Antonia. Jenny could hear her humming to herself in the kitchen. Gail, on the other hand, had a face like thunder. Antonia's mood might be about to change.

Antonia came back into the lounge to join them with an open bottle of wine and three glasses. 'Fancy a glass whilst we wait, ladies?'

In the circumstances, Jenny definitely didn't want to stay up with the two of them, but she couldn't possibly go to bed until they'd heard from Ruth. *Might as well have another glass.*

'I will.' Gail's tone was decisive.

Was she building up to tell Antonia everything? It wouldn't be surprising after Antonia's bitchy 'single mother' comment on the way home. Should Jenny leave? Was there time?

Gail stood behind the chair in which Jenny was sitting, her hands on the back of it. 'Antonia, I need to speak to you.'

Too late.

Antonia held up a hand and walked slowly to a chaise longue that was under the window, almost draping herself on it, like a heroine from a Fitzgerald novel. 'Hang on, darling. I need to be sitting down with a glass of wine in my hand when you tell me that you've been sleeping with my husband.'

CHAPTER THIRTY-SIX

Before having The Boy, I was adamant that I would never let the baby sleep with us. I was almost sanctimonious in my declaration that our bed was for us and that it would be damaging to our relationship to have a baby in between us. Clearly, I had no concept of the fact that exhaustion, breast pads and the aroma of poo would be such an effective anti-Viagra that the baby in between us would be merely a formality.

Affairs are surprisingly common in the first couple of years after a new baby. Posh says her mum advised her quite clearly that it was important that she remember to keep her husband happy, too.

I've employed a much better tactic: Mr Baby does just enough of the night-time getting-up to ensure that he's too tired to even remember a chat-up line…

From *The Undercover Mother*

✦

Jenny was speechless for the second time that evening. How did Antonia know? She tried to dart an 'I didn't tell her' look at Gail. Gail blinked twice but didn't lose her composure. She looked directly at Antonia. 'How long have you known?'

'I had my suspicions from the moment you walked into that antenatal class. It didn't take a genius to decode the look on Geoff's face. That's one of my husband's amusing qualities – he thinks that he's the king of espionage, when actually he's as transparent as a small boy.' She sipped her wine. 'I told myself I had imagined things. But when you failed to produce even so much as a picture of the elusive "Joe", I had to face up to it.'

Jenny's mind was going crazy. She had thought Gail was the Queen of Cover Up, but now Antonia, too? Ignoring her plan to stay out of it, she asked, 'But why didn't you—'

'Say anything? Who to? Him? You? The other girls? The leader of the group? "By the way, Sally, you can put one less chair out tomorrow as I think my husband might be the father of that woman's little bastard."'

Gail flinched. 'Don't you dare say anything about Jake.'

Antonia put her hand up. 'Okay, I take it back. It's not his fault. Must be hard for you to look at him sometimes, seeing as he's the image of Geoff.'

Jenny surreptitiously scrolled through the photos on her mobile to find the last group shot of all the babies together. It was true! Jake looked exactly like Geoff. Why had she never noticed before? There was no way she could slink off to bed now; this was too dramatic to miss. She had assumed that Gail would be the one with the jaw-dropping news. Antonia was supposed to be shocked, hurt, angry and bitter. Not just sit there, serenely sipping her wine as if they were all on a lunch date.

Gail seemed to have the same thought. 'How can you be so calm? Your husband has fathered another child and has attempted to keep it from you all this time.'

Antonia laughed. 'Attempted to keep it from me? I'm afraid that's not true. He told me about you our first day at antenatal class.'

Gail almost staggered backwards, sinking down onto the sofa. 'You're lying.'

Antonia shook her head. 'We had a huge row the whole way home in the car. When we got back, it was worse. I was screaming at him and he actually got quite distressed because he was worried my frantic state might hurt the baby.' She smiled sarcastically. 'Jessica is the one female he seems to actually care about hurting.'

'What did he tell you?'

'That the two of you had only slept together a few times, but you'd got pregnant. He also said he wasn't planning to have anything to do with the baby except financially, and that he had no intention of ever seeing you again.'

'And you believed him?'

Antonia snorted. 'Of course not. But once he had told me, I could feel sorry for you. Geoff was going nowhere.'

Gail put her arms around herself. She looked very cold. Jenny wouldn't have expected to feel sympathy for an 'other woman', but Gail looked so lonely sitting in the middle of that vast settee. Vulnerable, even.

Antonia was studying Gail, as if reading her thoughts. Was she even telling the truth? What did she know for sure, and what was she hoping to trick out of Gail?

'Did you get pregnant to make him stay?'

Gail shook her head. 'No. Did you?'

Antonia laughed. 'No. I think the universe was having a bit of fun with the both of us.'

Gail stood up, walked towards the fireplace and, leaning against it for support, turned to face Antonia. 'You seem pretty confident that he won't leave you.'

Antonia shrugged. 'He never has before.' Antonia appeared to be positively enjoying herself, torturing Gail slowly. She didn't even look angry. 'Surely you didn't think you were the first?'

'Or the last, obviously, if the nanny's knickers are anything to go by.' Gail bit back.

Antonia wrinkled her nose. 'Hmm. A little fib, I'm afraid. I thought you needed to be angry to get you to stick your head out of your shell. Seems you took the bait rather easily. I feel a little bit guilty, dragging poor Emily into it. Never mind, I'll make it up to her with a nice Christmas bonus.'

Gail's arms were poker-straight by her sides; she clenched and unclenched her fists. She was used to being in control, Jenny thought, manipulating conversations and situations as she chose. 'So he *hasn't* been sleeping with someone else?'

'I didn't say *that*.' Antonia took another sip of wine. 'I just said he hasn't slept with the nanny.'

Gail took a deep breath. 'I'm not sure that this conversation is going anywhere. I'm going to bed.'

Antonia pulled a mock-sad face. 'Oh. Giving up so soon? I thought you'd have a bit more fight in you. I was looking forward to a more heated discussion.'

Gail bristled. 'There is no point in a "fight", as you put it. I've never fought over a man in my life and I'm not about to start now. I have no idea whether you are lying or telling the truth, but my life is fine, with or without Geoff. If he chooses to join Jake and me, and I think he will, then he is very welcome. By the way, when Jessica comes to visit at our house, I will be very kind to her.' She smiled at Antonia with a saccharine sweetness.

Antonia blanched at that and her eyes narrowed. 'You really think he's going to leave me, don't you?' She sank further down into the chair, as if she were deflating. 'He won't ever leave me.'

'I don't know how you can know that.' Gail moved towards her, almost circling her prey. 'Marriages break up every day. Why are you so sure that yours won't?'

Antonia looked up at her. 'Because Geoff has a plan for his life, and being divorced is not part of that plan.'

Gail smiled grimly. 'Plans change.'

Antonia got up to get the wine. 'Not Geoff's.' She held the bottle towards Gail, offering her a drink, but Gail shook her head. Pouring another large glass for herself, Antonia passed the bottle to Jenny and then sat down again, nodding at the sofa opposite. 'Why don't you sit down?'

Gail started to shake her head and then changed her mind. She perched on the edge of the sofa and crossed her arms.

Antonia continued. 'Geoff is a very clever man – he always was. He's also used to getting what he wants. Even when I look at the way we met, our early times together, I realise that it was not a fateful, accidental meeting of two people. I was exactly what he was looking for. A pretty, bright – but not too bright – girl who was ready to be moulded into what he wanted.' She flicked her hands slowly downwards. 'He didn't do too bad a job, did he?'

Gail cut in. 'I'm not actually interested in any of this crap,' she said. 'I am already aware that your marriage is far from perfect.'

Antonia laughed hollowly. 'But that's the point. It doesn't need to be perfect. It just needs to *look* perfect.' She took another sip of her drink. 'And that is why he will never leave.'

Jenny knew that Antonia was telling the truth and, despite the anger emanating from Gail, she could tell that she knew that, too. Imperceptibly, something had changed.

There was a long pause. The weight of it made Jenny feel more obvious as an intruder. Nevertheless, they had chosen to have this conversation in front of her, so maybe she had a right to take part. 'So why haven't *you* left *him*?'

Antonia shrugged. 'I was speaking the truth earlier. What would I do? Where would I go? At one point I almost thought I might, but then Jessica came along. She's my priority now.'

Gail sank back into the sofa. 'And Jake is mine.'

The three women sat in silence for a few minutes. Then Gail spoke. 'He told me you married him for money.'

'He told *me* you were known for trapping married men.'

'He also told me that you weren't coping with motherhood.' Gail looked Antonia in the eye. 'That was a lie, too. You are a good mum.'

Antonia sucked in a sharp breath and put her hand to her chest. *Was that a stifled sob?* She bit her lip, and it took her a while to reply. 'So are you. It can't be easy for you with your job to juggle, too.'

Gail sighed. 'I hadn't really ever seen myself with a child. I didn't know if I was even mother material. But Geoff was so confident. So stable. I let myself imagine this other life. The three of us. A house with a little garden. Rather pathetic, really.' She paused, but no one interrupted. 'I had two months of that before I found out that you were pregnant, too. I was so angry.'

Antonia nodded. 'You should have seen me the night of the antenatal class. There are calmer volcanoes.'

Gail shook her head. 'But I was angry at *you*, not at him. Isn't that strange?'

'Not really. Geoff is good at that. How do you think we've stayed married all these years?' Antonia put her head on one side and looked at Gail intently. 'I might have lied about the nanny. But there have been others.'

Gail looked exhausted. 'I really do need to go to bed now. I can't think about this any more.' She got up. 'Are both of you going to bed, too?'

Antonia curled her feet up onto the chair. 'I'm going to wait up for Ruth.'

Jenny looked at her mobile. At last, a message from her.

I've checked into a hotel. Speak to you tomorrow.

Jenny sighed. *Now she bloody tells me.* She held the screen up to show the others. 'No need.'

CHAPTER THIRTY-SEVEN

I envy the people who have the kind of home where you can drop in unannounced and they are always tidy. I need at least a half-hour warning from any impending visitors so that I can kick toys under the sofa, cram shoes into cupboards and scoop three days of kitchen debris into the bin/sink/dishwasher.

Both Posh and Scary have cleaners, so their houses always look tidy. Sporty told me that she has a 'thirty-minute blitz every evening'. I tried that for three days but the clutter just came creeping back by midday, so I gave in to it. Mr Baby says that at least we won't get burgled, as they'd walk straight back out, thinking someone else had already turned us over...

From *The Undercover Mother*

✦

The kitchen was large and sleek, in lime green and grey, the floor cold as Jenny walked across it barefoot in search of coffee. Hopefully, she opened the cupboard above the kettle and found a myriad boxes of speciality teas and, thankfully, a cafetière and half a packet of filter coffee sealed with a pink plastic food clip. Finding a spoon in a precisely organised drawer, she scooped a few heaped spoonfuls of coffee into the cafetière and waited for the kettle to boil.

Her own house was nothing like this. In her kitchen, she would have had to retrieve a cup from the dishwasher. That's if the dishwasher had even been turned on the previous evening. If it had been Dan's turn to stack it, chances were he would have left it open because there was still an egg-cup-sized amount of unfilled space and he was waiting until it was 'full'.

There was movement upstairs; at least one other person was awake.

Despite the drama, much of last night had been fun. The restaurant had been nice, if you ignored the last ten minutes; the drinking games had been enjoyable, if you forgot about the drink-throwing; even the walk home had been pleasant, if you managed to black out the sobbing, the barbed comments and the subsequent revelations of marital infidelity. It was all about perspective.

The kettle clicked as it boiled and Naomi appeared at the door, her hair wet from the shower. 'Morning.'

'Good morning. Would you like some coffee?'

'Is there any herbal tea?' Naomi started randomly opening cupboards. The fringes on the hem of her skirt were beaded and they rattled softly as she walked.

'The tea is in that cupboard over there.' Jenny motioned with her hand. 'How are you?'

'My head feels like it belongs to someone else this morning. Which, considering I only had about half a glass of wine, is rather unfair.'

Jenny brought the cups over to the table and took a seat. 'Look, Naomi, about last night and what the others said. I don't think you should make any rash decisions.'

Naomi sighed and sat down, too. 'I'm not a complete idiot, Jenny.'

Jenny was taken aback. 'I know you're not, I just meant—'

'Look, I know what you all think of me. I didn't need to read your blog to know you think I'm an airhead hippy with weird and wonderful ideas. I also realise that I don't really fit in with you all.'

'That's not true!' Jenny lied automatically.

'I used to feel bad about it,' continued Naomi. 'But now I've realised that none of us actually fits. Not even you.'

Jenny attempted to protest, but Naomi was right. They didn't fit. Jenny had spent the last six months trying to hold together a group of five very different women, at least two of whom had good reason to detest one another. *What a waste of time.*

So why was Naomi smiling?

'The thing is, I think that that's okay. We don't need to be the same. The fact that we are all completely different is a good thing. This weekend could be the making of our friendship.'

'Ah, yes, well…' How could she best explain why that might not be the case? That this might be the last time they would be together like this. Which was a little sad. Sadder than she'd expected.

Another set of footsteps was coming down the stairs.

Gail came into the kitchen, dressed in smart trousers and a shirt and carrying her leather overnight bag. She looked from one to the other. 'Am I interrupting something?'

Jenny got up. She would have to wait to tell Naomi about last night's main event. 'No. Would you like some coffee?'

'That would be great, thanks. Strong and black.' Gail sat down on a kitchen chair and checked her watch. 'What time are we going to the station? I'm all packed and ready.'

Naomi stopped blowing on her tea. 'You're in an awful rush suddenly. Something we said?'

Gail tapped her fingernails on the table. 'Just ready to go, that's all. As the least popular house guest, I'd hate to outstay my welcome.'

Naomi started to plait her damp hair. 'Why wouldn't you be popular? What happened after I left last night?'

Jenny put a mug of coffee on the table and waited for Gail to explain. But she didn't need to. An immaculate Antonia breezed in and took up the story.

'What happened, my darling, was that Gail confessed to shagging my husband and I informed her that I already knew.'

Naomi froze mid-braid and looked at Gail, who gave a small nod of affirmation.

Jenny couldn't face a rerun of the previous evening. She just needed to keep things going for a few more hours. 'So, now we're all up to date. Coffee, Antonia?'

'Wonderful idea. And then does anyone want to join me in going out to get some breakfast? I'm desperate for some bacon and pancakes. Anyone else?'

Once again, Antonia was not acting as would have been expected in the presence of her husband's mistress. Gail, on the other hand, looked shaken, and nothing like her normal confident self. Now wasn't the right time to mention that, though. Unless you were Naomi.

'Gail, are you okay? You don't look right.'

Antonia wheeled around. 'Is *she* okay? What about me? I'm the wronged wife here!'

There was a pause.

'To be fair to Naomi, you don't seem to be looking for a shoulder to cry on this morning,' said Jenny. Antonia always looked good, but there was a new lightness about her today. Wearing a brightly patterned linen dress and with bare feet, it was as if she'd just arrived home from a holiday in the sun.

Antonia laughed. 'You're right. I'm feeling surprisingly chipper. I made some decisions last night before I went to sleep. I'm not coming back with you. I'm going to stay here for a while. I called my friend and I can stay if I want. Emily, the nanny, is going to bring Jessica later today.'

This was quite a sudden turn around. How much of Antonia's 'I can't do it alone' speech last night had been an act for Gail's benefit? She was clever.

'Are you leaving Geoff?'

Antonia nodded. 'I've been thinking about it for a while. I hired a private detective to take some incriminating photographs in case I ever decided I wanted a divorce. He was a dad I met at a baby group – we got talking, he told me what he did and I thought, "Why not?" That day we went clothes shopping, Jen, I met up with him and he gave me the photographs he'd taken.' She turned to Gail. 'There're some gorgeous ones of you.'

The young man in the suit! So that's why Antonia hadn't told Jenny about him that day – no wonder they had looked so intense. Could she have got it more wrong?

If Gail looked shaken before, she looked like she might fall to the ground now. 'Have you told Geoff?'

'No. I think I'll let him work it out for himself. It should only take him a few days at most to realise that we're not there.' She looked hard at Gail. 'Why? Are you planning on running around there to tell him?'

Gail waited a few moments before shaking her head. 'No. I think he and I are done.'

Antonia sat down. Her voice softened. 'I should hate you, Gail, but I don't. I think that's what made up my mind.'

Neither of them looked like they were going to speak again any time soon, and Naomi was standing there with her mouth wide open. *Time to sort out the other problem.*

'Has anyone heard from Ruth?'

'Did she not come home last night?' asked Naomi. Antonia and Gail reflexively checked their mobiles.

Jenny shook her head. 'She sent a text to say she had booked into a hotel. I'll send her another message. If we haven't heard from her in half an hour, I think we should go and look for her.'

'But where do you suggest we look?' asked Antonia.

'I don't know… the shops, the beach, anywhere.' Jenny waved her hands vaguely.

'She could already be on a train home,' said Gail.

'She might be, but do you want to call David and ask him if she's there? I'd rather just see if I can find her first.' Plus, Jenny had an idea she knew where to look.

CHAPTER THIRTY-EIGHT

One of the many books I am consulting for guidance suggests that you should be able to discern whether your baby wants feeding, changing or comforting from the sound of their cry. I couldn't even pass GCSE French so I don't hold out much hope that I can translate the different tones in The Boy's persistent yell. Feed? Change? Comfort? Sometimes I do all three and he's still going at it. What then?

The whole responsibility thing has kept me awake more than once in the last few weeks. Mr Baby has already had to talk me down from taking The Boy to A&E because I thought his breathing pattern had changed. It was when I was trying to impersonate the said change that I realised how ridiculous I was being: Mr Baby suggested I supplement my maternity pay with a slot on an adult chat line for heavy-breathing fetishists.

Sometimes the fear of getting it wrong is overwhelming. And then I have to remind myself how lucky I am to have a baby to worry about…

From *The Undercover Mother*

✦

The breeze was cool, but the morning air was starting to warm up. Jenny slowed down as she got to the beach, took off her sandals and felt the cool stones under her toes. She was beginning to understand Naomi's fascination with the sea.

In the midst of the revelations of the night before, she was relieved to have finally told the girls about the blog. They hadn't seemed too bothered about it in the end; other events had rather overshadowed it. Ironically, it probably wouldn't matter much now anyway. As far as Eva was concerned, she would be stepping back into her 'Girl About Town' role next week, and that would be the end of *The Undercover Mother*.

Right then, all Jenny wanted was to be at home on her sofa, with Henry on one arm and Dan on the other. Despite the hangover beginning to manifest itself at the back of her head, she would have even swapped her lie-in this morning for an early morning cuddle. If she went back to 'Girl About Town', every weekend would be like this: juggling late nights being a party girl with early mornings being a mother, and trying to write in the middle of it. But Eva had made it clear that this was what she wanted her to do. If she didn't, she knew that she would have to kiss goodbye to her own column at the magazine.

Putting her hand up to her eyes, she scanned the beach. There were a couple of people out walking their dogs and a young man asleep, but other than that the beach was empty. What a disappointment. She had been sure she would find Ruth here; hadn't she told them that her teenage self had always gone to the beach to think? Maybe Gail was right, and she had gone home already. Feeling terrible again that she had persuaded Ruth to come at all, Jenny turned to go.

It was then that she saw her, sitting in the exact spot they'd found Naomi yesterday.

'Can I join you?'

Ruth hadn't heard Jenny coming and she started at the sound of her voice. Smiling automatically, she motioned for Jenny to sit beside her. 'Please, take a seat.' She seemed quite comfortable, picking up pebbles and throwing them into the sea. If she was irritated about being found, she wasn't showing it.

Still, Jenny wanted to make sure she wasn't intruding. 'You can tell me to go away if you want. We were just worried about you.'

Ruth shook her head. 'No, stay, please. I'm sorry for leaving and waiting so long to tell you I'd found a hotel. It was thoughtless. I just needed to get away, not think about anyone else for a few hours.' She looked levelly at Jenny. 'Is Naomi okay? I feel guilty about throwing my drink over her. What a stupid overreaction.'

'She's fine. And she completely understands why you were so upset.' Jenny was relieved. This was the Ruth she recognised. Kind, thoughtful, not given to unpredictable reactions.

Ruth frowned. 'Didn't need to throw my toys out of the pram like that, though, did I? I'm not normally so dramatic.'

Jenny shrugged. 'If I were you, there would have been several toy-throwing incidents by now. To be honest, Naomi has brought out the tantruming toddler in me on many occasions. I've grown to love her, but it's taken some work. Do you mind if I text the others to say that I've found you? Everyone is out looking.'

Ruth nodded. 'Yes, of course. Please do. I don't want to worry anyone. I need to go back and face the music at some point, anyway.' She put her hands up to her face. 'I'm so embarrassed.'

Jenny started to tap away at her mobile. 'You don't need to be. Naomi will just be happy you don't hate her. She feels terrible for blurting out the pregnancy like that. She's a bit mixed up.' She stopped typing and looked at Ruth. 'Speaking of feeling guilty, I'm sorry if I did the wrong thing persuading you to come away. I didn't want to make you feel bad.'

Ruth put her hand over Jenny's. 'Don't be silly. And don't apologise. I'm glad I was invited. It's been good for me.'

They sat in silence for a few minutes, just listening to the sea. After a while, Ruth turned to Jenny. 'It's not like me, you know, losing my temper like that. And I have certainly never thrown a drink over someone before.'

Jenny shook her head. 'Really, don't worry about it. Everyone understands.'

Ruth carried on as if she hadn't spoken. 'And the feeling sick. That's not like me, either. I really wanted to have a good drink this weekend, but I haven't managed more than a sip of anything.'

'Well, you've got a lot going on and—'

'—and last night, lying in that hotel room on my own, my mind began to turn over. Feeling sick. Temperamental outbursts…'

Jenny stopped talking and stared at her. She didn't want to jump to conclusions, but Ruth was looking at her intently and it was hard not to. 'What are you saying?'

A smile started to spread across Ruth's face. 'I'm saying that I did a pregnancy test this morning. I've been trying to keep it in because I wanted to tell David first, but I must tell someone before I burst. I'm pregnant!'

Jenny almost dropped her mobile in her rush to throw her arms around her. 'That's wonderful, Ruth! So very wonderful! I can't believe it.'

Ruth grinned. 'Me, neither. I'm still scared, but I'm so excited, too. I know I haven't got a good track record, but I feel exhausted, sick and hormonal. That's got to be a good sign, right? I'm trying to keep the terror locked away for now and enjoy this moment. I can't wait to get home and tell David.' Her words spilled out in a rush of enthusiasm.

'Oh, Ruth, I can't imagine how you must feel! The doctors will watch you and this baby like hawks this time. Nothing will happen. Everything will be perfect. Oh, I am so, so pleased. This has made the whole weekend!' She hugged Ruth again. They were laughing happily when Jenny's mobile beeped and she looked at the screen. 'Ah, they got my message. They want to know where we are.'

'I suppose we should put them out of their misery. Maybe I'll pretend I went home with a strange man. Shall I take my knickers off and leave them hanging out of my handbag?'

Jenny groaned. 'Please don't. I don't think I could cope with any more revelations this weekend. Come on, let's go.' She stood up and held out her hands to Ruth to pull her up.

When their eyes were level, Ruth kept hold of Jenny's hands. 'Please don't mention my pregnancy to the others yet. I'd rather as few people know as possible until I've had the first scan.'

'Of course not.' Jenny paused. 'Whilst we're on the subject of secrets, though, I have a little confession of my own.'

It was easier telling Ruth than the others. For a start, she hadn't been writing about Ruth's parenting idiosyncrasies for the last few months. Plus, Ruth was barely listening to a word Jenny said: she had far more important things on her mind. Which was fine by Jenny. Anyone would be happy for Ruth.

But Jenny's happiness was bigger than that: Ruth was her friend.

When she'd first met these four women, they had been so far removed from her existing friends that Jenny could never have imagined that she would feel as she did now. But somewhere along the way, through a sea of nappy changes, sleep regimes and undigested milk vomit, they had somehow, unbelievably, become her friends. This was both wonderful and terrible: wonderful, because she had new buddies; and terrible, because she couldn't continue to write about them.

The Undercover Mother had been a stop-gap. A smokescreen. A means to an end. All she had wanted was to show Eva that she still had it, that she could be a mother and a writer. Once that had been established, Eva would have had no reason not to give her back 'Girl About Town'.

The problem was, she didn't want it back. It wasn't that she didn't want to write; there were plenty of ideas fluttering about her brain. But they were all ideas for *The Undercover Mother*. Writing about the restaurant, the bar, the social scene for 'Girl About Town' didn't interest her at all.

But no one wanted her to write *The Undercover Mother*. Not Eva, not Mark, and not the four women she now realised were her friends.

CHAPTER THIRTY-NINE

It's a pretty weird thing, being thrown together with a bunch of other women just because you have your babies around the same time. With normal friendships, you have a certain chemistry which attracts you to someone: they might make you laugh or have really interesting ideas; they might read the same books as you, like the same restaurants or secretly enjoy watching World's Strongest Man (you know who you are).

Scary, Sporty, Posh, Ginger and me – we never actually chose each other. Someone at Antenatal HQ stuck us in a class together and we've just made the best of it ever since. I was pretty sure that it wouldn't last. Like the blind date who turns up wearing a cagoule, the signs of lasting friendship between an earth mother, a lady who lunches and the businesswoman of the year were not looking good.

But all these months on and we're still together. Somehow, through a haze of weaning, changing and lack of sleep, we have slowly become friends. I'm not sure how it's happened, but it kind of has…

From *The Undercover Mother*

✦

As the sun climbed higher, the day got warmer. Antonia and Naomi were seated outside a café, underneath a large blue parasol. They made an incongruous pair: Antonia in her designer sunglasses and Naomi with her two long plaits.

Naomi jumped up and threw her arms around Ruth. 'I am so, so sorry. I was completely thoughtless.'

Ruth hugged her back. 'It should be me apologising to you. I don't know what came over me.'

'Where's Gail?' Jenny automatically looked at Antonia and then quickly switched to Naomi.

'She went towards the shops, looking for you. She's on her way back now.'

'Maybe she's calling Geoff to give him the good news.' Antonia looked at them over the top of her latte. 'He could be moving my things into the front garden as we speak.'

Jenny brought Ruth up to speed on the events of the night before. She had thought that no one could open their mouth as wide as Naomi had that morning. Turned out, she was wrong.

'What do you want to drink? Geoff's paying.' Antonia waved a credit card.

'You'd better make the most of that,' warned Jenny. 'I'm sure he'll get that stopped pretty quickly.'

Antonia smiled smugly. 'Actually, I have an account I've been transferring money into for the last couple of years. Just had a hunch I might need it someday.'

Naomi raised her peppermint tea cup. 'Well, I say good luck to you. I really hope you'll be happy. I'm jealous you're going to be living here. I'd love to live by the sea. Any chance your friend could be persuaded to open up her house as a respite centre for single mothers?'

'Not you, too?' Ruth's mouth fell open again.

Naomi sighed. 'No, I'm going home. I just can't see how much longer John and I can go on pretending everything is okay. I also have no idea what he's going to say about this pregnancy.' She looked glum, then glanced up sharply at Ruth to make sure she wasn't upsetting her. It was one thing to have wine thrown over you, hot tea was quite another. Her phone rang. 'Oh, bugger, that's him now. Excuse me.' She pushed her chair back and left the table to take the call.

'Well, the weekend hasn't quite turned out as I planned,' said Jenny. 'I think I need a coffee. Ruth?'

'Yes, please, a decaf cappuccino. Oh, here's Gail.'

Jenny waved at the young waiter, who came straight over to take their order. Ruth was apologising to Gail and Antonia for necessitating a wild goose chase all over Brighton.

'Don't worry about it. Naomi's news must have been a shock,' said Gail.

Antonia nodded. 'Yes, it's been quite a weekend of revelations, hasn't it? I suppose our Undercover Mother has told you her big secret?'

'She was just telling me.' Ruth smiled at Jenny. 'I need to take a look at this blog. Maybe I'll get a guest appearance one day?' She shook her hair. 'I'm pretty sure I'm only a couple of shades away from being ginger.'

'Unsurprisingly, I couldn't sleep last night,' said Gail. 'So I read your blog. It's actually pretty good.'

'Thanks. I appreciate that.' Much as Jenny was grateful, she just felt sad.

'I read it, too,' said Antonia. 'It was funny. Even the bits which took the piss out of me. You made me sound such a snob, darling.' She nudged Jenny.

'Thanks. You've all been so understanding. Honestly. But it doesn't really matter now. It's over.'

'What do you mean?' Antonia lifted her sunglasses. 'I know that we were a bit cross last night, but we've read it now. It's fine.'

Jenny had a mysterious lump in her throat. 'It's not just that. I can't get anyone to take it on. My editor hasn't wanted it from the beginning. I hoped I could change her mind, but I can't.'

The waiter arrived with their drinks and passed them out. Gail took her black coffee from the tray and then turned to Jenny.

'Why do you need someone else's approval? Why can't you carry on doing it yourself?'

'Oh, I know I can keep it up as a hobby. I meant I can't do it as a job. A *paid* job.'

'Ridiculous. Of course you can.' Gail sat up straight, reached into her handbag and pulled out her mobile.

Jenny sighed. 'No, that's what I'm saying. I've tried. My boss doesn't want it.' She didn't tell them how she had even tried her ex-boyfriend in her desperation.

Gail was tapping and swiping her mobile screen. Then she turned it towards Jenny. 'Look. Read this. *Monetising* your blog. Everyone is at it.'

Jenny took the phone and scanned the page. There were pages and pages of advice about how to make money from websites and blogs. Advertising. Affiliate programs. But she knew all this.

She handed Gail's phone back. 'I know about those things, but it takes an awful lot of time to build that up. And I doubt I could make it cover my entire salary.'

'Maybe not,' said Gail. 'But what's to stop you picking up some freelance work at the same time? Much more flexible than a full-time job. Plus…' She was tapping her screen again. She found what she was looking for and gave the mobile back to Jenny.

It was a comment on one of Jenny's posts, added last night:

I love this blog! It's made me feel sane again. Pleeeassseee can you write a book to get me through the bad days?

The comment already had about 200 likes and replies agreeing with the idea: *Yes!* and *Please do!* and *I'll buy it for me and all my friends!*

A book? Was there a journalist anywhere who didn't secretly dream of publishing a book? Could she do it? Going freelance was a risk, but what was the alternative? Jenny felt a flutter in her stomach. The same flutter she had got on the day she'd published her first 'Girl About Town' column.

Gail sat back in her seat confidently. 'Obviously, we will start charging a fee for our words of wisdom.'

'And I will not be happy if I start getting papped. Unless I look gorgeous, obviously.' Antonia flicked her shades back into place.

Before Jenny could answer, a wonderstruck Naomi rejoined them, sat down beside Antonia and started mechanically stirring her peppermint tea. The others watched her, waiting for her to speak. When she started to sip her drink, uncharacteristically quiet, Antonia prompted, 'Everything okay?'

Naomi looked up, a little dazed. 'It seems we might be going away.'

Jenny nearly spat her coffee across the table. 'What?'

Naomi's eyes shone. 'We might be moving to Canada. Or not. Or somewhere else. Like here.'

Ruth frowned. 'You're not making sense. What do you mean?'

Naomi put her tea cup down and looked at them properly. She was bubbling with excitement. 'It's all John's idea. He started off asking me if we'd had a good time, then told me that Daisy was fine, which I already knew because I've been texting him about every hour to check on her.'

'Yes, yes. Please get to the point before you force me to shake it out of you,' said Jenny.

Naomi giggled like a young girl. She flicked her plaits from her shoulders. 'Well, he was silent for a few seconds and then kind of launched into it. He knows I'm not happy, but he loves me and Daisy and can't live with the thought that we might leave.' She paused for breath. 'So, he's been thinking about what's changed and he spoke to your David' — she nodded at Ruth — 'at Antonia's house yesterday, and he's realised that he lost himself a bit. He's been trying so hard to be a good dad and provide for both of us that he's ended up being someone completely different. He also admitted that he knew dealing with his mother had not been easy and that I must be feeling lonely. He said he thinks if we go away for a while and spend some time just the four of us, we might be able to get back to the way we were – and make it work this time. He has an uncle in Canada with his own gardening business and—'

'Back up, back up – the *four* of you?' asked Ruth.

Naomi smile seemed to get even wider. 'He found the pregnancy test box in the recycling bin and put two and two together with the fact that I've been so emotional lately. It was that, coupled with not having me around for the weekend, that made him realise he needed to do something.'

'So you're having this baby?' asked Antonia.

'We're having this baby,' nodded Naomi.

'And you're moving to Canada?'

'He has lots of ideas. Backpacking around Asia when you're six months pregnant might be a little impractical, so we've agreed that just a change of scene would do us for now and then, who knows? One day we might buy a camper van and take both kids on a tour around Europe.'

'I'm so pleased for you.' Ruth put her hand over Naomi's. 'And I'm so glad you're happy about the baby.'

Naomi covered Ruth's hand with her free one. 'I am. It'll happen for you, too, Ruth, I know it will.' She looked around at the others. 'I'll miss you all, though.'

Jenny glanced at her watch. 'Speaking of which, we'd better get a move on or we'll miss our taxi.'

✦

Jenny stood with Naomi and Gail at the bay window. What a weekend. She still didn't know if she had done the right thing by bringing them all here.

'I feel quite sad.' Naomi had tears in her eyes.

Jenny put an arm around her. 'It's the hormones. You'll be all right when you get to twelve weeks.' But hormones didn't explain why she felt the same way. Was this an ending? Or a beginning?

The taxi came into sight around the corner. Naomi played with her bracelets. 'Do you think we'll all stay in touch? You know – with Antonia down here, me moving somewhere, you getting stuck into promoting your blog and maybe writing a book. And then there's the, the—' she glanced at Gail '—other situation…?'

Gail shrugged. 'Who knows? We will if we want to.'

'I'd like to stay in touch.' Ruth joined them, carrying her overnight bag. 'I'll need lots of tips if David and I do manage to have another baby.' Jenny reached over and squeezed her arm conspiratorially. If she had it in her power to do anything right now, it would be to guarantee the safety of that foetus. *Keep growing, baby. Keep growing.*

Antonia appeared in the doorway. 'Your ride is here. Are you all ready to go?'

'Naomi wants us to make a pact to be together for ever.' Jenny was pretty sure Antonia would be moving on sharpish. Brighton must be full of Antonias, just waiting to meet each other for afternoon tea.

'Well, I'd like to,' said Antonia. 'It's been good to go through this with you all. The babies, I mean.' She focused on Gail. 'You do realise that our children are half-siblings? If neither of us have any more children, they might be the only family each other has one day.'

Jenny hadn't expected that response. Judging by her face, neither had Gail. But Gail nodded. 'I'd like to stay in touch, too.'

'Give it a while and maybe we can start going to events for single mums together?' Antonia winked and smiled. 'Too soon for jokes?'

Gail's eyebrows shot up and then she spluttered a laugh. 'Why not? This year has been crazy enough that that might actually happen.'

Jenny nudged Naomi. 'Looks like we will.'

✦

New baby. New friends. New job. Sometimes, when people tell you that your life is about to change, they are absolutely right.

EPILOGUE

Today, in the midst of having Weetabix wiped in my hair, realising I didn't have one single pair of clean knickers and discovering that Mr Baby had eaten the last of the biscuits I was saving for nap time, I had a bit of an epiphany. So, just for a moment, please indulge me.

In those first few months of motherhood, a group of friends with babies the same age can be the difference between a thin grip on sanity and being tipped over the edge. Being able to confide in someone that you're worried that the small pimple on your baby's cheek is actually the beginning of bubonic plague, especially when your pragmatic husband has suggested that you may as well add the NHS advice line to your Friends and Family phone package, is vital. As is that ever-comforting phrase, uttered after you tearfully admit the latest stage of horror you have encountered with your small baby: 'Oh, yes, mine is doing that, too.'

Although other friends with children are valuable, it is amazing how quickly they forget the bittersweet joys and terrors of those first few months. A handful of women going through the same experiences at the same time can give you reassurance, a reality check and a really good opportunity to get everything off your chest.

No one wants to be lunching with the Super Mother who tells you she has everything under control and proceeds to lecture you on the 'right' way to bring up your child. No, far better to have a group of L-plate parents to accompany you on the journey: those who haven't slept in the last day because they have kept a twenty-four-hour vigil over the baby that rolled off the sofa the morning before; who confess that they haven't actually had sex with their husbands in over six months because they are just so damn tired; who admit that they feel like they have been run over by a very long steam train on a daily basis. These are the mothers with whom you should be spending your time to ensure that you keep that fingernail grip on the hope that you're doing okay.

Sometimes, these women may become life-long friends; sometimes you will barely remember them by your child's second birthday. It doesn't matter. For the first few months, they will be the people you will spend most of your time with, in the bubble known as maternity leave. Whilst your 'real' friends are at work, lunching in places that don't have high chairs and staying up past 9 p.m., these 'baby' friends will be there.

Posh, Scary, Sporty and Ginger, these last six months have been a rollercoaster of exasperation, exhilaration and exhaustion. We've experienced the highs and the lows, and had a few loop-the-loops, but I'll be forever grateful that I had you to share it with. Sometimes it's the friends you don't choose who turn out to be exactly what you need.

Now, before I go commando to the biscuit shop, can anyone tell me how to get Weetabix out of my hair?

From *The Undercover Mother*

A LETTER FROM EMMA

I want to say a huge thank you for choosing to read *The Undercover Mother*. Did you like it? If you did, and want to be kept up-to-date with my future releases, just sign up at the following link. Your email address will never be shared and you can unsubscribe at any time.

www.bookouture.com/emma-robinson

Like Jenny, I thought I had parenting sussed. And then the baby arrived. For the next six months I spent half my day adoring this tiny human being and marveling how we could have made something so perfect. The other half was spent sobbing about the lack of sleep, moaning that no one had told me the truth, and rubbing my nipples with ice cubes. *The Undercover Mother* was the novel I wanted to read. I couldn't find it, so I wrote it.

I know you're busy, but please help me to tell others about *The Undercover Mother* by writing a quick review. (And if you do it now, you won't even have to add it to your no-doubt giant to-do list!) This is my first book, so I'd love to hear what you thought of it, whether you'd like to hear more about Jenny and the Spice Mums and which of them you most identified with (please do not say that awful woman on the beach!). On a serious note, reviews make a huge difference in helping other people find my book and I am grateful for every single one.

I also love hearing from my readers. Come and join the fun on my Facebook page Motherhood for Slackers. They are a friendly bunch and we even let boys in. You can also find me on Twitter or my website. Chatting to you will make a lovely change from persuading teenagers that Shakespeare isn't boring, listening to my son talk about Minecraft or being bossed around by my six-year-old daughter.

Stay in touch!
Emma.

www.facebook.com/motherhoodforslackers

@emmarobinsonuk

www.motherhoodforslackers.com

ACKNOWLEDGEMENTS

I'd like to say a hugely grateful thank you to my amazing publisher Isobel Akenhead for her enthusiasm and support and to Kim Nash and the whole Bookouture family for making me so welcome.

Everyone on the Writer's Workshop Self Edit Course 2016, especially the incomparable Debi Alper and the best beta readers in the world: Kate Machon, Elizabeth Symonds, Martin Ross and Marie Dentan.

All my friends who read early versions, particularly Carrie 'Queen of Punctuation' Harvey. The readers of my blog – Motherhood for Slackers – who are an unending source of encouragement and kind words. Your likes, comments and shares have given me more pleasure than you can ever know.

My wonderful husband who makes everything in my life work and who never moans when he comes home on my day off to find the house in the same state as when he left. My hilarious children who give me the best one-liners and the best cuddles. My mum and dad, who brought me up to believe I could do anything I set my mind to and have been reading, and keeping, my stories since I was five. I love you.

And lastly, a huge thank you to all the parents out there who tell it like it really is: the good, the bad and the downright awful, so that the rest of us can breathe a huge sigh of relief and know that it's not just us.